TAL
AVALON

Wisdom of the Ancient Marshes

By
Walter William Melnyk

Co-Author of
The Apple and the Thorn
a Timeless Tale for the Ages

This Book is a Sequel to
The Apple and the Thorn
Written with Emma Restall Orr
and Published by Thoth Publications

Ancient Marshes Press

On the Cover:
Lady of the Lake portrayed by Anita Shaw
Cover Design and Map by Avey

ISBN: 1451566069
EAN-13: 9781451566062

email the author at: william.melnyk@verizon.net

For Glyn

*My best friend and companion in life,
who inspired the character of Enaid,
and who surpasses the wonder of the
Gwragedd Annwn.*

Affalon

In the Era of the Marsh Tales

To Llan y gelli
of the Silures

Bryniau'r Mendydd

Bryn
Llyffaint

Ynys Mawr

Ceunant y Gawr

✿ Prydde

Ynys Burtle

Ynys Llefrith

Cysgodion

Ynys Bragwair

✿ Pentreflyn

Ynys Calchfaen

Lynn Hydd

Bol Forla

Ynys y Niwl

Bryniau'r
Pennard

Crib Pwlborfa

To
The Stone Henge

To Cornualle,
and the Tin Mines

The Meaning of Myth

There are many ways of telling the truth.
This story is not true,
in the sense that most people use that word.
Yet it is deeply and profoundly a bearer of truth,
told within the story of Cethin, a young Celtic herbalist,
and Fianna, a priestess of Avalon,
as Roman legions consolidate their hold upon Britain.

The Marsh Tales are a collection of thirteen myths,
symbolic stories of people and gods
at the changing of the world.

Part of what follows
is historical, part is mythical, part is flight of fancy.
But all of it is truthful about what it means to be human,
the search for a deeper understanding,
and the intimate connectedness of all things.

Walter William Melnyk
Co-Author of *The Apple and the Thorn*
The Feast of Samhain, 2008

The Marsh Tales

These are the Marsh Tales,
being the ancient Wisdom of Affalon,
told by Vivian to Eosaidh of Cornualle
in the days before the Romans came,
and taught to Cethin the herbalist
by Fianna, at the changing of the world.

Prologue
A Memory of Magic

At the passing of Vivian of Affalon, in the first year of the Roman occupation of the Brythonic lands, when Sianed began her duties as Lady, it was decided that Sianed's daughter, Cariadh, would be sent for safety to Ynys Mon with Caldreg and his druids. Fianna, teacher of the daughters of Affalon, went with her as her guardian. There Cariadh grew to womanhood and gave birth to Elen, who was to follow her as Lady, even as Cariadh was expected to follow Sianed. On Mona, too, Fianna passed from maturity to elderhood. Though she never bore children of her own, Cariadh and Elen were as daughters to her. In the relative peace of Ynys Mon, far from the advancing Romans, Fianna taught them the ways of women and the mysteries of Affalon. She shared memories of Vivian, who had been Lady in her day, and of Eosaidh, the Iuddic stranger from the east who played a greater role in the fate of Affalon than any man before him. The tale of *The Apple and the Thorn*, Fianna called it, and it was a timeless tale for all the ages. As Fianna wove the magical words, Elen would nest in her mother's lap. Leaning her head back upon Cariadh's breast, she could see in her mind the wondrous scenes of Affalon as Fianna called them forth. In this way, both mother and daughter learned the Marsh Tales, the mythic wisdom of ancient Affalon once entrusted to Fianna by Vivian herself.

"Tell us again, Fi," Elen urged. "Tell us again how it all began!" She took her mother and Fianna by the hand and danced with them in circles on the sandy beach. Gentle waves washed the shore of Mona, as waterfowl wheeled their own circles overhead. Across the narrow strait lay the region of Eryri and yr Wyddfa. Beyond that, the marshes of Affalon that Elen had never seen. Between, in ever increasing numbers, were the soldiers of Rome.

The three at last gave in to the dizzying dance and collapsed in laughter on the sand among stalks of sea grass. Elen, as always, was the first to regain her breath.

"Tell us again, Modryb Fi! Tell us about when they met!"

"Alright, then," Fianna laughed. "I wasn't there, you know. I had not yet come to Ynys y Niwl to be a priestess. But Vivian told me the tale not long before she left the world. It was her favorite story, and these are her very words as she told them to me . . ."

~

I was stretched out on the branch of an old oak that hung over the marsh water when I saw him, a young man, ten summers or more younger than I was then. I rested my head in the palms of my hands to gaze at him through a mist spell that hid me from his view. His hair was thick and dark, but his beard had not yet lost its softness. He wore a simple tunic in the summer sun, and a trader's sandals. And his skin was a golden brown.

Who is he? I murmured to the spirits in the trees. He seemed not entirely real, so strange it was that he should be there at all. Without thinking, I let go of the mist, and suddenly he saw me there on the branch. He blinked his eyes in surprise, but then took a step toward me. And his question was the same as mine!

"Are you real?" he asked. He used the common tongue of the marshes, but his words were thick with a strange accent. I sat upright on the branch, my feet trailing in the cool water. *What right do you have to be here?* I had not yet spoken aloud.

He stepped back absently, then bowed low, then frowned, clearly unsure of what he was seeing. And I laughed out loud! The spirits of the marsh laughed with me, I remember. I stood, and walked along the branch to the trunk, then jumped lightly to the ground. The leaves of the old oak continued their laughter in the wind. He stood still, a strong young man, as I walked toward him. Slowly I reached out and touched my fingers to his face.

"Why are you here?" I whispered, speaking for the first time.

"You *are* real!" he said, gazing into my face.

"Almost," I murmured, teasing him. He was carrying a brown, woven bag. I lifted it from his shoulder so quickly he was too amazed to object. I emptied it on the grass and sat down to see what it had held.

I looked up at him, standing there, bewildered.

"Sit down and eat with me!" I smiled at him then, and took a big bite of his round barley bread. And he did sit, and eat.

Did we talk that day? Lying in the grass in the sunshine, with the hum of honey bees and dragonflies, we did speak, of marsh tales and nature's beauty, of how high the sky truly is, and other magical wonders . . .

~

Fianna was interrupted in her tale by the stern old druid, Caldreg, who was hurrying up the beach. He took her aside, and the two spoke quietly, their heads close together and their faces grave with somber news. Caldreg hurried away to the cluster of huts that was their community. As Fianna turned back to the young women her face was ashen.

"The Romans are a day's march south of the straits," she said quietly. "They will be here when the sun sets tomorrow."

Chapter One
Death In the Forest

The old druid muttered a menacing oath under his breath, his foot slipping yet again on the rain soaked path. They were nearing the top of what seemed the hundredth rise since leaving Pen Dinas on the coast three days before. A wild wind from the northeast drove into his face, blowing cold rain under his hood and down his neck. It had begun raining in earnest as they crossed the last stream, until the climbing path itself became a treacherous waterway beneath the gold of fallen beech leaves. It was getting dark. Between the drumming of rain and the rush of wind in the bare branches, it was becoming as hard to hear as to see. Caldreg bent his gaze to the ground, letting the path carry him as it would to the top of the rise.

In single file, also drawn into hooded cloaks against the weather, the others followed. Morfran, the only other druid in the small party and younger than Caldreg by nearly four decades, kept to the rear. Between them, three women: Cariadh, daughter of the Lady of the Lake, her own young daughter, and Fianna, priestess of Affalon. They would likely not meet Romans this far south, this close to Llan y gelli, thought Caldreg. He hoped not. They would be no match for a Roman patrol. Again Caldreg muttered a curse under his breath, and pushed on up the pathway. They were well inside the lands of the Silures, and the Romans were busy elsewhere. Perhaps only a few more ridges to cross before they reached the old hill fort that was the Silure capital. Yes, surely they would make it safely, and end the long flight that had begun so many days ago from the Roman carnage at Ynys Mon.

If it were possible, the rain came down harder yet. Caldreg pulled his hood closer around his face, shutting out all sound but the beating rain, all sight but the mud and leaves at his feet in the growing darkness. The wheezing of his breath rose as the incline steepened toward the summit. His ankle ached from slipping in the mud, and he whispered a charm against the pain, hoping it might work. But pain was a normal thing for a body of sixty-five years. Charms could not long hold off the inevitable.

The old druid risked a look ahead. They were nearing the top of the ridge, where the path bent around a large granite outcropping before dropping down again into the next valley. Behind him were the footfalls of his companions, softened into near silence by the blanket of wet leaves. No voices. It was too wet to talk, too cold. He looked up again as his left shoulder brushed the big rock. They were at the top. The path was curving around to the left. It seemed for a moment that time paused, the great forest spreading around him in the driving rain. And then the world changed.

~

If not for the storm, the horror might not have happened. The two parties approaching each other on the wooded path might have had warning. If the leaves underfoot were dry, the evening silent, the refugees from Mona might have heard even such a small Roman patrol and taken shelter in the underbrush. Or the patrol, left out of the glories of the attack on Mona, and the Iceni revolt far to the east, might have opted out of meaningless engagement altogether and swept wide around the travelers to avoid contact. Or yet, alerted to each others' approach, both might have perceived no real threat and simply greeted each other on the path. If there had been no slaughter at Ynys Mon. If Boudicca had not so recently taken up arms. If there had been no storm. If Fianna had been leading them instead of Caldreg. If the Roman had not lost a son with Vespasian's II Augusta Legion in the Exmoor. If only.

Caldreg felt the Roman before he saw him, for as the path bent left around the outcrop at the top of the ridge, suddenly it was blocked by the heavy movement of leather and steel. The exclamation of surprise, in provincial Latin, left no

11

doubt. Caldreg acted instinctively, in defense of himself, in defense of the priestesses in his charge. He reached deep into the folds of his cloak, drawing a short Celtic sword. But he was no soldier, and he was no longer young. Before his weapon was half drawn a Roman gladius gleamed for an instant, wet with rain, and disappeared, itself, into the druid's robes. A bright red wetness spread over Caldreg's cloak as the Roman thrust upward, through the belly and under the ribs, severing the great artery. Caldreg had no time to understand what had happened. Sightless eyes stared into the Roman's face, a lifeless body sagged at the end of the Roman's sword, dragging it toward the ground as Caldreg left the world.

Morfran had looked up at the sound of the impact. With a cry of rage he pushed past the women, throwing them off the path, with his own blade high advancing on the soldier who was still pulling his sword from Caldreg's lifeless body, Roman boot hard upon the old druid's chest for leverage. Morfran had the advantage of left handedness. In a sweeping arc his blade came from the sinister side and found its mark between the neck and right shoulder of the Roman. Blood sprayed from the severed artery, covering all three men as the Roman went down. But Morfran's rage left him open. Three remaining members of the Roman patrol came around the bend, already prepared to fight. It was three swords that struck him at once. He lost an arm, and his head, before he went down across the other two, adding his blood to theirs.

The women were heavily cloaked, off the path, and might have escaped notice. But Elen, granddaughter of the Lady of the Lake, was too young. At the sight of Morfren falling she let out a loud cry, and the Romans saw the three of them. Dark forms only in the growing shadows, they also might have been armed men. The patrol, frightened and enraged by battle, took no chances. Elen's cry was choked off as a gladius pierced her belly and severed her spine where it emerged, run completely through her small body. Cariadh, trying to save her daughter, was caught by a second blade which came crashing down from above, cutting deep into her unprotected skull, spilling red blood and something pink and gray across the shoulders of her cloak. She fell with her daughter in her arms, and they both died on the path.

Fianna, only, stood motionless. No stranger to Romans, or to death, she alone of her company felt no anger or fear, but only the deep, sad resignation that comes from an understanding of the sorrowful foolishness of men. Slowly she let down her hood, and looked quietly into the face of her attacker. For a moment the young soldier was caught in her gaze. He looked into the quiet eyes of a woman beyond the age of his own mother. More than that, he looked into quiet eyes that saw into him, through him, and understood. The rain fell around him, his comrades cursed, and the air was filled with the liquid silver smell of blood. For an instant the young Roman was almost changed. Then the blood lust of the moment overcame all. He thrust his sword slowly and intently into Fianna's belly, and her world went dark. On the path, the only sound was the rain.

In silence the three soldiers cleaned their weapons, wiped the blood as best they could from their battle leathers. They lashed the dead decurion to a litter fashioned from saplings, and returned quietly down the path toward their camp. At the crest of the ridge, near the rock outcrop and the twisting path, it was silent but for the rain and a soft hush of wind in the beech branches. Bodies lay scattered, on and off the track. So much blood. It lay pooled darkly in the dark of night, unseen, but the harsh metallic scent of it was everywhere. Scavengers of the forest, driven into dark dens by the storm, had not yet made their discovery.

~

Far away to the south, on a mist shrouded island in a low, inland sea, the Lady stood still as stone, blood drained from her face, heart nearly stopped. Her eyes looked off into the distance, and their terror told of the sight they saw.

"Priestess," she whispered to the young girl at her side, "They are dead. Cariadh and Elen. What will become of us?"

The young girl placed a caring hand upon Sianed's arm. "My Lady," she said, and sat long in silence.

~

The clouds parted over the last ridge before Llan y gelli. In the young night the first crescent of a winter moon hung low over the western hills. It was now truly silent, save for the slow, soft breathing of the bearer of the tales, the priestess of Affalon who once knew Sianed, and even Vivian. Fianna yet lived.

Chapter Two
In the House of Healing

She awoke to the dark smell of wood-smoke and thatch. Before she opened her eyes she knew she was lying on a rough cot in a small roundhouse, and memories of Ynys y Niwl came flooding back. She was on the Isle of Mist, in the house of the priestesses. Outside she could hear a goat naying, chickens complaining loudly, perhaps disturbed by the running children whose playful laughter burst over all else. She stretched, the long, slow stretch of age upon waking, and a sharp, screaming pain cut through her left side. Suddenly she remembered, her eyes opening wide with fear even though her body remained paralyzed by the pain. It was not Ynys y Niwl, nor the dark, wet trackway in the forest where she had fallen, and there were no children. There was light, though dim, and overhead the shadows of a thatch roof tilted and turned in her delirium, ghostly white smoke from damp firewood hanging beneath the straw before seeping into it and filtering out into the air. She tried again to move. Again the pain tore into her side, blinding pain that cheated what sight she had. As the small room swam sideways above her, all once again went dark, and she fell back into a fitful sleep.

The dream came again. Women, naked and painted, screaming, and dripping oaths. Men waiting silently, in the brush line behind the sand, with what blades they could muster. Rushing forward to meet the boats as they landed . . .

How long she lay in the balance between dream and reality she did not know. Over and over the scenes of massacre swirled before her, the ringing of steel, the sickening slice of sundered flesh, the crack of bone; shouts of anger, and cries of fear.

"Cariadh!" she cried out. Where was Cariadh? "Elen!" She thrashed about wildly on her cot, and the movement brought back the tearing pain, waking her from the horror. Suddenly she sat up, eyes wide open. "Cariadh!" she shouted, and screamed with pain.

"Lady," said a male voice behind her. A strong arm went about her shoulder, holding her upright, keeping her from falling.

Her breath came in ragged gasps, tears filling her eyes and flowing down her face. Though her eyes were open she did not see anything except the vanishing dream. "Caldreg," she said, "Caldreg, is that you?"

"No, my Lady," came the soft reply. "I know not this Caldreg, but I am Cethin, the herbalist. And you are in my care, such as it is." A young, strong hand came into her struggling focus, holding a wooden goblet. "Drink, my Lady," Cethin offered. "The sword injured no vital organs. You may drink. The water is cool, mixed with a little chamomile, and some lavender."

Fianna lifted the goblet to her lips, sipping slowly. A priestess of Affalon knew about healing draughts, and the way to drink herbal water. Yet it was a discipline she barely managed to accomplish. Her throat was raw and dry, her thirst anxious and desperate. Moments passed as she slowly returned to the world about her. Cethin sat quietly by her side on the edge of the cot. From outside the sound of goats broke the silence, and Fianna smiled. At least that part she had not imagined. Finally she turned to the young man whose arm still held her steady, and looked into his face. It was the color of olives, his eyes and curly hair a deep brown. The thin white line of a battle scar cut across his right cheek from just below his temple nearly to his chin. His nose was a bit askew. Not enough to be ugly, but endearing, perhaps in the eyes of a mother. Fianna had cared for many young boys on Ynys y Niwl. She knew a broken nose when she saw one. Again she smiled.

"It has been a long time since I have been held by a young man such as yourself," she said. Her quiet laugh troubled the wound in her side, and she winced with the pain. But the joke lightened her spirit, and she continued it. "Don't get any ideas, though," she smiled. "I am a helpless woman, and," with a wink, "old enough to be your mother!"

Embarrassed, Cethin dropped his arm and moved quickly from the edge of the cot to a low stool beside it. "Do not fear, Lady," he said, though he noticed a strange beauty that lay underneath the years, and the dirt and the pain. "It is only your wound I am interested in."

She touched his arm. "Oh, I know, Healer. Only it is also a long time since I have smiled."

Abruptly a shadow came to her eyes. She looked around the single room, where shelves filled with jars of many sizes and shapes lined the walls. There were several other cots, apparently for more patients, that lay empty. She thought the sob in her heart might be loud enough for the herbalist to hear.

"I knew you could not be Caldreg," she said. "I saw him go down. And Morfran as well, I fear." There was a deep silence for the space of many breaths. "But Cariadh. Where is she? And Elen? Are they in another roundhouse?" In her eyes Cethin could see she already knew the answer. He began to speak, but it was important to Fianna that she say it herself, not hear it from a stranger. "Dead, then," she whispered. "All of them dead."

"I am afraid so, Lady," he said, and they were silent.

"Can I see them?"

"Lady, you have been in a delirium for nearly three days. When you are able to walk, I will take you to their burial place."

"So be it," she said, with a deep sigh. *I must seek Sianed,* she thought, and already her mind began to reach out toward the mists in the south. *I must bring her comfort.* "Her mother will be distraught," she said, mostly to herself.

"Is there someone to whom you wish to send a messenger?" Cethin asked.

"No. Thank you for the kindness, but it will not be necessary." *When you leave, I will find her soon enough.*

Cethin rose quietly and busied himself with preparations among the shelves of herbs, to give Fianna time alone with her grief. Easing herself back down on her cot, she gazed at the roof of the roundhouse, letting her eyes lose focus in the hypnosis of radial beams, thatch weave, and white wood-smoke that swirled below the roof, sifted into the straw, and disappeared. *We are all of us like the smoke of a hearth-fire,* she mused. *Disappearing into the underside of a roof, and emerging above into the high crystal air.*

Cethin took down a clay jar from a shelf on the wall, and shook a bit of dried leaves into a cup. Lifting a small kettle from its hook above the fire, he poured simmering water over the leaves, and a pungent, insistent odor filled the roundhouse.

"Valerian," Fianna sniffed. "I am not yet ready to go back to sleep, Healer."

Cethin came back to her cot and held out the cup. "It will help you relax," he said, "I have to change the dressing. I see you, also, have some knowledge of herbs."

Fianna took the cup and sipped reluctantly. "I was once a teacher for the children of our community. Part of my task was to teach them herb lore." She thought back to a summer morning, many years before, when she and her young charges were picking sunwort on the slopes of Wirrheal on Ynys y Niwl. They had laughed with Vivian, who was Lady then, and the strange tinner from stranger lands, named Eosaidh. It brought a smile to her heart, though a tear formed in her eye. She fell silent, and slowly drank the calming tea.

Cethin sat on the stool beside the cot and watched the movement of memories across her face. At last he said, "It is a strange community in which all the children learn herb lore. Do you have a name, Lady?"

She stared into the cup. As if reading an answer in the dark leaves she breathed, "Fianna. Fianna, I am called, of Affalon."

18

For a moment the goats in the yard made the only sound. The wonder in Cethin's eyes changed to respect, and then to honour. "You are a priestess, then," he said, "A priestess of the mysteries."

"Yes," she answered. "I had almost forgotten."

He pulled the rough blanket up, covering her hips, and then reached for the softer woolen shift in which the young women had clothed her when she was brought in. "Mother," he said, "with your permission?"

She accepted the honour without thinking. So often had she been like a mother to the children of Affalon. For so long she had been like a foster mother to Cariadh on Mona. And to Elen, who had left this life before discovering her own motherhood.

"Only be gentle, Healer," she said as he pulled away the shift. And she drew inside herself, letting the valerian do its work to ward against the pain.

Cethin slowly pulled the shift up past the edge of the blanket until the bandage was fully exposed, dark red with dried blood, and still damp with a mild tincture of rosemary and sun's-bride, to help ward off putrefaction. He poured more of the tincture from a small jar onto the cloth, to moisten it further and soften any scabbing before pulling back the dressing to remove it. As the dressing came away Fianna stirred and moaned quietly, but she seemed to be moving even more deeply into a trance. It was a deeper swoon than the valerian would have produced, Cethin knew. She must have been using her magic. The wound looked good. The Roman's thrust was skillful and clean, but Fianna's heavy woolen cloak had turned it from its mark. It had gone completely through the flesh of her left side. He turned her gently so he could see both wounds at once, and this time there was no sign that she was awake. Both wounds were open. He could not risk closing up something so deep, for fear of festering. But the cuts were clean, and the sun's-bride had kept down the swelling. Deep within the wound he had used a hot iron to cauterize the larger blood vessels. Only where absolutely necessary, for fear that too much seared flesh would do more harm than good.

He used an infusion of sunwort and soldier's woundwort to clean deep inside, then sprinkled a small amount of garlic powder over the exposed area as a strong aid against festering. Finally, a paste of honey spread around the opening of the wounds, and a fresh dressing treated with the rosemary and sun's-bride tincture, and bound loosely around her waist. The wounds would heal from the inside out, slowly. It would leave dramatic scarring that would remind her of the ordeal for the rest of her life. But it couldn't be helped, and indeed she would heal. Cethin smiled. Battlefield medicine was seldom successful. He was glad his skill was helping this priestess of Affalon, but how much was due to his skill or her magic he could not know. Gently he turned her over on her back, pulled the shift down over the new bandage, and the woolen blanket up to her neck. At a cauldron set beside the fire he washed his hands in warm water, and stepped outside into the cold morning air. Silently, in her heart, Fianna was singing the songs of Affalon . . .

~

In a small hut far to the south, on Ynys y Cysgodion in the dark, hidden waters of the Affalon marshes, Sianed stirred. For fifteen years, ever since the leaving of Vivian, she had been Lady of Affalon. For fifteen years she had held the community of priestesses together, hidden in the strange mists that surrounded them, though they were also closely surrounded by the Romans, and abandoned by the druids. Shortly after Vivian and Eosaidh of Cornualle had disappeared forever into the marsh, Caldreg had taken the remaining druids and left for Ynys Mon in the north, the Mother Isle. He had said it was to find a better way to fight the Romans. Vivian had bitterly accused him of simply seeking his own safety. After all these years, Sianed had no idea which one of them had spoken truth. And now it hardly mattered. Sianed's daughter, Cariadh, was a blood heir to the role of Lady. Sianed had reluctantly sent her

20

with Caldreg, and the priestess Fianna, to share in the safety the druids had sought. Shortly after, Elen had been born, also heir to the obligation of Lady of Affalon. But it had been futile. Nearly a fortnight ago Sianed had seen her vision of blood and turmoil, horror and death. First on the shore of Mona, then in the forest of the Silures. It was there, she knew, her daughter and grand daughter had died, ending her line. But she had not seen Fianna, nor could she see her yet.

Now a song of Affalon was singing in her mind, and the voice was Fianna's.

Fianna? Oh, Fianna, is it you? Sianed's thoughts reached northward, seeking the source of the song. She felt the mind of the younger priestess, and then the pain of the wounds, and then the gentle, healing touch of the herbalist.

Yes, Lady. Yes, I live, though for a time I feared I would not. Is it well with you?

The dark shadow returned to Sianed's heart, and tears formed in her eyes. *No child,* she answered. *I have seen the death on the Mother Isle, and the death in the forest, and I know that Cariadh and Elen are gone from us. I thank my Lady that you are saved.*

Tears choked Fianna's heart. *Sianed, I am so sorry. I thought I had managed to keep them safe when Caldreg got us off the island. We were so close to the shelter of Llan y gelli . . .* her thoughts fell silent, but Sianed could see her remembering it all again.

You did well, Daughter, came the calming voice, *as did Caldreg. You both did all that could be expected. But there is no safe place in the world from these Romans except here in our mists. Fianna, I want you to return to Affalon.*

Lady? Fianna asked, searching for Sianed's meaning, for her feeling. She had not thought to be welcome again in the ancient marshes, after her failure to protect the Lady's daughter and heir.

I feel the weariness of age, Sianed continued. *Already I have stayed too long, and have no idea how many cycles are left to me. Morfrenna is still by my side, but I need you here, Fianna, with me, now that Cariadh will not return.*

I am not well, my Lady, Fianna replied. *I cannot return for some time.* Vaguely she felt Cethin's touch through her trance, saw in her mind the deep, open wound that had only just begun to heal.

Rest, Fianna. Rest and heal. And then come to me . . . And Sianed was gone into the darkness. Rest and heal. It was all she could do.

Chapter Three
Memories

The days that followed were quiet at Llan y gelli, for immediately after the massacre of the druids on Ynys Mon, Seutonius Paulinus had begun moving his forces to the east to deal with the uprising of the Iceni under Queen Boudicca. The few Roman units that remained had been withdrawn across the mouth of the Hafren for the winter, out of the Silure lands altogether. That was the last gift of Caldreg to the tribes, for Paulinus wished to lose no more soldiers to a troublesome people. And so began a respite of nearly twenty years, during which time the Silures would live in the illusion of peace and the fear of war. Then, too, winter began to settle into the valleys and bogs. The hill fort drew warriors and cattle into itself. The dark time of the year had arrived. And in those quiet, dark days, Fianna began to heal.

One morning, when a cold frost still clung to the roundhouse eaves, Cethin had just added wood to the fire and passed a goblet of warm tea to his patient. He sat in silence, watching her slowly drink. Though he could reach out and touch her on the cot, her eyes were in some distant place. There was no sound except for the soft crackle of the flames, and the slow wakening of the animals in the yards. She was his patient in name, for he was the village herbalist. Yet her healing progressed at a rate far beyond his skill and he knew this priestess from the old mists had more than a hand in her own recovery.

~

Priestess, how are you healing? The words of Sianed, Lady of Affalon came to Fianna's mind from the far isle of Cysgodion.

This wound of the flesh does well, My Lady. Young Cethin is an attentive healer, and the power sent by the

23

priestesses on Ynys y Niwl is strong. In another two cycles, when the ice melts and before the honeysuckle awakens, I may be able to travel.

Sianed's thoughts were gentle in Fianna's mind. *"Do not rush, Priestess. You are needed here, but you are needed here fully healed.* And then, even more gently, *But what of the wounds of the spirit, Fianna?*

For long moments Fianna could not answer. From his seat against the wall Cethin could see a shadow fall across her face, a shadow he had seen upon her often since the day of terror. He knew she was seeing again the Roman swords, the death in the forest.

He leaned back against one of the hides covering the roundhouse walls and closed his own eyes. He had come to know something of healing herbs in the ten years since his father had died, enough for Cadael, the Silure Chief, to appoint him healer for the settlement. But real healing came rarely, especially when the wound was as wide and deep as Fianna's. As the fire's heat began to warm the room, Cethin drifted into that mysterious place between waking and sleeping. He saw the horror of another Roman ambush and his fingers went to the long white scar across his cheek. That had been nearly ten years ago, and his own wound had healed poorly, and slow.

It was late in the cycle of Vespasian's occupation of the west country that Cethin had arrived in Llan y gelli. Corio, the Dubh-bunadh Chief, had swiftly capitulated, hoping for Roman preferment and perhaps a stake in the lead mines. Cethin and his father had followed the hero Caradoc across the Hafren to the Silure lands, unwilling to surrender to Rome. Only just coming into his manhood, Cethin looked forward to the time when he would stand against Vespasian's soldiers, and help to free the tribes. That time came eight years later when, as a young man of twenty summers, he joined his father on one of Caradoc's raids. Instead of a Roman patrol they encountered the army of Publius Ostorius Scapula crossing into Silure territory to punish the tribe for harboring this Caradoc of the

Trinovantes. The battle was fierce and bloody. Cethin remembered how his father had kept him close, how they had fought back to back as the Romans closed in and swept by them in pursuit of the fleeing Caradoc. Only in the sudden quiet had he realized his father was no longer at his shoulder, and that there was blood all over his tunic. His own blood. His hand went slowly to the side of his face. It was wet with the flow, and numb. His finger tips felt the open wound, went through the opening, and touched broken teeth. The forest wheeled around him in a great arc; he was unconscious before he hit the ground.

When at last Cethin had awoken the sun was low in the trees. There was a fierce pain in his jaw, but though his cheek was still wet the bleeding had slowed to a trickle. In the deep silence that follows battle he heard only the wind in the trees and the twitter of birds looking for an evening meal. The world, continuing to turn, had like the Romans moved on. A groaning by his side drew him out of his reverie, making the pain in his jaw worse. Struggling to remain conscious he turned slowly to his left and saw his father down, his tunic, also, soaked with blood and torn in a great diagonal slash from his left breast to his right hip. At first Cethin thought the buzzing in his ears was part of his dizziness, and he almost fainted again. But then in horror he saw the flies, everywhere, swarming around his father's torn body, crawling into the gaping wound. Ignoring the pain, Cethin took off his own tunic and swung it in anger to chase the flies, then laid it gently across his father's body. But he saw the broken ribs and the deep belly wound, and knew he did not have the skill to keep his father in this world.

Alone, through the night, Cethin had sat by his father, keeping away the vermin, washing his brow with water from a nearby stream. Sometime in the night his father had died. Cethin, succumbing to his own pain, had drifted into unknowing. In the morning they found him and brought him back to Llan y gelli. The herbwise did his best to treat Cethin's face wound, but it had been open for too long, and festered, and it never did heal properly. It was then that the young man vowed to learn the practice of herbs, to become himself a healer so that, having failed to save his father, he might save others.

~

Cethin opened his eyes and looked at Fianna, who was still in some other place, her eyes seeing what his could not. Cethin's eyes were a deep dark brown, set in the rich olive skin of the Dubh-bunadh, framed by dark locks of long, curly hair. He would have been strikingly handsome. But though the name "Cethin" meant one who is dark, it also meant "ugly," and this is why he had been so named: for the ugly scar that would always remind him of his father's death, and of his vow to become a healer. His real name was all but forgotten, lost along with the loss of his Dubh-bunadh heritage. His eyes closed once again.

"Where are you, Healer? Do you also have the Sight?" Fianna's words brought him back to awareness. She was sitting up on the cot, finishing her tea, smiling at him. "Perhaps there is more to this young herbwise than I thought," she said.

"No, Lady,' he answered, "I have no gift. I was only," he paused a moment, "remembering."

"Remembering is a form of seeing," Fianna said. "And you have more gifts than you know, Healer." She touched her side, covered with a dressing of sunwort and chamomile. "It is more than the magic of Affalon that heals this wound, you know."

Cethin stretched and stood. He looked down on her as she sat on the cot, but was aware that in some way she was larger than he. He was the herbwise, the healer, but she seemed to be healing, itself. "Then perhaps we are a matched pair, Lady," he grinned.

"Perhaps we are," she answered. And her eyes once more drifted, briefly, to another place and another time. Cethin was alarmed.

"Lady, are you unwell?"

Fianna opened her eyes and smiled at him again. "I was remembering another matched pair I once knew, many years ago. The memory brings me peace, and helps me to heal. Do you know of the name Vivian?"

Cethin sat beside the cot. "She was the great Lady in Affalon, before the Romans came."

"Yes," said Fianna. "She was *my* Lady, when I served as a young priestess caring for the children on the Isle of Mist. I taught them all about sunwort, you know, and other herbs. You have done well with this dressing on my poor side."

"Thank you, Lady," Cethin answered, blushing as if he were one of her young charges rather than the Chief's own healer. "But you spoke of a pair?"

Fianna gave a quiet sigh. "Perhaps you have also heard of someone we called Yashi?" She could see by the puzzle in his eyes that he had not. "His real name was Eosaidh, a trader in lead and tin. His family had long owned mines in Cornualle and among the Mendydd hills. He came to us on changing currents at the turning of times, just before the Romans, and those who called themselves servants of the Christ."

Sensing the beginning of a tale, Cethin poured her more tea, and some for him, and settled on the low stool beside Fianna's cot.

"We knew not then that he and Vivian had met years before. Nor that they would become the 'matched pair,' of which I spoke. They had grown old, but years are different for a Lady of Affalon. As cycles of the moon passed during those strange days they seemed to regain the spirit of an earlier time, the youth of a past meeting. They left us at the turning of the moon on a cold night so many winters ago. It is a strange and wonderful tale."

Cethin was lost in the eyes of the older priestess. "Tell me this tale," he said quietly.

"The tale of Vivian and Yashi is lost in the mists," Fianna whispered. But her eyes brightened and her voice filled once again with life. "Yet there are tales that survive, tales it is

27

said they told one another in the days of their first meeting, the Marsh Tales of Affalon, and other wonders."

Fianna reached out and took Cethin's hand. "Come," she said. "Trust in the gifts you have, Healer, and come with me, for I have something to show you." Her eyes closed and her face, her face, softened. That was the word Cethin would have used. Her features had not been hard, but now they seemed softer still, as if surrounded by a fine mist, which began to swirl, and grow, and deepen. Without willing it so he closed his own eyes, yet still the priestess and the mist were visible before him. Something strange was happening, a shift in his balance, a dizziness that slowly resolved itself as if he had stumbled and regained his footing. As the mists cleared he found himself no longer in the house of healing at Llan y gelli, but in another thatched roundhouse, smaller, strewn with hides upon which he found himself sitting. A small fire burned in the center, its drifting smoke disappearing into the thatched roof above. Over the fire hung a small kettle, and there was the scent of chamomile and blessed thistle, and other herbs he could not recognize. Fianna was still with him, her back turned as she faced another woman whose face was like the strength of the earth, and the darkness of ancient marshes.

Hush, Cethin. It was Fianna's voice speaking in his mind. *Hush and fear not, for this is Vivian of the Lakes, Lady of Affalon.*

Eosaidh has come upon a current, my Lady, Fianna was saying. *Why do you fear his presence here?*

It is not fear, the older woman answered. Her voice was like deep and slow moving waters. *He has been here before; he and I are tied together. It is a strange thing to feel old ties reborn at this turning of the ages.*

The women sat facing each other across the fire. Fianna glanced toward Cethin and looked questioningly at Vivian.

Do not worry, the Lady said, *It is well for this young Dubh-bunadh to be here. If you have chosen him to bear the*

28

tales into his time, then I trust your instinct. Let him listen, and watch with us.

Once again ancient mists swirled around Cethin. When they parted, he saw Fianna and Vivian walking along a marshy shoreline. A grove of oaks grew along the marsh, a long, low branch of one old tree hanging out over the dark waters. Vivian was speaking in low whispers, seeing something under the oaks that was dark to his eyes.

Did we talk that day? Vivian asked, as if to herself. *Lying in the grass in the sunshine, with the hum of honey bees and dragonflies, we did speak, of marsh tales and nature's beauty, of how high the sky truly is and other magical wonders.* Suddenly Cethin realized he could feel the warmth of sun on his face, hear the drone of bees and other insects. Vivian and Fianna were gone from his sight, and in their place were a young woman and a man, seated together in the grass beneath the ancient oak, their heads together, their faces animated in conversation. The young woman leapt up, laughing. *Don't move,* she said to the lad, *Wait here!* There were apples growing beyond a hedge of thorn. She ran to them, gathered an armful, and ran back to the young man, laughing and singing like a mischievous child. Suddenly she was silent, and the wind blew through her dark hair. She took a large bite, her eyes never leaving his, and then gave it to him, and he ate as well, the juice of the ripe fruit running down into his beard. Suddenly she pushed him over on his back, rolled with him in the grass and came up sitting on his chest. She laughed out loud again, and dribbled the juice of the apple from her lips onto his, and they kissed . . . and the vision was gone.

~

Cethin found himself again in Vivian's roundhouse with Fianna. *Tell him, Fianna,* Vivian was saying. *Tell your healer the tales as I have told them to you!* And they were no longer in the roundhouse, but in a small clearing in the moonlight. Off in the distance, near the edge of the forest, stood a man, strong yet filled with age, his face a rich copper color, his dark hair and

29

beard mixed with gray. Vivian looked to him for a moment, then back to Fianna. *We must go now, Fi,"* she said quietly, *Eosaidh waits for me.* She turned and reached her hand out to him, and the two vanished into the trees. Cethin and Fianna stood together in the soft moonlight, the breeze dancing around them, as the mists rose once more.

~

When his mind cleared Cethin was sitting on his low stool, Fianna had let go of his hands and was resting against the wall on her cot. The world as he knew it had returned.

"But, but I thought . . . " he began, as if to himself, "I thought Vivian and Eosaidh had died."

"Nothing dies, Healer," said Fianna, "and no one is ever completely lost from us." She opened her eyes and took a sip of her tea, grown cool during their traveling. "Vivian showed you more than I would have imagined. She bids you know not only the tales themselves, but the meanings they held in her heart, and the truths they bear for all who will hear them anew. And there are other wonders besides."

Cethin's instincts as a healer took over. "Rest now, Lady," he said, "and we will save tales for another day." He bent low over his patient to get a close view of the long, ugly wound in her side. Just to the left of her stomach. Had it been an inch further to the right she would have been found dead on the path. As it was, he marveled at how well she was mending. Left open to avoid festering, it had begun healing well from the inside out. Soon he would be able to bind the outer edges more tightly together, and the final stages of recovery would begin.

"That is the closest look any man has ever had of my belly, Healer," Fianna ventured with a wry smile. "I hope you appreciate it. I'm afraid it looked much better many summers ago!"

Cethin finished covering the wound with a light compress soaked in a tea of chamomile and sunwort. "I imagine it looked much better just before it met that Roman sword," he answered. "I have seen many bellies, Lady,"

Though he kindly stopped short of adding, "and one is pretty much like another." He pulled a light blanket over her and she sat up carefully, leaning back against a pile of furs on her cot.

"Stay, Cethin," she said, "and I will tell you a tale of bellies, if you will make some tea for the inside of my stomach as well as the outside."

Cethin smiled at her remark, for she well knew he had kept chamomile tea hot on the fire for her always since her arrival. He served them both, and sat on his old stool to hear the first tale.

"It is the oldest of tales," she began, "as old as the marshes . . ."

Chapter Four
I. Morla's Belly

A small rounded hillock still rises out of the mists to the west of Bryn Fyrtwyddon on Ynys y Niwl. In all but high summer it is separated from the isle of the priestesses by a narrow but deep channel. Bol Forla, it is called; Morla's Belly. Its story is the oldest of tales, as old as the marshes themselves.

~

Ages ago, yet not so many that the marshes were not already ancient, there lived a girl who was young and very beautiful. Her name was Morla, which some say means bitter, and some, woman of the marsh. Either would be true. Morla had been given in marriage to a tribal chieftain. He was old and leathery, kept his thoughts to himself, and was given to snapping at people when he wanted something or when he was feeling out of sorts. And so he was called Crwban, which in the common tongue means Turtle. The marriage had not been Morla's idea, for she had been a youth of only eleven summers and dreamed of love and adventure. There was no adventure in Crwban's roundhouse. He was too old for war, and, it was said, too old to please a young woman. Morla warmed his meals, and his bed at night, without feeling warmth herself. During the long days when Crwban drank with his fellows and bragged of ancient conquests, Morla would wander alone in the cool darkness of the Bitter Marshes. Her companions were marsh hens, and eels, and she learned the cycles of marsh marigolds, and the secrets of the ancient currents. Crwban did not care that she was gone all day, as long as she had his dinner ready each evening, and offered him the spreading of her thighs should he chance to be capable, though this was not often. So cycles of the sun went by, and Morla began the flow of her moontide, and became a woman.

It was early in the warming of the year, and Morla was wandering the bog paths west of Bryniau'r Pennard, near Llynwen and the Bitter Marshes. Most considered the old bog impassable, but Morla had befriended the lands and waters; they shared the same solitude. The myrtles that surrounded the marsh were more numerous then, and they were just coming into bloom. The sun was low in the sky, its light gilding the waters of the shallow lake. Humming bits of old marsh tunes, Morla sat on a fallen log, pulling and plaiting reeds into a small basket.

The sudden flushing of several marsh hens alerted her that she was not alone. Ceasing her own tune, she heard it faintly echoing back to her from out beyond the reeds in words of an old marsh tongue. Her own clan had not spoken that language for generations, but she knew most of the words from the folk she had met in her wanderings.

> *Dark waters, deep, slow,*
> *secret paths among the reeds;*
> *dark paths where none may go*
> *who know not where the waters lead . . .*

> *Then I laughed, danced and sang,*
> *when I dwelt with tribe and clan;*
> *now dark waters are my home,*
> *because I went where currents ran . . .*

Through a gap in the reeds, out on Llynwen, Morla saw a small flatboat. A young man was standing in it, poling it through the shallow waters, and singing. Morla had never seen anything like him. Her people were short and dark. She had never seen any other. Compared to those of her clan, the young man in the boat hardly looked human. To begin with, he was tall. It was hard to tell from a distance, but Morla thought, were she standing next to him, she might barely reach his breastbone. It was curious that the thought of standing next to him warmed her blood. She peered closer, and listened as he sang.

Because I went where currents ran . . .

His skin was fair. In the setting sun it looked almost pure white. His hair was wild. It seemed to stand out from his head in spikes. And it was red. He seemed almost otherworldly as his boat glided silently on the lake and the words of his song faded into a soft hum. Then he was gone. At the same moment the sun set. Dusk began to envelope her as if it emerged out of the reeds, and she turned for home and the roundhouse of Crwban, her mind still wandering in the reeds of Llynwen.

~

Often thereafter she returned near day's end to the same spot. Mostly she saw only marsh creatures, but sometimes she saw him, out on the lake or poling through a channel. She invented stories about him, and began to imagine what it would be like to share his bed rather than Crwban's.

In the waning of the year, as the waters rose and flooded the bogs and geese flew overhead, Morla tucked her long tunic around her waist and waded out to the small rise from which she was used to watching for her young stranger. Her eyes were downcast, taking care for the perilous footing. As she stepped onto the rise she looked up. Her heart paused in its beating and she uttered a cry of surprise, for there he sat, on the overturned bottom of his little boat, looking up at her with eyes as blue as the harvest skies. He blinked once or twice. A dragonfly flew between them, hovered for a moment, and then sped off. She could hear the soft hush of the currents at her feet and, when it began again, the beat of her own heart.

"Hello," he said.

Morla stared. He was tall and angular. As he sat there on the boat bottom his feet were flat on the ground and his knees came nearly up to his shoulders. His skin wasn't actually white, but pale. She could see thin blue veins pulsing at his temples. His eyes were a pale, clear blue, and they stared curiously back at her. She saw up close in the shadows that his hair was coppery, rather than red, but it really did stand up from his head in several spikes, greased, perhaps, with animal fat. His nose and ears were pointed, almost sharp. He had freckles high on his cheekbones. She stared for many moments, and then started as he spoke again:

34

"Hello. I am called Crika. Who are you?"

Morla surpressed a laugh. Crika was a strange name. Not really a word, but sort of a sound that represented the phrase, *a sharp poker made of red marsh reeds.* "It fits," she thought in amusement. And yet she knew instantly there was more to him than a frivolous nickname that made fun of his appearance.

"I don't remember my real name," he said, sensing her need for an explanation.

"I am Morla." That was indeed her real name, but she had never realized how well it actually described her. Bitter as the Bitter Marshes.

"Sit with me, Morla?" he said, more like a question. And added, "Please."

No one had ever asked her "please" before. Indeed, no one had ever asked her to do anything. She had always been told. Morla sat at the end of the boat, keeping her distance, not taking her eyes off him, and together they shared silence as the sun lowered toward the marsh.

"I've seen you watching me from the reeds," Crika said, after a time.

Morla quickly offered the apology she knew was expected.

"No," he said. A broad smile revealed sharp teeth stained with the greens and browns of a marshweed diet. "No," he repeated, "do not be sorry. It has made me feel less lonely, as if I had a friend."

Crika told her the tale of his banishment from the dwellings of the lake people. At first they had found him to be merely a strange child of a wandering stranger. But as he grew, his appearance became less and less that of his lake village mother, more and more that of the stranger from the north with whom she had lain. Still this would not have been impossible, but the changing shape of his ears and nose was troublesome. Put all together, the signs were seen to be ominous.

"They said I was possessed by a water-spirit," Crika said, "a child of the *tylwyth teg*. When I reached my twelfth summer they gave me a boat with provisions for a cycle of the moon, and sent me away. I have not seen my people since." He had wandered the marshes, living on marshweed and eels, and little else. Once or twice he paddled close to the village, hoping to peer through the reeds for signs of his family. But he never saw them. "And so I have learned to be alone," he concluded.

"I, too, have no friends," said Morla, thinking of Crwban's hearth, of lost memories of childhood. She lowered her eyes, struggling with choices. The sun had set, and darkness was spreading quickly in the reeds. "I must go," she said, and stood, turning toward the shore.

"Wait! Please." He took her hand in his, then stood beside her and she saw she had been correct about his height. Nearly half again as tall as her, but almost as slight. "Wait, Morla. Stay with me. It will be dark soon and you will lose your way through the bog."

Morla knew she could not lose her way, even in the deepest night. The bog and surrounding marsh were more home to her than the tribal camp. But Crika wanted her to stay. Perhaps that was reason enough. "Where, Crika?" she asked. "We cannot spend the night on a tussock of marsh reeds!"

"Come, I know a place," he answered, tipping his boat upright. The first quarter moon was already high in the sky. Its light cast a glow upon the marsh mists as they swirled slowly in the breeze. Briefly, across the marshes and to their left, the high tor of a fog shrouded island appeared in the moonlight. Crika gestured. "Around the other side of that island," he said.

"Ynys y Niwl? But no one goes there! Crwban says it is an enchanted place."

Crika slipped the flat bottomed boat into the water. "Just another island in the marsh," he said. "No one lives there except thrushes and hares. How can it be dangerous? Besides, we're not going there. Just to a little island around the other side, where I stay sometimes. Ynysig, I call it." The look in his eyes told her it was more dangerous than he said, but he was hoping against hope she would go with him.

Morla stood in the moonlight and mist, between Crika's boat and Crwban's bed. And she decided.

~

The soft rushing of the water and quiet hiss of reeds along the side of the boat seemed like music. Crika hummed as he poled the boat around the east end of Ynys y Niwl through marsh that was for the most of the year wet bogland, heading for the Bryw channel. Crwban would never come looking for her, Morla knew, but he would be furious when she returned.

I'll tell him I was lost in the marsh, she thought. He would not believe her, but would pretend to in order to save face in the camp. It was not a thing of honour for a chieftain's young wife to go missing for the night. He would back her story publicly, but she shivered when she thought of how he would punish her inside his roundhouse. *Perhaps I will not go back at all*, she told herself.

The boat scraped to a stop on solid ground. "Here is Ynysig," said Crika, and he helped her step out onto the soft earth.

Ynysig was a small island, a slight rise in the marsh bed, really. In summer it was merely the raised end of Ynys y Niwl's long western arm where rose Bryn Fyrtwyddon, the hill of myrtles. But then, and through the winter, it was separated from the larger island by a marsh channel. Willows ringed the shore, between open stands of marsh sedge. On the western flank a small spring offered fresh water. The crown of the island rose as a small grassy hill, looking bare in the moonlight. Crika stopped at a weathered lean-to and found a fur to wrap around Morla's shoulders against the night chill. Apparently he came here often enough to keep shelter and supplies, she thought.

"Come," he said, taking her hand, and together they climbed the small rise to the center of the islet. Though it rose only slightly higher than the surrounding marsh, it was enough to lift them above the evening's ground mist. Spread out before them in all directions under the moon was a smooth white sea of cloud. The willow crowns formed a ring around them and Morla could see Ynysig was tiny indeed. Not more than two hundred of her paces across. Straight ahead, beyond the Bryw channel, rose the hills of Ynys y Niwl, including the high and mysterious tor. To her left, the tops of marsh isles grew here and there above the mist, finally reaching the tor of Bryn Llyffaint, which some said lay at the edge of a vast and deep sea. The whole was surrounded at a distance, as if by the rim of a bowl, by the hills of Mendydd, Pennard, and Pwlborfa. A light breeze came from the northwest, whispering through the dry quaking-grass at her feet.

The crown of Ynysig seemed to shimmer in the moonlit breeze. Here and there among the tall grasses were the year end remnants of knapweed and trefoil, and the bare tangles of dog roses. Near the crest of the hill the naked branches of an ancient whitethorn raised to the sky. Morla followed their pointing fingers upward and gazed at the stars, finding the Hunter low in the sky, the Sisters a bit higher overhead, and, from horizon to horizon the long bright Cowpath. She felt Crika's arm enfold her waist, the gentle warmth of his slight body. She turned to him, but his eyes were still on the heavens.

"There is magic here," she whispered.

He bent and kissed her lightly on her forehead. She raised her head, seeing the moon over his shoulder, and his lips touched hers. Softly, then more intently, and then with the growing passion of need that came from years of loneliness. Morla knew of the relentless insistence of male passion from Crwban. Something to be endured but not shared. But this was something different. In this kiss, Crika gave as well as took, and a warmth Morla had never known spread through her body. She raised her arms to encircle his neck, drawing him more deeply into the kiss, closing her eyes to the turning stars overhead.

And then she was lying with him on the moss and soft loam of the hilltop amid the high grass, drawing him to her, drawing him in. They spent the night in the intense sweetness of discovered love, until the sun rose over the ridge of Bryn Pennard in the morning. As she lay in Crika's arms, their covering furs damp with dew, she knew they had done what she and Crwban had been unable to. With the certainty a woman understands and a man finds unfathomable, Morla knew she had conceived a child.

~

"No!" she cried, great shuddering sobs shaking her body, her face wet with tears. "Crika, how can you say such a thing?" She turned from him, fell to her knees, and continued to cry.

The days and nights since their first time on the top of Ynysig had been delightfully happy for Morla. She had helped him to repair and enlarge the old lean-to. During the day she went with him in the boat to gather marshweed and sometimes a fish for food. In the evenings they would sit atop Ynysig, telling each other imaginary tales of Ynys y Niwl across the marsh. At night she would lie with him under the furs, and they would make love, and she would fall asleep in his arms. All the while, within the warmth of her belly, a child began to grow.

Then came the morning, when frost was on the grasses and the curve of her belly had begun to show, that Crika told her of his fears. They had not yet risen from their sleeping furs. She lay in the crook of his arm, and he was stroking her long hair.

"Morla, I am afraid."

She shifted and looked at him, his usually spiked hair curling around his face in morning disarray. "Afraid?" she asked.

"It is lonely and dangerous out here in the marsh," he said. Our shelter is poor, the cold is coming. Already we eat only marshweed. Soon there will be little of that. It is not a good place for a pregnant woman. I fear for you, and for the child."

She shifted closer, pressing her breasts and growing belly against him, reaching out and drawing his face to hers for a kiss. "I am safe, here, with you," she said.

Crika sat up, raising his knees to his chest, folding his arms across them, drawing himself into a tight ball. He pretended to look at something out in the marsh, fighting to withhold what he knew must be said.

"I think you should go back to Crwban."

"What!"

"Just, just until the baby is born. You'll be safer with your clan. Then I'll come back for you, in the night.

"No!" she cried as she turned from him. "Crika, how can you say such a thing?"

~

But in the end, with the growing awareness of an expectant mother, Morla knew the wisdom in his words. She had been carrying the child for three cycles of the moon when he returned her to the mainland, poling his boat slowly back through the night marshes. Their hearts broke as one while they held one another in the dawn mist. Then she turned on the path to Crwban's village. Crika pushed off the bank into the marsh, and headed he knew not where.

~

Crwban had finished his morning meal and was already sitting with the old warriors around what they pretended was a council fire when the ghost of his young wife, disheveled and dirty, walked into camp. She walked right up to him where he sat, his mouth open, drinking gourd dropped at his side. She reached out her hands to him.

"I am home, husband," she said. "I have missed you so much."

Under the watching eyes of all the camp he stood silently. Without a word, his face a blank, he lifted her in his arms. With her arms about his neck and her head resting on his

40

shoulder he turned from the fire, and slowly crossed the common area of the camp. They disappeared through the door of his roundhouse.

He did not beat her, as she had feared he would. But he put her down in one corner and retreated to another, as far from her as he could get. He stared at her, his face filled with cold rage.

Morla knew it would be best to begin her tale before the profanity of his questions could begin. She told him of setting out on one of her walks in the bogs the day he last saw her, taking great care to remind him of the joyful passion of their lovemaking the night before. It wasn't true, of course, but his arrogance would supply the needed belief. She had lost her way and spent the night in the bogs, pulling reeds and grasses over her for warmth. The next day she tried to find her way back, but got turned around and headed farther north. Several days of this wandering had left her weak and hungry. She collapsed on a small rise of dry ground and lay unconscious while the sun traveled across the sky, then through the dark of another night. In the morning a hunting party found her. They took her to their village among the wells that border the north marshes, where she spent many days recovering her strength and health.

"As I regained my strength I knew I was with child. I came home as soon as I could" She smiled at Crwban and moved toward him across the floor of the roundhouse. His face was still flushed with anger. He retreated further into his corner as she approached. Morla came to him, sitting beside him. Putting a look of love into her eyes she said, "Dear husband, I remembered the passion of our last night together, and I knew at last I would bear you a son." She took his hand and placed it on the curve of her belly. He began to soften then, and she kissed his face. "Crwban," she said with tears in her eyes, "It is so good to be home, and to be carrying your child." She drew his arms around her, sinking back against him. When she felt him tighten the embrace, and the touch of his face in her hair, she knew it had worked.

~

Cycles of the moon passed in the camp. Morla's belly grew, as the cold of winter came and went. Crwban often walked her around the encampment, arm proudly around her shoulders, showing her off to all.

"Look at Morla," he would crow. "She's giving me a big, healthy heir – the new chief!"

Then, just before midsummer, the marsh flush began to appear on her belly. It began on the underside as a small, dull patch of blue-green, just below her navel. At first she was able to cover it on her dark skin with an ointment of oak bark and walnut hulls ground in sheep's fat. But the flush grew and spread until it completely covered her abdomen. By her final month it was too obvious to hide any longer. During a particularly callous and inept attempt at lovemaking, Crwban wiped away some of the ointment, and discovered the rash. With a scream he leaped up and backed away into the shadows. There was only one way for marsh flush to appear on the belly of a pregnant woman. The child was not his! Morla had lain with a spirit-possessed outcast of the marshes! The child in her belly was *bendith y mamau*, a "mother's blessing" spawn of the fairies. In the dead of night Crwban dragged his young, pregnant wife into the reeds, dumped her in a flatboat, and cast her off into the marshes, there to die of exposure. He would find some excuse to tell the people in the camp. Bandits had come in the night, perhaps. Anything rather than admit the child was not his.

~

But as usual Crwban was not thinking clearly. Even in the marshes it is hard to die of exposure in midsummer. Heavily pregnant in her final days, Morla pulled her boat through the reeds, cutting her hands on the sharp sedge. She headed for Ynysig, where she had been with Crika so many moon cycles ago. When she arrived, the island was empty and quiet, save for the calling and scuttling of marsh creatures. The lean-to had fallen into disrepair. There were no supplies. Crika had left, and there was no sign of where he had gone.

Morla was utterly alone. She sank dully onto a willow root hanging out over the water, not knowing what to do or where to go.

She sat for days, neither eating nor sleeping, staring into the marsh, becoming weaker and weaker. When her grief overwhelmed her, she cried to the sacred spirits of the marsh to take her soul, and that of her child, that she might die in peace. Finally she waded into the waters, calling her prayer, and the waters took her soul, allowing her the peace she needed to die. She slipped beneath the marsh waters. All was still.

In that peace her body was washed up on Ynysig, beneath the willows. It was there that Crika found her. His heart breaking with love, he held Morla in his arms and cried out to the goddess of the water.

The goddess, hearing his cries, sent spirits of the marshes to whisper Morla's song in the trees, guiding her back.

Come, child of the whispering reeds,
marsh daughter, wand'ring alone.
Back from the call of the ancient seas;
from where the dead have gone.

Daughter of chieftains, bride of the fens,
lost on a distant shore,
come to us through the watery glens,
back to your home once more.

As she awoke, her body began to pulse with the power of birth and, with the marsh spirits around her singing the songs of the goddess, her daughter was born.

~

Now the marsh folk speak of the daughter as a wild dark child, half sprite and half human, with coppery hair. So do they bring all such children, born with too much marsh power, to

Ynys y Niwl for the priestesses to raise. But among the priestesses Morla's daughter is described in all her beauty, as a child crafted by love.

The rest of Morla's tale is lost to memory. She and Crika, and Anwyledd their daughter, faded into the marshes and were not seen again.

Ynysig, the tiny islet in the marsh, became known as Bol Forla, Morla's Belly. It has ever been a sacred place, wrapped about with this tale. Women go there for their unborn children to be blessed, for the goddess to ease the birthing, and to heal the damage wrought in the tide of giving birth. Some, who have courage, seek its shores when their hearts are broken for they have fallen in love with men they should not love. But always, it is said, through the willow branches and the quake-grass the song of Morla can be heard across the little isle in the whispering of the wind.

Daughter of chieftains, bride of the fens,
come back to your home once more.

Chapter Five
Boudicca's Revolt

The news reached Llan y gelli even before the arrival of its messengers, for men must stop along the way to rest, but news is under no such compulsion. By the time Rys and Cledwyn stood, filthy and exhausted, before Cadael in the chieftain's hut, the latter had already heard reports from three traders and several Dubh-bunadh farmers from across the Hafren. Cadael was not happy with the delay, and had already summoned his council, which included the herbalist healer. Cethin sat in the shadows, having no desire to be a part of the unfolding drama.

"Three days!" Cadael thundered. "Three days it has taken my own men to reach me with news of her defeat, while all the countryside has been buzzing with the tale for two sunrises!"

The travel weary messengers stared intently at the rushes upon the floor. It did not do to answer Cadael yea or nay when he was in such a mood. Not unless he looked you in the eye and asked a specific question. Rys and Cledwyn were hoping to avoid such a misfortune, steadfastly keeping their own eyes downcast.

"Look at me, you fools!" he bellowed. His head, as well as his beard and belly, was filled with barley beer. But if he was not sober enough yet to fully grasp the catastrophe, he could certainly deal with the two idiots he had once called messengers.

For fifteen years Cadael had led the Silure resistance to Rome. For fifteen years he had been surrounded first by the II Augusta Legion under Vespasian, and then the XIV Gemina under Seutonius Paulinus to the east and north. The hills and heavy forests of the Silures favored their tactics of small raids with quick, highly mobile bands of warriors. In all this time

Cadael had managed to avoid head-on conflict with full sized Roman units. As a result, the Silures were still nominally free, while most of the other tribes had long since capitulated through treaty, or been defeated in battle. Now the II Augusta seemed content to consolidate it gains in the south, while Seutonius, having gotten word of a growing druid presence on Ynys Mona, cut off his forays into the Silure forests and headed north where he could use his legion in direct conflict. It was Seutonius and the XIV Gemina who was responsible for the slaughter from which Fianna had escaped. He would have scoured Mona and destroyed the druids entirely to the last woman and child, had not the Iceni and Trinovantes chosen that moment to begin their revolt in the east of the Brythonic island under Queen Boudicca. Seutonius and the XIVth were summoned to the new Roman settlement at Londinium to stop Boudicca's forces, which had reached perhaps 250,000 warriors. He saw at once that Londinium, like Camulodunum, was lost. The IX Hispana Legion had been routed at Camulodunum, and the rebel army had so far slain nearly 80,000 Roman sympathizers. So Seutonius turned back west into the midlands. He took a stand near the Roman fort of Manduessedum, near the capital of the Catuvellauni tribe to await Boudicca's advance. It was there that warriors from several other tribes, including a handful of Silures sent by Cadael, joined the rebel ranks.

Cethin's mind had been wandering, in the shadows of the chief's roundhouse. Most in Llan y gelli knew these broader details of the revolt. After the horror on Ynys Mon, it was exhilarating to learn of one Roman defeat after another. True, Boudicca's march had been taking a ghastly toll on Celts as well as Romans, for collaborators were given no mercy. Tales had reached Llan y gelli of burnings and crucifixions. Noblewomen who had become too Romanized, it was said, were impaled upon spikes, and had their breasts cut off and sewn to their mouths. That was the way with the Romans, Cethin reflected. When they did not have the numbers to defeat a tribe outright, they turned the tribes upon one another with a savagery even the Romans loathed and feared.

"The XIV Gemina took up a position in a narrow defile on the side of a hill," Rys was saying. His voice brought Cethin's thoughts back from the shadows. "There was a dense forest to their rear and, in front of them, a broad stream we would have to cross before attacking uphill."

"Fool!" Cadael said. "They think to win battles by standing in line." There was a sneer of derision on his lips, even if the shadow in his eyes betrayed his respect for the disciplined troops.

"They formed their ranks there," Cledwyn added, waiting for reinforcements from the II Augusta, which never came. Our scouts told us to expect no more than 10,000 to stand against us. We outnumbered them twenty-five to one."

Cethin listened as Cledwyn and Rys went on with the report. It was early morning when Boudicca's forces drew up across the stream from the Roman lines. Mist swirled in ragged wanderings along the line of the stream. Here and there, where the rising sun was able to break through, it glinted off polished Roman armor. Boudicca, standing at the stream with her chieftains, immediately saw the problem. Her numbers were overwhelming, but she would not be able to use them. The Romans might not be able to escape from the defile, but its steep sides, and the woods to the rear, prevented any flanking movements she might try. All she could do would be to meet them head-on, with a front rank no broader than theirs. Boudicca had the numbers, but the Romans had training and discipline, and she knew that counted for more. She stared up the hill to the Roman line. A swift breeze had begun to scatter the mists, and both sides could see one another clearly. Roman shields and gladii. Inceni and Trinovante pikes and spears.

Even to the Romans Boudicca was an imposing sight. Queen of the Iceni, her royal bearing was obvious. She was taller than even most men. Long, red hair that fell to her hips flew and swirled like war banners in the fresh breeze. She wore a tunic of red, yellow, and blue, covered by a red woolen cloak that was fastened at her shoulder with a golden knotwork brooch. A heavy gold torc, sign of her authority, circled her neck.

She reached into the folds of her cloak and pulled out a large gray hare, holding it high for her battle line to see, her left hand around the long ears, her right under the creature's buttocks, so the hare was presented upright. Only Boudicca was close enough to see the fright in its eyes. Crossing the stream to the Roman side, to the nervous response of Roman armor, she set the hare down in the grass. Instantly the creature raced along the stream's bank, stopped, paused a moment looking around and sniffing the air. Suddenly it turned, leaped across the stream on several rocks, and took off toward the rebel line as though it had wings, finding refuge in some tall grass and brambles on the right flank of the line.

Boudicca's shout was harsh, sending shivers down the backs of all who heard. "Victory is ours!" cried the Queen whose name itself means "Victory." And the rebel lines cheered. One of her chieftains drove to her side in her chariot. She climbed in and rode back and forth before her ranks, exhorting them to victory. By her side were her two daughters, whose brutal rape by Roman soldiers had helped to spark the revolt. She addressed the battle line not as an aristocrat seeking to recapture her lost wealth, but as one of them, seeking to regain lost freedom. Seeking revenge for the flogging she had been given, and the lost chastity of her young daughters.

"Men of the Iceni and the Trinovantes," she shouted. "It is a just cause we serve this day, and you have seen by the divination that Andraste has promised us the victory! Though I am a woman I am prepared to fight. If men wish to be slaves, it is their own business!" She turned and charged the Roman line, and her army followed, slowly pressed into a narrow front by the steep sides of the valley.

The mistake was quickly obvious. The rebels had no skill in the tactics of open field combat with broad lines. They had no room to maneuver in any case, and could not bring

48

overwhelming numbers to bear at any point along the line. In the opening charge, thousands fell to the Roman javelins. Gaining quick advantage, the Romans formed a battle wedge and advanced into the rebel ranks. When Boudicca's forces tried to flee, they were boxed in by their own supply wagons, including the camps of their own families which they had formed in a circle at the rear. The slaughter was massive and quick. Nearly eighty thousand of the rebels fell that day, compared to less than four hundred Romans. Boudicca managed to flee the battlefield, but the tales say she died by poison at her own hands, to avoid capture. None in the battle, nor among those hearing of it in Cadael's roundhouse at Llan y gelli, knew that in far-off Rome the Emperor Nero had nearly been convinced by the early successes of Boudicca's uprising to withdraw all Roman forces from the Brythonic lands. As it was, her fall at Manduessedum marked the end of freedom for the tribes, and the beginning of Roman rule.

Rys and Cledwyn finished their report of the battle and were given leave to find food and drink. Cethin left the gloom of the roundhouse for the cold sunlight of the late winter day, seeking a high place along the wooden palisade atop the south embankment where he could breathe fresh air again and clear his mind. What little interest he may once have had in strategy and tactics had disappeared during the night he sat in the forest with his dying father. It was life and death he had come to care about. The healing of the injured in body or in spirit, or the granting of a gentle death. He found a quiet place on the palisade, away from the sentinels, and leaned upon the rough hewn logs. Rolling hills stretched away into the distance, the broad mouth of the Hafren flashed silver in the sun. It was not the success of the opening campaign that held his thoughts, nor the tragedy of the final blunder. It was the horror wrought in the lives of individual people, those who were insignificant in the eyes of generals or historians.

The final tale of Boudicca had begun with such horror, he knew. Had begun with the death of her husband, Prasutagus, only weeks ago. The first wave of Romans had hardly come ashore when Prasutagus capitulated, realizing the Iceni were no match for the Legions on the open plains in the east. This decision supposedly made the Iceni an independent ally of Rome. As was expected, Prasutagus revised his will to make the Emperor co-heir to his kingdom, along with his wife and daughters. But Rome did not recognize the inheritance rights of women, especially the daughters of a Brythonic tribal chieftain. The lands of the Iceni were summarily annexed by the Roman governor as if they were conquered territory. When Boudicca objected, she was brutally flogged, and her daughters raped before her eyes. All family property was confiscated. Prasutagus had lived well on money borrowed from Roman lenders, all of whom called in their loans upon his death in support of the Imperial claim. Boudicca and all the Iceni leading families were left destitute, little better than outlaws. Bristling with desire for revenge, Boudicca accepted the tribes' request to lead them in revolt, but she and her daughters would bear the scars of injury and humiliation for a lifetime.

"There are herbs for treating lash wounds," Cethin muttered into the air, "and for dealing with the unwanted offspring of Roman scum."

But, and this he said in the silence of his heart, *there is no medicine for a ruined honour or a broken heart.* Had he given Cadael more credit, he might have understood how deeply the Silure chief felt the same way about his own people and the settlement of Llan y gelli. He watched a circle of buzzards wheeling slowly overhead. *How long before the rape of Llan y gelli, now?* he wondered. Perhaps Fianna would have wisdom to help him understand the sorrow in his heart. He looked once more to the glint of the Hafren in the distance and the misty shadows of the nearer Mendydds beyond. In his heart he felt the marshes of Affalon that lay beyond the hills, out of his sight. He left the palisade, and headed for the healer's hut.

~

Fianna was stronger every day. The sword wound was

50

healing well after the first setbacks. In midwinter, not long after the wound had closed over, the skin around it began to redden, and became hot to the touch. In spite of all the care Cethin had taken, there was a danger it would putrefy. He had to reopen it, cleanse it, and let the slow healing begin all over again. Now at the approach of the equinox all seemed to be well. With the healing of her flesh, Fianna had begun to feel a lifting of her spirit and sometimes even a lightening of her heart. She was well enough to walk a bit in the forest, and there to visit the graves of the friends whom she had not seen die. Once grief was able to take its course, true healing began to follow.

So it was that Cethin was surprised, upon entering the hut, to find Fianna sitting in the shadows, her face gray as ashes, tears in her eyes and on her cheeks. Having seen the massacre on Ynys Mon with her eyes, she had now seen the slaughter at Meduessedum with the sight of a priestess. Fianna was the only person in Llan y gelli that morning who understood the full tragedy of Boudicca's defeat. Rome would not now be leaving the Brythonic shores. The Imperial Eagle had come to stay.

"While you were at the council," she told Cethin, "Sianed came to me in my mind, and Boudicca with her, bruised and bleeding, and feeling the first effects of poison." With Cethin's help she struggled from the floor to sit on the edge of her cot. Then, thinking better of it, she lay down, still favoring her side where she had been pierced with the Roman sword. "I am weaker again, Healer," she said.

"Rest, Mother, I will make some tea of chamomile and valerian." As he set the water to boil over the small hearth fire, Fianna reached out, and shared the meeting of the three women, in his mind.

Priestess, Sianed had said, *it is all the more important now that you return to Affalon before the frosts.* The Lady turned to look behind her, and it was then Fianna saw Boudicca as she had died. The Queen had not escaped the battlefield unharmed, to die in peace. There were deep gladius wounds across her left thigh and the side of her face. Blood no longer

51

flowed, but caked on her opened skin like black mud. It was then Fianna had slumped against the wall of the hut and fallen slowly to the floor. Boudicca did not speak in words, but in her eyes was deep grief. Just visible behind her were shades of the XIV Gemina; So powerful had been the energy of their attack that they had found their way into this vision with her. She seemed not to notice, or was beyond caring.

Boudicca was nearly successful in saving us, said Sianed. *Her march from Camelodunum to Londinium very nearly convinced Nero to withdraw his legions and leave the Brythonic tribes to themselves. Now they will stay, with their arrogance and their violent gods. Already they plan to return to the west country, Fianna. By winter we must draw Affalon deep into the mists. You must return to us by then.*

Fianna's heart grew heavy. *My Lady,* she answered, *if what you see is true, the Silures will stand alone. I will be well enough to travel by midsummer, but I need time to teach the Marsh Tales to Cethin.* She paused, hesitated, looking to the shade of Boudicca standing beside Sianed. *My Lady, it is worse than you know in the countryside. Our own people become as savage as the Romans.* She let her mind wander through the tales from Camelodunum and Londinium, sharing with Sianed images of burning homes, of Brythons crucified by Brythons or burned at the stake. The agony that filled her shook even Sianed in far-off Affalon. *She is not completely a hero, My Lady. She has slain more among the tribes than among the soldiers of Rome.* Again Fianna turned her gaze upon the Iceni Queen. Her agony turned to anger, the anger of a young priestess who for many years cared for and taught the young children on Ynys y Niwl. And in that anger judgment wrestled with compassion. *You are courageous Boudicca Queen, she said evenly. But you have brought the end upon us.* As if in response, the once powerful Iceni leader faded from the vision, as she would for many generations fade from Brythonic memory.

Fianna turned again to Sianed. *My Lady, give me more*

time with Cethin. I need more time if I am to leave the wisdom of the Tales in the world.

Sianed's voice was soft, bearing concern rather than command. *Only do not tarry overlong Fi,* she said, *if you wish to find Ynys y Niwl once more.*

~

"Mother, here is your tea,"

Cethin's voice roused Fianna from her reverie, and she rose to sit again on the edge of her cot. The vision had taken much from her. She was tired, and cold. The tea warmed her hands as well as her belly. For some time she sat, sipping quietly, Cethin sitting on the low stool beside her where he had so often sat to tend her wounds. Would the wounds within ever heal, she wondered? And what wounds awaited Cethin, the young Dubh-bunadh healer in service to the proud Silure tribe?

In the silence of the hut Fianna said, "Cadael wants to avenge the Iceni defeat." At first Cethin thought it was a question, then remembered he often could not explain how she knew things. "It is a foolish hope," she said.

"Cadael has stood alone in the west since the defeat of Caradoc," Cethin offered. It has been along struggle. He knows he is not strong enough to take the fight to the Romans. He fears he is not strong enough to defend his own lands. The hills and forests are his best allies, and he uses them well against the small Roman units able to enter. But for a man who would lead armies in battle, forest skirmishes are an unsatisfactory substitute."

Fianna sighed quietly. "Cadael is motivated by pride. Or at best by patriotism, which is another form of pride. You, Healer, are motivated by compassion. That is perhaps nobler, but equally as unhelpful. Cadael looks at Boudicca and sees the next battle to be fought. You look at her and see individuals, on both sides, whose lives have been destroyed. In Boudicca My Lady sees the land, which was from the beginning and will be always, seeking to be at peace, to remain unstained by the violent blood and tears of hatred, to be left in peace to bring

53

forth life, and to shelter the dead."

"But, Mother, surely that is all connected?"

"Surely it is," said Fianna, "but those with responsibilities seldom see it. Nor do they wish to have it shown to them"

"My responsibility is herbs," Cethin answered. They work well with individual patients," his gaze went to Fianna's side, "but are of no avail in the struggle of tribes and empires."

"Cethin," she said, using his name rather than his title, "You are a greater healer than you know, but you will soon need more than herbs for the healing of your people." She handed him her cup. "More tea is needed, young Healer, if you are to learn the Marsh Tales of Affalon."

Chapter Six
Marsh Mallows and Marsh Tales

"We will not find marsh mallows in these hills, I suppose," said Fianna. They grow everywhere along the shores of Ynys y Niwl."

"Later in the year, when they come into bloom, I collect some in the salt marshes along the Hafren channel," Cethin answered. "Sometimes we find a few in the bogs nearby, when their seeds have wandered north. Not enough to gather for healing purposes, but the children love to spy out their pink blossoms at midsummer."

The days had begun to warm, and Cethin allowed Fianna to roam farther afield from the gates of Llan y gelli. They shared healing knowledge, gathering herbs together in the woods and clearings of the old forest. Fianna enjoyed their talks. Some of her earliest charges on Ynys y Niwl would have been as old as Cethin now, so it was like seeing them actually grown up. She thought of little Marni helping to collect sunwort on Bryn Fyrtwyddon. He would now be . . . No, she realized, he would still be ten summers younger than the young healer at her side. Had it been only fifteen summers since she had last been with the community on Ynys y Niwl? It seemed to her as lifetimes ago. And Cethin, she knew, seemed young to her only in comparison to the age settling into her own heart. Yet he was to her very much like a son of her own that she never had.

In a sheltered clearing warmed by the noon sun they sat down to eat and sort their early harvest.

"Mallows are usually not much help to me," said Cethin, continuing the thought. "They are good for shallower cuts, not the sort Silure fighters usually come home with." He was separating new, green sunwort leaves - perhaps that is why she had thought of Marni - from their stems, and placing them in a small bag. "When the Romans return we will need all the sunwort we can find."

"Or comfrey," Fianna suggested, "if only it could heal the spirit from within, as it does the flesh."

When they had done with their sorting they lay back against the bole of a giant old oak, listening to the wind in the branches, watching gathering clouds in the west that promised a storm soon.

"Tell me about the Marsh Tales," Cethin said. "Are they all like Morla's?"

"Yes and no," answered Fianna. "For they come from different times and many places. Some are happy, many are sad, but they are remembered because they bear the ancient wisdom of Affalon.

Cethin leaned forward, resting his arms upon raised knees, his head in his hands. "Wisdom *about* Affalon, or wisdom *from* Affalon for others? We need much wisdom of our own these days."

"Both," she said. "The wisdom of Affalon is timeless and knows no earthly boundaries. But the tales are truly tales of the old marshes, and have their origins there.

"I am now the last person in the wide world outside of Affalon who knows these tales, Cethin. They must not be lost forever. You must learn them, and pass them on to others, if you will. No one from outside the marshes has ever heard them before. You are the first."

It had been growing darker as they spoke and, finally, the first drops of rain began to fall through the bare tree branches. Cethin looked down at the ground, watching the drops splashing upon the dry leaves.

"Why me? Why a Dubh-bunadh herbalist living among the Silures this far from the marshes?"

"One might say it is because you are available," Fianna smiled. "Or that you are in the right place at the right time. But in the marshes we understand the meaning of currents, Cethin. You were brought to Llan y gelli on one such current, I on another."

Cethin rose and offered her his hand. "That is good enough explanation for me, I suppose. But first we must keep you warmer, and much drier." She stood, with his help, and they headed for the gate.

As they came out of the forest they passed a small bog.

"Look, Cethin, there!" Fianna pointed to the edge of the bog, but Cethin saw nothing save the brown tangle of last summer's vegetation. He followed her off the path, looking to the clouds and trying to determine how far away the heavy rainfall might be. Her hand on his shoulder brought his gaze back to earth.

"Mallow," she said, simply, and squatted before the matted tangle of brown stems. Cethin knelt beside her, but still could see nothing.

"See," she said, lifting some of the dead stalks. "They die back in the autumn. But see, the young green shoots are just starting to come forth." She brushed aside the old vegetation and fallen leaves, and there among the brown tangle were the new shoots. Brushing a little deeper into the soil, she uncovered the tell-tale mass of yellow roots. Carefully, avoiding the new growth, Fianna covered the roots and broke off part of a brown stalk that still bore several leaves and a hollow crescent seed pod.

"Come, Healer," she said, standing. "I will tell you about marsh mallows, and then about marsh tales."

The rain began falling in earnest as they entered the gate of Llan y gelli.

~

When they had dried themselves and restored the hearth fire, Fianna spread the old marsh mallow plant out on Cethin's cutting board.

"In the marshes we call this plant *cwbl-iechyd* for its powers of healing," she said. "They say whoever eats a bit of mallow leaf shall that day be free of all illness."

Cethin sat next to her, bringing the hot tea.

"I know of its healing uses. But there are many other

57

plants that do the same work. Why do you find the mallow so interesting?"

Fianna picked up a dried leaf and crumbled it into their tea. "Its power has lessened over the winter," she said, "But still it will help the chamomile."

"You are right, healer.," she continued. "There is more to this plant than its healing powers." She picked up another leaf and showed it to him. "The leaf is pointed, like a spear head. Higher on the plant, like this, the point has a small lobe on either side, three lobes for the three-fold nature of the goddess."

"Are there not many goddesses?" asked Cethin.

"There are many goddesses. But when we speak of them all at once, we speak as of one. And her three-fold nature is that of all women; Maiden, the life-bearer; Mother, the nurturer; and Crone, the guide between the worlds. The mallow leaf is sweet to the taste, as the presence of the goddess is sweet to the heart. For these reasons many women carry a mallow leaf with them always, to remind them of the presence of the goddess in their lives.

"Look at the edge," she said. "The many sharp teeth around the edge remind us of the many hardships of life. But as we seek the goddess within, we are empowered to face those hardships. Most healers know of the power of marsh mallow to heal the skin outwardly. Few have learned that drinking mallow tea brings healing from within, in the flesh as well as the spirit."

"It does sweeten the tea," said Cethin.

"As it also sweetens the spirit," Fianna repeated. "And as marsh mallow brings healing from within, so also do the Marsh Tales."

"How is it that stories can heal?" Cethin asked.

"Perhaps," said Fianna, "they make a connection between what you carry inside and the experiences of others. Shared joy is more joyful, shared pain finds more comfort. Stories of hope lighten despair, and tales of triumph inspire endurance. When you hear a story you become part of it, and when that happens, you are no longer alone. Perhaps, and this is most important, stories enable you to share a healing experience you might not be able to have on your own."

Cethin rose to pour more tea, then sat down again, his eyes searching for more understanding. "So a woman hearing or remembering Morla's Tale might find encouragement in childbirth, even if she could never go to Ynys Bol Forla?"

"Not only encouragement, Cethin, but physical strength and ease. And, if needed, even healing. The Marsh Tales are ancient myths, symbolic stories that carry power in their very message. You might say they do what they talk about, in the life of the storyteller as well as the one who hears."

"It sounds like magic," said Cethin.

"If you choose to call it so. It is a way of connecting with the sacred."

It was raining harder, and the wind seemed to drive the wet and cold through the wattle sides of the healer's hut. Darkness of later afternoon was settling in. Cethin built up the small fire and found furs for their shoulders. All thought of an evening meal was forgotten.

"Tell me, then," he said. "Tell me, Mother Fianna, about the Tales."

"*Morla's Tale* you already know," she said. "It is the oldest of tales, for the sorrows of women and the birthing of children are the oldest of memories. Old as the marshes themselves. Yet it comes first in the telling, for the truth of the other tales emerges from it. In time, as time exists in the tales, it lies midway between the birth of the Lady and her coming to Ynys y Niwl. *Morla's Tale*, the Tale of *The Dark Lady of Llyn y Cysgodion*, *Doeth and the Marsh Sedge* and *The Lost Land of Iwerydd* are tales of beginnings. Yet they tell not the true record of how things came to be, but the truth of how things are. Together they tell of the lot of women, the nature of the Lady, the settlement of the marshes, and the meaning of the stone temples. But those are the themes of the tales only. Each has deeper truths buried within.

"There follow tales of living, and there are six, bearing lessons of life.

"*The Lights of the Ellylldan* is a tale of courage and trust. It tells of the origin of our community of priestesses. *The Visit of the Bendith y Mamau* is a tale of hope. *The Old Frog of Bryn Llyffaint* is a humorous tale of the power of humilty. *The Tinner and the Coblynau*, a story of the coming of the ancestors of Eosaidh of Cornualle to these shores, is a tale of faith in the midst of darkness. *Hiraeth's Tears* tells us of the sorrows of love denied, and the failure of old and new traditions to find common ground. And the tale of *The Gwraig Annwn* does much the same. In the joys and sorrows, humor and tragedy, of these six tales lie deep lessons for the living of life.

"Finally, there are tales of completion. *The Coming of the Lady* is about the creation of the community of Priestesses on Ynys y Niwl, and their emergence from the ancient shadows. *The Dragon's Womb* is a tale of power.

"These then are the Marsh Tales:
Morla's Belly
The Dark Lady of Llyn y Cysgodion
Doeth and the Marsh Sedge
The Lost Land of Iwerydd
The Lights of the Ellylldan
The Visit of the Bendith y Mamau
The Old Frog of Bryn Llyffaint
The Tinner and the Coblynau
Hiraeth's Tears
The Gwraig Annwn
The Coming of the Lady
The Dragon's Womb

"The tales were told by different peoples, in other times and from many places. We know not their origins, but tradition has drawn them together. And together the twelve form the unwritten body of lore that bears the ancient wisdom of

Affalon."

Indeed, Fianna wove her story with many more words than these, and with deep silences, so the telling lasted into the middle darkness of the night. The hearth fire had nearly gone out. Shadows were deep in the hut, and it was cold.

Cethin rose, feeling the stiffness in his body, knowing it must be even worse for the woman before him.

Fianna knew his thoughts. "It is late for both of us," she said, "and the tales need time for telling. Build up the fire for me, Cethin. These bones need some warmth in them before I sleep." She sat on the edge of her cot and drew the fur closer around her shoulders. Cethin put a few sticks on the fire and a few more beside her cot, should she want them in the night. A desire to learn the tales burned in his heart. This strange woman of the marshes whom he had brought back from the edge of death was about to lead him into a new life. Perhaps she might bring healing of a kind to the healer. He took his leave and stepped out into the cold night, drawing his furs about him as he headed towards his sleeping hut.

In the flickering shadows Fianna stretched out on her cot. Its feel had become familiar to her, the healer's hut almost seeming like her home. She let her mind drift, alone with her thoughts.

So this is why, my Lady, the currents have carried me here to the forests of the Silure. A young man of the Dubh-bunadh peoples seems such a strange choice to be the bearer of the sacred tales. Not twenty summers ago he might have been leaving my charge to dance before the fires at Dolgwyl Waun. Instead he was already fighting the soldiers of Rome. Surely there is a young woman in Llan y gelli who would make a better vessel for the ancient lore?

Sianed drifted into her thoughts, speaking to her. *It matters not, priestess, whether there is a better vessel. Doubtless there are many. But the currents have brought you together, and he is the choice. You have through the summer to teach him, but return to us here before the frosts.* She raised a

61

hand in blessing, and the calm gift of sleep washed over Fianna's heart. Outside, in the Silure forest, came the single cry of an owl, and the music of the night.

Chapter Seven
II. The Dark Lady of Llyn y Cysgodion

It was a time beyond the memory of times. The marshes were vast and dark, and the boundaries between earth, sea and sky were less certain than they are today. The Dark Lady was a rumor that haunted the reeds, hovered above the black waters, sank into the deep mud. All was empty and silent, save for the soft whisper of changing currents. For the marshes always were, but it was the Dark Lady who brought them to life.

The Mendydd were towering hills in those days, for no hand had begun to take their ores, and they cast their long shadows across the low marshes. Under those hills, in a place where land became bog, and bog became marsh and then open water, lay the reed ringed darkness of a shadowed lake. High above all, the changing cycles of the moon marked the slow passage of time, her silver face reflected unseen in the quiet waters. And so it went for cycles without end, and there was no change. The same turning of the moon. The same flowing of currents. The same silence. The same flickering patterns of light and dark. The same ancient lingering marsh.

But then the currents began to shift and change in the growing and dying reeds. Endless turnings of tides carved new channels in the black mud. Eddies became currents, currents became flows, flows turned and twisted back upon themselves. One moontide as the surface rippled beneath the full silver face in the heavens, the face reflecting back from the depths looked up, and recognized what it saw, and the waters were living and aware, and they called themselves 'She.' She saw the marsh water that surrounded her, and she called it Llyn y Cysgodion, and it was her home. At first the marsh knew her only as Llyf, which means *Current*, but with the coming of the first folk she was called Morwyn. In later tales she and those who followed her were often called Vivian, *Giver of Life*.

She rose from the depths as a darkly shimmering mist. Her face was as the reflection of the silver moon on the dark rippling waters of the flowing current; her eyes not so much black as deep, fathomless. She was short, little more than an arm span in height, and slightly built. Her skin was the color of shadows. Her long black hair fell to below her knees, where it disappeared rather than ended, and it swirled about her like the flow of the currents. She was clothed in marsh reeds, and her song was the sound of deep waters. Llyf was one with the water, and standing reeds, and the black mud. In that moment she knew she was the Dark Lady of Llyn y Cysgodion, though that was her only awareness, and she felt nothing but the slow passage of time.

In the ages that followed, the slow, inexorable flow of the marsh currents stirred something inside Llyf. Her awareness began to grow, and she knew of things that had not yet come to be; living things that would crawl and swim, walk and fly.

From the waters and the mud she called forth the marsh spirits: fur and feather, leaf and fin. They each bore within themselves the power to beget and to conceive, and they called forth more of their own kind, and the marsh swarmed with the new currents of Llyf. They danced with her in the channels of the marsh as the silver moon waned and grew, and the ancient stars shone overhead. As they came forth, from the first, simplest folk to very last, Llyf sang to them the same knowledge, and invited them to the gentle dance.

~

Deep in the waters of the flowing channels, where the primeval reeds stood in rich black mud, a new plant appeared and opened itself to her song. Llyf bent low over the dark waters. She reached forth a gentle hand to touch the tiny shoots, and she knew in herself it was Bog Moss. The new stems twined themselves around her fingers, growing in a soft green along the length of her arm, with thin mossy leaves like the finest thread spiraling around each stem. Finally small pink

64

flowers appeared, and Llyf welcomed Bog Moss to the marsh. Then, for the first time in the countless ages of her existence, Llyf spoke to another being.

"Welcome, Mwswgl," she said. "The marshes rejoice in your presence. But they do not need you. Learn what that means, and join us in the dance of life." Mwswgl loved the song of Llyf, and took her place in the way of things. Mosses and ferns, flowers and shrubs came forth from the marsh earth. They lived together, and they sang the same songs.

Above the quiet waters, hovering upon the tips of reeds, flashes of blue and green appeared in the summer sun as it filtered through the new branches of island trees. A blur of beating wings darted through the air. Llyf raised a cupped palm, and a flying thing landed upon her slender fingers. Within herself she knew it was Dragonfly. It sat gingerly in her hand; tiny legs tickling her olive skin. The soft, clear wings fluttered with the notes of her song, and Llyf welcomed Dragonfly to the marsh. She was getting used to speaking, for spirits were appearing here and there all around the Lake of Shadows.

"Welcome, Draig Athar," Llyf said. "The marshes rejoice in your presence. But they do not need you. Learn what that means, and join us in the dance." Draig loved the song of Llyf, and took her place in the way of things. Butterflies and beetles, spiders and bees came forth among the reeds. They lived together, and sang the same songs.

Other ages passed. Under the blue sky and white clouds there was a wild cry. Talons and feathered wings crossed in front of the sun, the shadow frightening those who swam in the waters or walked upon the bogs. Into Llyf's voice fell the tone of command. "Hush, loud one, be still." She lifted a dark forearm over her head and raised her shadowed eyes to the heavens. The bird dropped in slow circles and landed upon her arm, stretched and folded its wings, and stroked its beak upon her skin. In the depths of her being, Llyf knew this was Marsh Harrier, and felt what she had not felt before: a sense of power set apart to itself, and a scent of danger. But there was a beauty and nobility in Marsh Harrier as well. "Welcome, Gwalch," Llyf said. For a moment she hesitated, sensing something strange, then continued, "The marshes rejoice in your presence, but they do not need you." Gwalch cocked her head, and scratched under her wing with a long, curving talon. Llyf's voice tightened. She had never known this strange feeling in all the long eons. She was discovering emotion.

"They do not need you, Gwalch," she said. "Learn what this means, and join us in the dance." Gwalch flew off to the top of a nearby tree. She did find the song of Llyf lovely, and decided she was willing to take her place in the way of things. Sparrows and cormorants, ravens and corncrakes came forth in the clear skies. They lived together, and sang the same songs. But Gwalch brooded.

"Do not need me?" she said aloud. "The marsh itself bears my name!" And she felt the marshes needed her indeed, and it made her feel important. And somewhat lonely.

Through the turning cycles of the ages Llyf walked upon the waters of the marshes, changing the seasons in the bogs and upon the land. The marsh folk grew in number, and came to love her. They no longer called her Llyf, but Morwyn, which in the old tongue means "Maiden." For she had become one of them, and learned to love as well as they. Even Gwalch would visit from time to time, but she continued to brood, and her eyes were always veiled.

One day Morwyn was sitting on a tussock of reeds talking with a family of Marsh Hens, when she saw a glint of silver on the surface of the water. It was not a fish, for it had no fins or scales. Nor did it have feathers, or beak. It was covered with hair, like Morwyn's, but from head to toe. The hair was short, and a shiny sort of silver brown. It had long whiskers sprouting from both sides of a tiny nose. It was swimming on its back, and it seemed to be smiling. Slipping from the tussock, Morwyn swam out to the strange creature. She stroked its slick fur, and they laughed together. In her heart, Morwyn knew this was Otter.

"Hello, Dwrgi," she said as tread water beside the newcomer. "The marshes rejoice in your presence. But they do not need you. Learn what this means, and join us in the dance."

Dwrgi loved the song of Morwyn, but found her words too serious. She swam to the great mud bank, climbed to the top, and with a cry of delight threw herself over the edge, landing on her belly and sliding all the way down to the water, which she entered with a loud splash. Dwrgi didn't much care whether the marshes needed her or not. Yet Dwrgi took her place in the way of things. Foxes and deer, bears and badgers came forth upon the earth. They lived together and tried to sing the same song, but it was becoming stranger to their ears.

And time still passed. More and more, each of the marsh folk were drawn to their own kind. They began to sing their own songs, and they danced together less and less. Often they ignored, sometimes they feared, other folk. They no longer truly understood one another's speech, and sometimes, when food was scarce, they began to prey upon one another. For the veiled look in Gwalch's eyes had spread across many; the careless look in Dwrgi's across others. Morwyn grew sad and quiet. She walked less and less upon the marshes or over the bogs. She spent more and more time on the tiny, shadowed island of Ynys y Cysgodion in the midst of the lake. Shadows drew around the Dark Lady, and the marshes, too, grew darker.

~

Through the ages that followed Morwyn often saw her own reflection in the marsh waters. But although the marsh folk each carried something of her nature, she noticed there never was one who looked quite like her. Then, one day, near the end of this tale, the world changed. Morwyn was sitting on a branch of a marsh alder that hung out over the mossy bank, reclining back against the old trunk, softly humming her song and watching water spiders play, when,

"Are you Morwyn?"

The voice was so soft she thought she had dreamt it.

The water spiders knew her name, so it could not have been one of them. She was still puzzling over it when the voice came again, a bit louder and a little closer, from just behind her.

"Are you Morwyn?"

There stood a being Morwyn had never seen before. There had not been a new one in such a long time, and she could not remember having called this one forth. It looked very nearly like her, yet . . .

The new creature stood a head taller than Morwyn. Her skin was the color of starlight. Curling silver hair fell across her shoulders and over her breasts. She was not clothed in marsh reeds as Morwyn had been. She was naked. Her eyes were blue and piercing. Her voice was swift and light, like the waters that fell along the slopes of the Mendydds.

Again she asked, "Are you Morwyn?"

Morwyn reached out with her mind for a name, but heard only her own. *I am like you*, came a voice to her awareness.

"I am Morwyn," the Lady of Cysgodion finally answered. But there was a questioning in her voice. *Who are you, strange one?*

"I heard your name in the marshes," was the reply, "and I have come seeking you."

"But what is your name?" asked Morwyn. "I cannot feel it."

The creature smiled. "I am Enaid," she said. "I am a Woman."

~

For many days Enaid stayed with Morwyn on Ynys y Cysgodion. She had come from the east, she said, where the lands were high and the earth was dry. She had heard rumors of a dark lady who lived alone, among the folk of the ancient marshes, and whom some said was the giver of life.

They sat together under the old alder drinking a tea of marsh herbs. "For years we have heard the tales of Morwyn," she said, "Though the people of my clan call you Vivian, for we believe you are the giver of life."

This new name sought a resting place deep within Morwyn's being. But she let it remain quiet, more intrigued by other parts of Enaid's story. She had never seen another human before, did not know she was human herself now, and was curious to hear there were others, somewhere out beyond the marshes.

"Clan?" Morwyn asked. "Is that like a flock of Graylag Geese that gather in the marshes?"

Enaid laughed. "Indeed it is" she said. "And sometimes they make as much noise when they are all gathered together!" She sipped her tea and leaned back against the alder trunk. "It is so quiet here. And safe." Enaid told her tales of giant animals called mammoth and aurochs, and winters of ice. Of long migrations in search of food. Of men who hunted game, who fought with each other, who gathered women to them. And of a way of begetting that was strange to Morwyn.

The tales stirred currents of unrest in Morwyn's spirit. "These 'men' sound like our tales of marsh monsters," she said. And a shiver went through her body as if from the cold lands of Enaid's tales.

"Sometimes they are." Enaid looked over her tea gourd into the distance, seeing beyond the marshes to the high eastern land that was her home. "But on cold nights it is good to have company, and warmth."

"Company?" Morwyn asked.

Enaid looked into the eyes of the Dark Lady and saw loneliness. "Someone to be with you," she said.

Morwyn stood and stretched her arms out to the waters. "The marshes are filled with company," she said. A marsh hen roused itself from a reed tussock and flew; Morwyn called in greeting.

Enaid came to Morwyn and circled her arms around the Lady's waist from behind in a gentle hug. Softly, she kissed the back of Morwyn's neck. "Like this," she said. "There is another kind of company, Morwyn."

For the first time in all the long ages tears ran down Morwyn's cheeks. At last she understood she had become truly human, and was completely alone. The two women sat together at the base of the old tree, all forgotten but the warmth of the other's presence and the gentleness of enfolding arms.

The marshes have always rejoiced in my presence, Morwyn thought, *But they do not need me.* So Morwyn learned the heartlonging that would one day be known as love, and the need for the nearness of another of one's kind. In the presence of Enaid she became Vivian, for both were givers of life.

After several cycles of the moon Enaid left and returned to her own lands in the east. Vivian, who had been Lady since before the memory of times, did not again depart from the dark waters of Llyn y Cysgodion. She became a memory, and finally a rumor. But it was always her spirit that enlivened the marshes at their heart. One day others would come after her, who would journey beyond the borders of the ancient dark. But they are a part of other tales.

Chapter Eight
III. Doeth and The Marsh Sedge

Before the first memories of the marsh folk, the vast Brythonic sea began to withdraw, leaving shallow waters, fens and marshes in the broad levels between the Mendydd Hills and the Pwlborfa. Marsh reeds grew in abundance, and died, forming peat in raised bogs. On the borders of bog and marsh, in the wet black mud, grew the great sedge meadows. There the Dwrtrygydd came to be, the water people. And life for them was as sharp as the sedge.

~

Heavy gray clouds hung low over the marsh. It was raining, as it had been steadily all morning. Gobaith and Dyfrgi paddled their marshboat to the edge of the flooded sedge meadow that bordered the south side of Ynys Calchfaen. The meadows were growing. For countless cycles of the sun, Gobaith's ancestors had lived on the islands in the great marsh. The waters had always been unpredictable. At times they had become a wide shallow sea, engulfing many of the smaller islands. Then the people would retreat, sometimes for many generations, to the highlands of the Mendydds or Pwlborfa. But they were not a land-loving people and, when they could, they returned to the water. Throughout Gobaith's life the waters had been low and the marshes rich with life. Ynys Calchfaen had remained dry, home to several clans who raised sufficient sheep and pigs to barter a few for grain from the mainland. They traded pottery for tools and trinkets of bronze, copper, and tin. Gobaith's father had been a weaver, producing coarse wool cloth which, heavily oiled, kept one relatively warm and dry when hunting and fishing in the marshes. But the waters were rising once again; much of Ynys Calchfaen had been lost to the marsh. The clans had to move most of the livestock across the wooden trackways to pasture and stables on Crib Pwlborfa. And in the areas between island and marsh the sedge meadows were growing. Gobaith pulled his wet woolen cloak closer about his neck and stepped out into the shallow water and muck. He hated the sedge. It grew in dense tussocks in the black, waterlogged earth. To step in between meant sinking sometimes up to the knee, inviting encounters with leeches. To step on the tussocks risked deep, painful cuts from the sharp spikes that grew on each sedge stalk.

"Keep your hands in the boat, Dyfrgi," he warned. Gobaith's young son of four summers sat in the back of the marshboat, wrapped in a wool blanket. In the summer he would be reaching for butterflies and Gobaith would worry he might grab a handful of sedge. But in the cold rain of year's end there was no danger of the young lad wanting to escape the warmth of his wrap. Instead he laughed, and urged his father to pull faster, as Gobaith drew the flat bottomed boat into meadow.

Dragging a boat through the southern sedge meadow was not the usual way to approach Ynys Calchfaen. Ordinarily Gobaith would have returned from fishing to the north coast, where channels of open water led through the marsh to the island at several points. It was at these landing points that the families of Gobaith's clan had their huts. But the fishing had not gone well that day. After sitting in the rain for what seemed like ages and catching only a few small pike, Gobaith decided to try his luck with bigger game. Once in a while a roe deer would stray too far out into the bogs from Crib Pwlborfa and become mired in the sedge meadow, weakened from struggling in the muck, losing blood from the deep sedge cuts. Gobaith prayed to the goddess of the marsh for luck. But the rain came down harder, and he cursed when he stumbled and grabbed a handful of sedge to steady himself. Prayers and curses often mingled in Gobaith's heart in those days; neither seemed to move the gods to stem the rising waters. In spite of the pain, Gobaith grinned. *I ought to have worried about me rather than Dyfrgi*, he thought.

He moved slowly forward, pulling the boat behind, stepping on the tussocks because he preferred to lose blood honourably to the sedge than have it sucked from him by the horrid leeches. A shiver went through him at the thought of their fat, slimy bodies . . .

Gobaith was almost upon the roe buck before he saw it, maybe about thirty paces away. In the summer sunshine he would have seen it clear across the meadow, its russet coat flashing against the green sedge. But its winter gray matched everything around. It was nearly invisible. He dropped his rope and moved back to his son,

"Hush, Dyfrgi," he whispered, pointing to the buck that was still struggling to free itself from the muck. "The goddess has blessed us. We will eat well tonight."

Dyfrgi's eyes went wide. He had been on hunts with his father before, and he knew what was coming. "Can I help, Tada?" he asked with excitement.

"Shhh. Here, take this." Gobaith handed him a blanket roll from the front of the boat, then turned his back and bent over for the boy to climb on. "Jump up, lad," he said. "And mind the sedge spikes."

Together they approached the mired buck, being careful not to startle it badly enough that it should leap free. When they drew near they could see the animal was badly frightened. It stood still, eyes wide with fear, shudders rippling through its tensed muscles. It made one more attempt at a leap, but the muck held it fast. Red blood ran down its legs from the sedge cuts.

Gobaith could feel his son's rapid breathing on his neck, nearly matching the rhythm of the buck's tremors. It was a small roe, not as tall as his waist. But it still had its summer weight. This would be a good catch. He stepped forward, slowly taking the blanket roll from his son. "Ho, there, Iwrch," he said, as if calling the creature by name. The deer struggle again and let out its barking cry of distress. "Easy, Iwrch, easy." In one movement he threw the blanket over the animal's head and, as sudden blindness confused it into stillness, he drew his long iron knife and slit its throat. Blood flowed from the wound, steaming in the cool air, and the buck lay dead.

"Now," he said, as he swung his son down to stand by the carcass, "you can help me get him ready to take home."

"Tada, why did you throw the blanket over the deer's head?"

"The gods will that we eat their creatures in order to live," my son. "They give them into our hands, and they grant us skill to have a successful hunt." He put his hand on the boy's head and Dyfrgi looked up at him. "But it is up to us alone, little one, to show a bit of kindness."

~

That evening Gobaith and Doeth stood side by side on the bank of Llyn y Aberthau, their son Dyfrgi between them. Several other clan members made a solemn semicircle, all facing the lake of offerings. Doeth lifted a long bronze knife blade, old, but smoothed and polished to look like new. It glowed softly in the rays of the full moon.

"Goddess of the waters," she called, "Goddess of the marshes, hear our prayers . . ."

Gobaith was impatient. *It would be good to include the goddess of the sedge meadows too*, he thought.

"Mother, we call upon you to still the rising of your waters," Doeth continued. "Spare our home of Ynys Calchfaen, and the islands of the other clans across the marshes." She held her arms out over the waters of Llyn y Aberthau and reverently let go of the blade. It dropped into the water almost without sound, and the water accepted it from her hands in expanding ripples with the brightness of the moon reflected at their center. All was quiet.

Our women have performed this ritual every full moon since I can remember, thought Gobaith. *As their mothers did before them, and their grandmothers' mothers before that. There is more silver and bronze at the bottom of Aberthau than in all the homes of our people, yet still the waters rise.*

And still the waters did rise. Ynys Calchfaen grew ever smaller, while more and more of the Dwrtrygydds were forced to make it their home. Isle after isle was inundated. Ynys Llefrith and Ynys Burtle were already gone, as was Ynys y Llynhydd across the marsh. Nearby Ynys Bragwair was no longer habitable, useful only for keeping sheep in summer. Of the isles remaining, only Calchfaen was available to the clans. The great Ynys Mawr to the north was held by the tribes of the Mendydds. Ynys y Niwl, where no one lived, was rumored to harbor strange things in its mists. And Cysgodion: older rumors told of an isle of shadows hidden somewhere in the north marshes that was home to the Lady of the waters. But no one had ever found it.

The ritual was over and the clan members were drifting back to their huts. Gobaith hoped for a good night's rest. In the morning he would help to sink new pilings to raise the Chweg trackway out of the water.

~

A fine mist came from the gray sky as Doeth sat by the shore of Llyn y Aberthau. Countless interlocking circles marked the fall of tiny droplets of rain. The whole surface rippled in a gentle breeze from the northwest. Several curlews circled overhead, calling to one another their plaintive *cour-lee, cour-lee,* then headed out over the eastern sedge meadow toward the marsh. Doeth sat on the large gray rock from which offerings were dropped into the waters. All around her was water. The lake, the grass, the sedge and marsh, the sky, her long dark hair and woolen cloak; all were wet, cold, and uniformly gray. Waters fell from the gray sky, mists rose from the gray sea. Doeth was caught in the middle.

"We have been making offerings to you for countless cycles of the moon," Doeth said aloud, looking out over the lake. "Yet you do not answer, and the waters rise. What are we to do, Goddess? How are we to live?" No sound answered her but the hiss of falling rain on the lake surface. "No, I did not suppose you would answer." She sighed, looking up into the clouds, falling rain mixing with her tears. Finally she rose and took the path that skirted the huts of her clan on its way to the north shore of the island. There marsh and sedge meadow framed the one short stretch of open shoreline, where the clan moored their marshboats. The sedge was spreading, the only living thing, it seemed to her, with the tenacity to survive in a world becoming more water than land.

There were the curlews again, swooping over the wet meadow. They were well suited to the sedge, she realized. Their long, curving bills were made for probing the soft mud, where they found crabs, mollusks, and lugworms. But even the curlews needed the drier moors and fields higher up on the island for breeding. Soon they, too, would leave Ynys Calchfaen for higher ground.

"Would you give us curlew-wings, my Lady?" Doeth asked. "We could fly then across the rising waters."

Silence.

"No, I suppose not."

She sat on the bottom of an overturned boat, gazing into the distance. In front of her the open water lapped the shore in gentle waves. To her right, sedge meadow gave way to marsh. Beyond that she could just see the suggestion of Ynys y Niwl, the upper reaches of its high hill lost in low hanging clouds. What shadows dwelt on that strange island, she wondered?

Several boat lengths out in the water she could see the top of a pole that in drier times had been well up on land, and used to secure her husband's beached boat. Perhaps out of habit, he often still tied it there and wadded in to shore. The boat sat there now, rocking slowly, turning in the current. Not much of the pole stood above the water. It was about mid-day. The full moon of last night would be about half way between its setting and its rising, so the tide was high. She watched the boat bob up and down, its slack tie rope letting it wander a bit from the mooring . . .

Suddenly she realized she had been staring at the boat for some time, and she blinked rainmist from her eyes. There was something about the boat, something that seemed important. But whatever it was eluded her as if it had vanished in the mist. *Time to think about an evening meal.* Gobaith would be famished when he came home from working on the trackway.

~

"Indeed it was hell, Doe," Gobaith said, stretching the aching muscles in his arms. They were seated on furs around a central fire in the hut where he was finishing the last of a deer haunch. He laughed and ruffled Dyfrgi's damp hair. "I kept the lad out of the water because we were in the sedge," he said. "But he was a great help to Gwrol carrying the ash poles to us along the walkway."

Doeth smiled at the boy. "You will be manly yourself soon enough," she said. The boy beamed with pride.

Gobaith wiped his arm on his mouth and drank some honeyed water. "Gwrol supplied us with enough poles from the ash coppices to raise a hundred paces of trackway," he said, "mostly at the edge of the sedge meadow." He rubbed at the bandage on his left leg where Doeth had cleaned and covered his cuts with a salve of chamomile.

The Chweg trackway ran from the south side of Ynys Calchfaen through sedge and bog to the north shore of Crib Pwlborfa. Most of the cattle and sheep had been moved over it to the ridge some time ago. On the ridge, below the slopes of the hills, oak and ash were grown to maintain the Chweg and other trackways of the marshes. So it had been for time out of mind. No one in Gobaith's clan knew when the tracks had first been built, but remains of old sections were often found buried in the black mud. They must have been ancient. Some of the trackways were nearly a day's journey in length. They were built mostly of crossed ash poles sunk into the mud, with oak planks laid end to end upon the crossed poles. A grove of ash trees on Pwlborfa was kept coppiced, cut nearly to the ground on a regular basis, to produce the long, curved poles needed for the supports.

That day, Gobaith and several others had raised twenty sections of trackway above the floodwater level by pounding new supports into the mud and pulling out the old ones. It was wet work, and cold at that time of year. But Gobaith preferred the cold to the biting gnats of warmer seasons. The problem with the trackways was that they were anchored in the mud. As the water level rose, and more of the raised bog reverted to marsh, deeper water threatened the usefulness of the wooden paths.

A shadow crossed Gobaith's face. "We are using the longest poles we can now," he said. "It won't be long before the Chweg track sinks below the water. Then likely we will have to leave Calchfaen."

Doeth had often used the tracks. In her mind she saw the poles anchored firmly in the mud, the unmoving oaken boards gradually reached, and then overcome, by the rising water. She thought of Gobaith's moored boat, bobbing on the tide.

Doeth.

It was as if someone had called her name. But no one was with her in the hut except Gobaith and Dyfrgi, and they had gone back to finishing their meal.

Doeth. It was the soft, deep voice of an old woman. *Doeth, think of Gobaith's boat.*

Without a word, Doeth stood and left the hut. Gobaith and Dyfrgi were too busy with deer bones to notice. Outside it had grown dark. The rain clouds had passed over with a chill northwest breeze. Stars shone overhead, the Hunter and the Sisters in clear view. Doeth followed the narrow path down to the moorings, visible in the light of the newly waning moon. She reached the shore and sat again on the overturned boat. The tide had gone out, leaving the old boat much higher up on shore than her earlier visit. There was Gobaith's boat, still bobbing in the water, just a bit offshore. Its tie rope now hung above it from the mooring pole which stood high above the water level.

"What is it, Lady? What do you want me to see?"

The pole stood perhaps an arms length out of the water, where earlier only a handsbreadth had been visible. Because of the slant of the lake bottom, the tidal effect was greater on the north side where she stood than over in the southern marshes, but the principle was the same. As the water level rose, the mooring remained anchored in the mud, and the surface of the lake climbed higher and higher up the pole.

"What do you want me to see?" Doeth asked again aloud in the moonlight.

Gobaith's boat. Look at Gobaith's boat.

Doeth stared. It was nearer the bottom of the pole than before, yet riding still upon the surface of the water, held fast by the length of rope. It was always that way. As dawn approached and the tide began to rise again, the boat would rise higher up the pole. But it would always be resting on the surface of the lake. *The surface of the lake!* Suddenly Doeth realized even if the lake level rose above the top of the pole and it disappeared from sight, the boat would rise with the water and keep its user dry!

"My Lady," she breathed, "If we cling to the land, the rising water is our enemy. But if we embrace the rising water, it will support us and keep us safe."

Doeth, came the reply. *It was not in vain that your mother named you "Wise."*

Doeth had always looked to the tenacity of the marsh sedge for hope against the water. But it was the changeful water itself in which the answer lay; the lesson of Gobaith's boat that brought them all hope.

~

"Well, that does it," Gobaith proclaimed, as he pulled tight the last of the lashings joining the hut of Bugail and Tresglen to the rest of the small floating island. Most of the clan was finally connected, with six huts resting upon logs lashed to a series of flat bottomed marsh boats. The whole was loosely moored to several large wooden pilings set in the lake bed, and sat on the water about twelve boat lengths offshore.

The clan's new island rose and fell twice a day, about an arm span, with the tide. More importantly, there was room for the general rise that would occur over time with the rising lake level. Nearby, up and down the shore, the other clans of Ynys Calchfaen had formed five more islands. One, to Gobaith's right, was the same distance from shore. The other four were farther out, but all sat close together. Two had walkways stretching between them, though they relied on flatboats to reach the land. A feast was held that evening onshore, with offerings and prayers of thanks to the goddess for the hope given through Gobaith, builder of the first floating island. But he and Doeth both knew it was to her the Lady had granted the gift of wisdom.

For generations after, the Dwrtrygydd made the lake their home, living on the floating islands when water levels left Ynys Calchfaen too small to sustain the community. To their old skills they added those of lake knowledge: fishing, and trading with tribes far off across the water. One day, when the tides turned again, the floating islands settled on the marsh bed and became the great lake village of Pentreflynn. There the clans would often tell this tale around their fires, debating whether old Doeth had used her own wisdom to solve the riddle of Gobaith's Boat, or the Lady of the Lake had truly spoken to her. But whatever that truth may be, it is because of Doeth that the Dwrtrygydd, like the sedge, remain to this day.

Chapter Nine
IV. The Lost Land of Iwerydd

This is a tale of the coming of the Wise to the Salis Plain beyond the eastern marshes. Drwyds, they are sometimes called in error, for it was thought they bore the wisdom of the ancient oak trees. Some say they came from an emerald isle in the west, others that they once lived in lands beside a great sea in the middle of the earth. Still others claim they had their origin in four mystical cities at the far corners of the world, and are children of the goddess Danu, or that they began along the banks of an eastern river sacred to that goddess, which flows into wide black sea. Here is the tale the people of the marshes tell, and no one knows from whence it comes, for the land it describes is forever lost. The marsh people call this lost land Iwerydd, for the great sea that circles our Brythonic island. But those who once lived there knew it as Atlandes, the Fatherland.

The realm of Iwerydd was an island to the east in the cold northern sea. It was several days' journey across on swift foot from north to south, and longer from east to west. Its central plain was circled by a ring of coastal hills, and cut in half by a high plateau. In the center of all rose the ancient city of Arian, whose solid walls stood on the plateau like the circling hills. Those who dwelt in the land were called the Iweryddon, and they were reputed to be wise. They worshipped the bright disc of the sun, who they called the goddess Huan, and in whose honour they built great temples of stone with tools of iron that were unknown in our marshes. In those days, Lisinde was 932nd in the line of the High Priestesses of Huan, serving the Great Temple at the heart of Arian.

There were also priests of Huan, but no High Priest, and they served no ritual function except to search the skies for omens and to trace the journeys of Huan as the seasons came and went. Countless generations of this work had made them scientists as well as priests. They gained great knowledge in the motions of the stars, the turnings of the seasons, and the movement of Huan through the circling star-pictures that stretch across the night sky. When they built the Great Temple to aid their observations, they became architects, a new kind of stonemason, free from mere labor, who understood the esoteric secrets of geometry and the mysteries of fitting stone upon stone. The Great Temple had been the first wonder of Iwerydd, with six hundred stone steps climbing nearly to the clouds. Its summit was an observatory for the priests, from which they traced the movements of Huan across the sacred peaks of the circling hills. In this way they marked times and seasons, proclaimed to the priestesses the arrival of festivals, and advised farmers and herdsmen in their labors.

But the summit of the Great Temple served a more sacred purpose than this. For there, high above the city of Arian, lay a great stone altar: the Marriage Bed of Huan where Lisinde and her ancestors before her carried out the most sacred of all their duties.

So it was that just before midday on the longest day of summer, Lisinde climbed the Temple steps, taking with her Eagil, Prince of Iwerydd. They wore brief loincloths of sheepskin, and their bodies glistened with sweat and sacred oils in the summer sun. For three great cycles of Huan they had made this ascent together, as had Princes and High Priestesses for generations before them. The fruit of their joining provided priestesses for the temples and officers for the fleet of seagoing ships. But of more import was the summoning of Iwerydd to the Marriage Bed of Huan, providing growing warmth for the land as the ancient wall of Ice made its retreat.

Indeed, Huan had blessed them with her warmth since before the time of Lisinde's great grandmothers. The high Ice of the old tales had withdrawn far to the north, no longer visible from Iwerydd's shores. But that had brought a new trouble, for with the retreat of the Ice came the rising of the circling sea. In only a few generations it had swallowed much of the earth, separating the Brythonic lands from the great continent to the south, and turning Iwerydd into an island.

As they climbed, Lisinde knew this would likely be her last Great Marriage as High Priestess. She had served with several Princes in the years before Eagil. Last summer their joining had produced no offspring, and she knew her time of bearing children was past. Her long hair still flashed its coppery blaze in the sun, sweeping over her shoulders and hanging loose about her hips. Her body was still strong, her breasts high, her proud countenance still took away the breath of even young men. But each summer it was harder to climb the temple steps. Her breath came shorter, her heart pounded a bit faster each summer. The ravishing beauty of youth had already turned to the regal beauty of maturity. Soon it would become the classic beauty of age, and then another High Priestess, one of Lisinde's daughters, would be needed for this task. She had borne several daughters. One, Miamir, would likely replace her before the next Great Marriage.

From the high top of the temple Lisinde looked out at the horizon. The old tales told of fertile plains as far as the eye could see, the ancient realm of Daggerlanden filled with game and fruit-bearing trees. But now there was only sea, sparkling in the high sun. To the south she could just see the dark coast of the great continent. To the west, our mist shrouded Brythonic shores. At the summit of the temple a stiff sea breeze dried the sweat off her body with refreshing coolness. Below lay the green fields of her people, and the circling hills. White gulls glided around her, calling their presence, diving to the blue waves for fish.

Eagil watched her and grinned. He was nearly young enough to be her son, yet old enough to be moved by her sensual beauty. He was dark skinned, with shining black hair nearly as long as hers. It was gathered and tied in the royal knot atop his head, with a stallion's tail hanging down his back to just below his left shoulder blade. Like all who were chosen Prince of Iwerydd, Eagil was trained for battle even though there had been no war in anyone's memory. His muscles were strong and hard, his loincloth hiding nothing. With the arrogance typical of a young Prince he mistook the response of Lisinde's breasts to the cooling breeze as a passion for him. His own flesh answering proudly, he removed his loincloth and dropped it to the floor. Far below, the sounding of trumpets and pounding of drums heralded their imminent union, as the people of Arian looked on and shouted their encouragement. Many of them began to pair off in quiet corners or in the open sunlight to copy the joining of Prince and Priestess, adding their own magic to the union of Huan and Iwerydd.

In recent generations this ritual had taken on new purpose and expression. The old tales told of days on end that were wild with the lustful celebration of Huan; the couplings of leaders and people encouraging her to grant the heat of her passion to Iwerydd for the banishing of the Ice. But now the ritual expression of lust was brief, followed by a dance of separation, and a bowing of respect. Huan had expressed her passion too well. The circling sea had risen too high and Iwerydd was in danger of being consumed. So when Lisinde's great grandmother had become High Priestess she declared the unbridled revels to be at an end. While the union of Land and Goddess was still useful for the fertility of herds and crops, Huan must be urged to propriety and circumspection for the sake of general survival.

As the sun rose brightly over Ing, easternmost peak of the circling hills, Lisinde lowered herself upon Eagil's loins to the shouts of approval from below. He thought of the old tales and envied his grandfathers, whose desires would have been indulged for days rather than the few brief moments he could expect as his due. He liked to imagine Lisinde feeling the same way, and perhaps it might have been so, if he had been a bit less arrogant.

~

That night Danien, Priest of Huan and Captain of the Fleet, stood in the moonlight on a long stone quay that moored the largest of his ships. He was ankle deep in the rolling waves of high tide where, as a child, he would have been well above the water. For too long he had argued this very point with Eagil. He allowed himself a sneer. To him, it was Eagil who was still the child. The old priest had served twenty-seven years in the fleet, the last seventeen as Captain. His face was weathered by the wind and salt, his hands calloused by years of ropes and helms. He may once have been handsome, before he gave himself to the sea.

The time had come for him to act on his own. Sailors were loading supplies on board, taking advantage of the fleeting darkness provided as scudding clouds flew across the moon. He thought back to the afternoon's council meeting which had, unknown to Eagil, brought the final parting of their ways. It had begun calmly enough, the two men seated across from one another in the stone room that served as council chamber. Leaders of the major Iweryddon families sat around the walls on either side, forming the High Council. Danien had been speaking with a quiet determination that masked his sense of urgency.

"We cannot stay," he concluded. "Already the sea overwhelms the quays at high tide in our one remaining harbor."

"What do I care of quays and ships?" retorted Eagil. "Surely the sea cannot break through the circling hills! Are you telling me all of Iwerydd is in danger of drowning?" His dismissive laugh was echoed by his followers among the council.

Danien was stone-faced. It was the same argument he had heard from Eagil time and again. "That is not the point, Sire," he answered with forced respect.

"Then tell me, please, *sea-captain*, what *is* the point?" The title was intended as an epithet. If the Eagil had been a stronger, wiser man, this exchange would have resembled a chess match. As it was, the Prince was merely being petulant. It was the same question he always asked, and Danien always gave the same stupid answer. The Prince was in no mood for further frustrations after the all too brief ritual with Lisinde on the temple summit earlier in the day. He thoroughly enjoyed the ceremonial of being Prince of Iwerydd. He did not cherish the responsibility.

Still Danien held his anger. He fixed his gaze upon a spot high on the opposite wall that had become his focus for calm whenever Eagil was unreasonable, something that happed with more and more frequency. "Of course we do not know what plans the sea may have for us in the future," he explained again. "But if we lose the last remaining moorings for our fleet we lose all hope of escape, should that ever become necessary."

Eagil's short supply of patience ran out. His chamberlain had secured a roomful of young women who awaited his presence and who would, if not with genuine enthusiasm, at least on his command relieve the frustration that had been building in his mind and his flesh. "No more talk of leaving Iwerydd!" he shouted, rising to leave the chamber. "I am tired of talk!"

"Sire," Danien urged in a final effort, "perhaps just a scouting ship to the wilds of the Brythonic lands to see where we might one day form a colony." He paused, then added as a caution, "Should we ever need one."

"No!" shouted Eagil toward the doorway as he stormed from the chamber. The council was ended.

So it was that Danien stood on the quay, ankle deep in the tide, and watched as a company of sailors, engineers, and priestesses boarded the ship. Among those who were heeding Danien's alarm was Miamir, heiress to the High Priestess Lisinde. The secrecy of their departure was painful to her, for she wished to have had the chance to reconcile with her mother, and to say goodbye. Disagreement between them had grown nearly to the point of estrangement. Lisinde believed her own calling to lie with the realm of Iwerydd, come what may. Miamir felt called to protect the welfare of the people. By the time of the sailing neither had been able to convince the other.

Neither had guessed at the finality of their last heated parting.

Danien had been planning the move since the previous midwinter, in anticipation of Eagil's intransigence. They would sail before the turning of the tide, even as the final days of Iwerydd approached, unexpected and unheeded by the Prince ...

~

It had been a full cycle of the moon since they had landed on the Brythonic shore, During those days they encountered only small bands of hunters, for the land was mostly uninhabited. Danien led his small band inland until they reached a high plateau of grassland stretching far into the distance. Sightings taken on the stars, and charts made on many sea journeys, told him they were near the center of the island, far from the sea, and this satisfied him. Salis Plain it was called, as they learned from local hunters. There they built roundhouses of sod thatched over with tall grass, and began to settle in for the dark of the year, hoping to find enough local game to supplement the stores they had brought by boat. Most of Danien's company would never look upon the circling sea again. Certainly none would ever return home, for it was during their first winter that Iwerydd met its terrible end, sooner and with greater catastrophe than Danien might ever have imagined. Miamir was chosen first High Priestess of the colony, severing forever her ties with the isle of her birth.

~

At midwinter came the celebration of Sunreturn in the city of Arian on the high plateau of Iwerydd. Fires roared in every hearth. Evergreen boughs and bright banners decorated the city, and there was feasting in every great hall. Eagil sat with Lisinde at the center of a long table in the palace, heads of the leading families and their wives or husbands spread out on either side of them. Eagil had an actual wife. But he considered her of no consequence for celebrations of state, so she was not present. And Lisinde was wed to Iwerydd, so it was she who sat beside the Prince. As usual he missed no opportunity to remind her of their midsummer ritual, graphically recounting the pleasure he had felt, asking if she also had been sated, suggesting several ingenious ways in which he might please her better next time. Lisinde smiled constantly and tolerated him as she would a child. Old Wattling, the Chamberlain, was seated on her left. She spent as much time as possible turned towards him, pretending to be engrossed in the minutest details of running the palace.

The wines of Iwerydd's southern plain flowed freely, and the night soon grew late. Eagil, knowing he could not command the affections of the High Priestess, summoned several young revelers to join him in his bedchamber. They left the hall singing bawdy songs about Princes, cattle, and courtesans. With the Prince's departure the celebrating quickly came to an end, and the palace sank into the deep darkness that comes before first light.

Lisinde wished not to remain at the palace, nor to return alone to her apartments. For a time, she wandered the empty streets of Arian. It was a regular practice for her, to the constant dismay of the Captain of the Nightwatch. But she was known to all Arian, and no one would dare lay hands on the High Priestess without her permission. Near dawn on the shortest day of the dark season she climbed the steps of the Great Temple and looked out across the sea. Far to the north, along the horizon, a strange band of silver flashed brightly in the light of the setting moon. She could not tell what it was, but it was something she had not seen before and it should not have been there.

That night, farther to the north than she could have seen even after several days' sailing, a cataclysm had taken placed that was about to change the shape of the world. Around the long curve of what mariner's tales called the Northland, winter seas raged in wild frenzy, lashed by storms that could not be imagined in Iwerydd. From steel gray skies came fierce winds and torrents of rain, frightful flashes of lightning thrown by a strange northern god named Thor, who wielded a great hammer and led the raging rout of winter through the air. Deafening explosions of thunder shook the sky as the giant waves hurled themselves at one another and ice fell from the heavens. Deep beneath the wild surface of the Northland sea, the cold, dark waters thrashed and churned upon old underwater cliffs. In the dark depths a crack appeared in the earth. In a mere moments a stretch of cliff nearly the size of Iwerydd broke away, and plunged down the long slope into the utter darkness of the sea, throwing before it a great wall of water higher than anyone living had ever seen. With rapidly increasing speed the wave raced across the northern reaches, leveling islands as it went, sweeping the ruins of human habitation before it.

As Lisinde watched from the summit of the temple, the strange silver band grew higher and wider, until it filled the horizon. With the sudden powerless clarity that comes from approaching death she knew what it was! The wind driven ahead of the giant tidal wave blew wildly around her, almost throwing her over the edge. She clung to the wide altar stone upon which she and Eagil had joined at midsummer. Her eyes grew wide with horror to see the giant wave crash through the circling hills as though they were sand. Moments later it rose over the city, seeming to hover for an instant to relish the kill.

"Mother! Mother!"

Lisinde looked up at the giant wave. In her mind she saw Miamir riding the crest, screaming out a warning to the people sleeping below. But there was no time for a warning.

"Miamir!" she cried, "Mia, Daughter! O Huan, help us!"

But Huan sat low in the eastern sky, a helpless goddess, as the great wave came crashing down upon the temple, sweeping Lisinde into oblivion, submerging the city of Arian and grinding it into the seabed with the churning, heaving waters of its ferocious power. In moments the ancient island of Iwerydd was no more, and the waves of the sea heaved to and fro over its grave.

~

In the middle of the Salis plain Miamir, the first High

89

Priestess of the Brythonic Iweryddon, had awoken with a start. She could see nothing in the darkness of her roundhouse, but she felt the earth tremble in agony. Her stomach twisted and lurched forward as if she had been thrown with great speed into a yawning abyss. She closed her eyes and saw stars flying by overhead into the north. As Huan rose in the east, Miamir rode the crest of a great wave, the realm of Iwerydd rushing forward to meet her. She flew over the circling hills on explosions of sea spray, and saw the city of Arian lying small and helpless beneath her. Her mother stood on the summit of the Great Temple, looking up at her in horror, and Miamir cried out. But hers was a seeing of what was already taking place; there was nothing she could do. Then she heard the cries of her people as they were swept away, and she broke free from the trance, trembling and sweating outside in the cold of the Salis Plain. When she could will her shaken body to move again, she awakened the other priestesses. Together they roused the rest of the colony. It was nearly morning as they all gathered, cloaks hastily pulled around them, in the center of the camp.

Light snow fell about them as they sought meaning in Miamir's vision.

"She saw true," Danien said. "I feel it. I have felt it coming for a long time. A sailor knows the waves, feels it in his gut when something strange is happening. The sea has not felt right since last midwinter."

"That's true," another man answered. "Fishing's been bad in the northern waters all year. It's almost as if the fish 'ave left for other waters." Others nodded assent.

"I tried to reason with Eagil," Danien said. "I told him constantly it was time for us all to leave." He drew his wife close to him, and she wept at the bleakness in his eyes. "I wish to all the gods I had not been proven right."

The snow stopped, clouds lifting and glowing red as Huan rose above the edge of their new world. Where Iwerydd once lay, she was already high in the sky, looking down upon unbroken waters black with silt, littered with the floating remnants of a lost people who were, in the end, not as wise as they claimed to be. But there on Salis Plain it was the beginning of a new day.

~

In early spring, when snowdrops began to appear, Danien and Miamir held council with those who had emerged as leaders of the colony.

"We now dwell far from the wealth of the sea," Danien began, "and we will be dependent upon crops and the movement of game for all our food. More than ever before, we will need to know the travels of the sun upon the rim of the horizon. No longer do we have the Great Temple and the peaks of the circling hills to tell us of Huan's times and seasons."

"So we must recreate the circling hills with what we have available," continued Miamir. And she began to explain plans for the building of a great circle. When she finished, men began gathering wood from the copses that stood here and there on the plain. From ash and oak they fashioned sharpened stakes the length of a forearm, and long posts, twice the height of a man and several fingers in diameter. They stripped the bark, dried the smoothed posts over a slow fire, and rubbed them with oil rendered from animal fat. Then they waited.

On the morning of the balance between dark and light, Danien stood with Miamir in the midst of a broad, flat portion of Salis Plain. Beside them was a long stake Danien had driven into the ground. Together, in silence, they watched the sunrise. Miamar greeted the goddess Huan, asking her for guidance in following the times and seasons. To mark the place on the horizon where Huan appeared, Danien strode eastward fifty paces, turned, and faced Miamir where she stood beside the first stake. Waving with one arm and then the other, she directed him to the spot where he stood directly between her and the rising sun. There he drove a second stake into the ground, the line between the two stakes pointing from Miamir, past Danien, to the sunrise on the horizon. The next day they did the same, and the day after. When clouds hid the horizon they would wait for the next visible sunrise, mark its place on the growing circle, and then fill in the days that had been missed. The whole process took a year to complete, with special reverence at midsummer, and the autumnal equinox. As each stake was set and the great circle took shape, each short stake was replaced with a tall, wooden post reaching toward the sky. At midwinter, to honour the anniversary of the dead of Iwerydd, two large poles were set side by side in the north of the circle, with a lintel joining them across the top. The rising sun cast its rays through the memorial arch, where Huan seemed to stand still in reverence as her light fell upon the circle's central pole. It had been painted blood red with ochre, for the blood of their people, and could be seen from far across the plain.

When spring came again the circle was completed, a broad henge of wooden posts rising into the sky from Salis Plain. What no one but the small band of Iweryddon refugees would ever know was that every so often around the circle a certain post, taller than the others and carved with special markings, represented one of the sacred peaks of the circling hills of Iwerydd: Ing, Elger, Miamar, Tidwell, and Ghent. Like the sacred peaks, now slowly eroding in the deep ocean currents, the posts were used for marking times and seasons. But they served a purpose more sacred to the hearts of the Iweryddon: they were a reminder of the circling hills of their lost home.

Of course the wooden posts were not as durable as the hills of Iwerydd, but stonemasons among the refugees had plans for that. Over three generations, as the new community flourished and grew in numbers, they quarried giant bluestone monoliths from the far hills beyond our western marshes and dragged them across the wide plain to the site of the henge. There they raised them in threes like the original northern archway: two upright stones joined by a lintel across the top all around the circle, forming a great stone henge. A semicircle of larger trilithons in the center represented the central city of Arian, and an altar stone in their midst was the memory of the

Great Temple. There the priests and priestesses of Iwerydd celebrated the rites of Huan in a new land, and remembered the lost island that had been the home of their ancestors in an age that was fading from the world. And so it was for many ages.

~

But the colony would not prosper forever. In time, the tides of many more generations swept over even their memories, and the last people of the lost land passed from the earth. Frosts of countless winters and the rains of as many summers took their toll upon the untended stones, left alone on Salis Plain. One by one most of the trilithons leaned, then tumbled, and were covered over with moss and lichens, bindweed and creepers. Sometimes a passing band of hunters would pause to wonder at the sight. But they always moved on, for the high plain was exposed to the elements. Its weather was harsh, and it was no place for a settlement of any kind. So the stones stood alone, touched only by the weather, and the passing of time. The day came when no one could remember who had raised the stones, or in what pattern, or what purpose they might have served.

So it was in the days when the Drwyds at last came from the southern continent, across the sea channel, to make the Brythonic island their home. They, too, wondered about the ancient stones: who had placed them there, and for what purpose. They told campfire tales of a race of giant men who brought them from a green isle in the west, and set them in place under the instructions of an old wizard named Merlin. "The Giants' Dance," they called the stones. But really they did not know. No one knew. There are tales today that say the first Drwyds used the fallen temple for their own rites, or even that they were the ones who raised the stones in the great circle. Indeed, it is often told that the Drwyds themselves came from the realm of Iwerydd, bringing ancient and arcane knowledge with them. In truth they came from lands far to the south, and dwelt in the great forests of Armorica before crossing to our Brythonic lands. They loved trees more than stones and worshipped rather in our ancient groves. It was they who brought the ancient oak knowledge to this land, as old in its own right as the stones of the Iweryddon, but of different origin. The Drwyds grew wise in the workings of the world, but it was the Iweryddon who had raised the standing stones. Few remember that today, for there is little of the ancient wisdom left in the world.

We will never know how much has been forgotten. But the wisdom of the times and the seasons remains yet. And Huan, now called by many names, still heralds the plantings and the harvest, while the ruined and fallen stones remain forever silent on the wide Salis Plain.

Chapter Ten
The Quiet Fires of Bel

Galan Haf came and went, and with it the celebration of the Fires of Bel. The long paddock on the southeast side of Llan y gelli was emptied of its winter residents. Passing between twin bonfires in token of fertility, the livestock moved out into summer pasture. The cattle found their way into the forest behind the fort, where much of the year they lived unsheltered and nearly wild. There young women, living in family roundhouses scattered outside the walls, wandered among the trees each day with milk buckets. The Silure cattle were small, no higher at the shoulder than even the youngest of milkmaids. The sheep had lambed in late winter, and the grassy meadow in front of the fort was filled with scruffy brown sheep of all sizes. Like the cattle, Silure sheep required little care and were mostly left to fend for themselves. The broad enclosure within the walls was still alive with fowl, and some pigs whose ancestors had been coaxed out of the forest several of their generations before.

Though the Iceni uprising in the east had been put down some time ago, Seutonius showed no signs of returning to the Silure region with the XIV Gemina legion. The once great II Augusta was without a commander, Vespasian having returned to Rome. So for a time, at least, there was peace at Llan y gelli. Men who had fought off Roman patrols for years spent their time repairing winter damage to the palisades, or plowing the small barley field before the gates. The older men were grateful for this gentler activity, while the young ones grumbled, and boasted of battles to come.

Fianna's wound had healed well, but she was still recovering her strength. Often she worked with Cethin in the healer's hut, where she taught him much, from the esoteric uses of hellbore to the daily salves and ointments of marsh mallow used for the gentler injuries of peacetime.

And she had begun two moon cycles before, in early spring, to teach him the Marsh Tales. It turned out to be a far greater task than he had imagined, for learning the tales meant memorizing them word for word so he could tell them to others.

"There is not enough space inside my head for all this!" he complained one day to Fianna.

"Nonsense," she said, laughing out loud. Such laughter still caused a pain in her side, but it was therapeutic, so she ignored the pain and laughed as often as possible.

"Nonsense," she said again. Among the druids there are bards who memorize many more tales than this! If you can keep dozens of herbal recipes in your head, you can learn a few old marsh stories!"

The tribes knew of writing, of course, but the advantage to learning by ear was that it took much longer, and was done with another person who had the time to answer questions that came up along the way. Cethin had never heard of Cysgodion or Ynys Calchfaen. Several times he had seen the great henge on the Salis Plain and walked among its fallen stones. But he had no idea who had built it or why. Indeed, Cethin often had so many questions that Fianna would accuse him of making them up in order to avoid the tedium of memorization.

One day after the last frost they were walking in the forest above the fort, looking for early stitchwort and toadflax, working on the tale of the Dark Lady.

"Now again," Fianna said, "beginning with the appearance of Gwalch, the marsh harrier."

"Under the blue sky and white clouds there was a cry," he began. Then, for a time, he was silent.

"Talons . . .," Fianna prompted.

"Yes, I know," said Cethin. "But I was wondering, what does she mean when she says 'The marshes rejoice at your presence, but they do not need you'?"

Fianna bent to look at some new cranesbill growing beside the path. "The Lady is speaking of the importance of every creature, and the interconnectedness of all. Each of us is a part of the dance of life, but if we were not here, the dance would go on without us. A different dance, to be sure. But the dance would nevertheless go on." She rose. "We'll come back here in the fall for the crescent seed pods. The mashed seeds make a good eyewash."

"It seems a shame to discover you are not needed," Cethin mused.

"Does it?" asked Fianna. Wanting to be needed means wanting another to be dependant upon you. Is it not better simply to be a reason for another's rejoicing? When you realize you do not need another, Healer, you understand you are complete within yourself. And when you know that, you are strong enough to love."

They walked farther into the forest as Cethin recited more of the Dark Lady's tale. When he came to the appearance of Enaid, he paused again.

"I think this pause is not for more prompting," Fianna smiled. You have another question?"

"Where did this woman come from?" Cethin asked. "All the other creatures, like the Lady herself, appear out of the marshes. But Enaid comes from somewhere else. Who is she."

"You will meet Enaid again in another tale," Fianna said. "For now, let her be a mystery, with no beginning and no ending. Perhaps she is a part of the Lady's self-awareness, a part of her growing from Morwyn into Vivian."

"But they are so different. Enaid is bright, and the Lady is shadow."

"We are each of us darkness and light," Fianna answered. "Now begin again, after, 'Is that like a flock of graylag geese?'"

~

Word came now and again of the Romans in the east. Seutonius was loath to return his forces to the treacherous bogs and ravines of the Silure forest. But the swarthy, battle tested Silure warriors were all that prevented complete Roman occupation. One day they would return, Cadfael knew. And when they did, he would be ready for them. Even when all else was quiet in Llan y gelli, the smithy was alive with the ringing of iron; spearheads being prepared, for the day when peace would end.

~

The tale of Doeth was even more perplexing.

"Why remember a tale in which the gods do not answer?" Cethin asked.

"What tale is that?" Fianna asked in reply. "I do not remember such a tale."

"Doeth is sitting in the rain," Cethin said, "and tells the Goddess that she has . . . ."

Fianna held up her hand to stop him.

"Recite it," she said. Cethin paused a moment, remembering.

"'We have been making offerings to you for countless cycles of the moon,' Doeth said aloud, looking out over the lake. 'Yet you do not answer, and the waters rise. What are we to do, Goddess? How are we to live?' No sound answered her but the hiss of falling rain on the surface of the lake. 'No, I did not suppose you would answer.'"

"And did not the Goddess answer?" asked Fianna.

"Not that I can see," answered Cethin.

"And what happens in the end?"

"Doeth watches the boat rise on its tether with the tide, and figures out the solution for herself."

"For herself?" asked Fianna. "Go, Healer, and think about what that means."

~

Finally, the eve of Galan Haf was upon them. Cethin stood on the south palisade overlooking the sheep meadow, where preparations were being completed for the fire festival that evening. The cattle and sheep were restless in the paddock, sensing their release to pasture was near, nervous about the campfires that had begun to burn before the gates. As with every fire festival before, people came in families and clans from all the nearby villages to celebrate the feast of Bel, the sun god whose time of year was beginning. The livestock in the enclosure at Llan y gelli belonged to all the villagers in common, and now the people were gathering on the green for the ceremony that would ensure fertility for another year. They had been arriving all day, laying fire rings for cooking, gathering wood, spreading hides for sitting on the ground or raising small lean-to's. But the center of all the activity was the laying of two great ricks of wood, side by side in front of the paddock gate. When the time came, as night's darkness covered the land, these would become the fires of Bel, ancient symbol of fertility and purification. In the meantime children played games in the grass, men told tales of ancient battles, and women wove stories about their men while preparing evening meals. In this way, the celebration beginning before the gates of Llan y gelli was just like every other ever held throughout the Brythonic lands for as long as people could remember.

But that night, Cethin knew, would be different from any Galan Haf that had come before.

"I wondered why my heart was breaking as I watched them arrive." It was Fianna, who had joined him on the palisade. "All those years on Ynys Mon we held this celebration on the flatlands near the beach. But here we are on a hill." She looked around at the rolling countryside, and the smoke from cook fires drifting into neighboring glens. "Here we are on a hill," she said. "It reminds me of Dolgwyl Waun below Fyrtwyddon, with the high Tor of Bryn Ddraig rising above us." There were tears in her eyes.

"I would not have thought you to be homesick, you who can travel where you will in your mind and see Ynys y Niwl as if you were there."

"Ah, Healer," she said. "The Sight is not the same thing as hearing the wind in the old yews above y Ffynnon Goch, or sitting under a tree on Bryn yr Affalau, or touching Vivian's hand." Tears came anew as she remembered that Vivian was

99

lost to her now. It would be Sianed, as the Lady, who would welcome her home. "Ah, Cethin, I have been away too long."

A shout rang out from below in time for them to see a ball flying toward them, escaping from a group of boys playing on the grass. Cethin caught it in midair and tossed it back, laughing. "It is like any celebration of Bel from my boyhood," he said. But then he looked at the shadow upon Fianna's face and was silent. Because in truth it was not like any such celebration that could be remembered. For that night, for the first time ever, there were no druids.

After the slaughter on Mona what druids were left had scattered across the waters, or into the forests and mountains around yr Wyddfa. Indeed it might has well have been a tomb they entered, for they disappeared without a trace. Now the feast of Bel had come again, and there was no druid to lead the ritual, to perform the magic.

As the great fires were lit, Fianna's heart took her back to the last fire festival on Dolgwyl Waun, before the great stone altar. She watched in her mind as Vivian and Caldreg raised their arms and called down the powers upon excited yet frightened young men and women prepared to leave childhood behind. She remembered when it was not Cethin, but Eoasaidh who stood beside her, frowning as Vivian stepped to Caldreg and kissed him.

"It is a ritual, and her duty as the Lady, Eosaidh," she had told him then, trying to assure him that Vivian was not taken with the young druid. But it was a young Dubh-bunadh herbalist standing beside her now, not an old tinner from Cornualle. And Caldreg had died in the forest, in the rain, trying to get her to safety. And because there were no druids in Llan y gelli to tend the fires of Bel, there would be no revelers in the forest, none to release their virginity to the gods.

"The fires of Bel will be quiet this night," said Cethin beside her. And suddenly the night was cold upon the palisade, and she drew a woolen shawl more closely around her shoulders. "You are cold, Mother," he said. "We should go down to the fires where it is warmer."

"Thank you, Cethin, but no, I would not join in what revels there are. I can watch the running of the cattle from here, and then I would like to go to bed." When he asked her leave to at least bring her some tea she agreed, and when he returned with it the warmth was welcome.

When the twin fires were fully ablaze, the wooden paddock doors swung open. Suddenly the night was filled with the lowing of cattle and bleating of sheep. Two young men emerged into the firelight, one leading the old bull on a tether, the other holding fast to a horn of the lead ram. As they drew them between the fires, the rest of the livestock came through the gate, following behind. In other years this moment was marked by raucous cheers from the crowd, the singing of songs and the thundering beat of drums. But the people fell silent, as did the animals, until the only sounds were the shuffling of hooves and the crackling of the great fires. And everyone knew they were present at a turning of the ages. When the animals had been let loose to pasture, the people drifted back to their camp fires and unrolled their sleeping furs. Perhaps in years to come the celebration of Beltane would regain some of its old glory, but that night all was quiet around the dying fires of Bel.

~

The next day, when Cethin and Fianna had tended to the last burned finger and scraped knee, and the people had gone home, each to their own village, the healer and the priestess sat together on an old wooden bench outside the doorway.

"I think, Mother," Cethin said, "it is like the Lost Land of Iwerydd."

Fianna smiled, for she saw the Tales were becoming a part of him. But she pretended not to notice.

"What do you mean?" she asked.

"When Iwerydd was lost and the refugees settled on the Salis Plain, they had to find a new way of relating to Huan, their sun god, a new way of understanding a new world. But the temple they built, the stone henge, was not entirely new. Rather

101

it was a new representation of the ancient encircling hills of their homeland. So as times change, old things are seen in new ways. But the old is never completely lost."

Fianna nodded. If she had ever borne a son of her own, she realized, she would have wanted him to be just like the young Dubh-bunadh healer.

~

And so the days of spring grew warmer as the world turned toward summer. In the meadows and forest glades around Llan y gelli wildflowers grew and bloomed as ever they had since long before such as the Romans had arrived on the Brythonic shores. Dog violet and moon daisy, celandine, cow parsley, and fox gloves. Fianna moved from the healer's hut to an empty roundhouse beside the sheep meadow, enjoying the freedom of being outside the confining walls. Often she would walk alone in the forest. Sometimes, gazing into the quiet pool of a brook, she would find Sianed, and they would speak in their hearts of the coming of Rome and the safety of Affalon. Always, Sianed would end with the same admonition. *Do not tarry, Fianna. Return before the frosts.*

Often, too, Fianna and Cethin would sit on the bench beside the healer's hut as she taught him the Marsh Tales. Tales of seekings and beginnings, tales of hopes and sorrows. And they would walk nearby in the forest, and she would ask him what he understood of what he had learned. Those were the gentlest of days at Llan y gelli, before the return of shadows.

Chapter Eleven
V. The Lights of the Ellylldan

At the edge of the ancient marshes, far from the open waterways, there are things in the darkness that are best left alone. So are the fens that surround the forbidden isle of Ynys y Cysgodion, where the Lady of Darkness is thought to dwell below the shadows of the Mendydd hills. From ancient times hapless travelers in those noisome waters have told of the Ellylldan, but only in daylight, for they dare not speak of such things in the darkness of the night.

~

Once there was a young woman of the Dwrtrygydd who was known as Tresglen. She was darkly beautiful, with a voice that sang like a marsh thrush. She was promised in marriage to Oriog the boatwright, a man of rough appearance and dangerous moods. Tresglen was a lover of the wide marshes, but Oriog hated them, and made it known at every turn. He came from a distant tribe that dwelt by the shores of the wide sea. His father had been a builder of proper boats, with deep hulls and sails that caught the wind. They would race through the blue waters like storm clouds that flew across the sky.

"You can't call this a boat," he said with disgust, ignoring the cold venison and birch beer that Tresglen had brought. "It's your damned marshes! Not enough water to float a tadpole." He dropped his stone adze, picked up the piece of venison and stared at it a moment, then dropped it as well. He snorted and walked over to a bush to relieve himself while Tresglen stood nearby in silence. When he returned to sit again on the ash log he was working on, she finally spoke.

"I don't know why you stay here when you are so displeased with us." He always ranted about the marshes, but clearly it was her people he hated. "Why don't you return to the sea and your own people?"

He looked with yearning for a moment to the west, then spit in no particular direction. "You know well the answer to that, woman. It seems our Chief desires an alliance with the Dwyrtrygydd, for what deranged reason I cannot guess. I am his nephew, you are the daughter of Gweledydd the seer." He spit again on the ground near his foot and picked up the adze. He hated the damned marshes, the damned marsh people and, she knew, he hated her only slightly less.

"No keel," he muttered, "no frame, no sail. Just a damned log." In truth there was a certain degree of skill involved in crafting a marsh boat, but not such that Oriog would acknowledge. He set to work attacking the tree's heartwood with the adze, his noon meal and his inconveniently betrothed woman both driven from his mind.

Tresglen did not cry. There were no tears left. Oriog's mumbled curses faded behind her as she followed the raised trackway through the marsh back to the island of huts. "I will not have this life," she said to herself aloud. A startled marsh hen flushed from a thicket of reeds to her left. She shouted to it as it flew off, "I will *not* have this life!"

~

At supper that night Gweledydd's eyes were sad but resolute. "It cannot be undone, daughter," he said. "Oriog is a skilled craftsman, even if he would rather not be making marsh boats. He will be a good provider, and we cannot insult his clan by backing out now."

Tresglen poked absently at the small hearthfire. Her father was a seer. Could he not see the grief in his own daughter's face? She imagined herself in Oriog's bed, saw the disdain in his eyes as he lay over her and took what was his due. *I cannot,* she thought. *I will not! He would not dare do this to me if Mother were still alive.*

And so the days went by. The grief in her heart turned to anger, and the anger to resentment. One day, as her wedding to Oriog drew near, her resentment turned to resolution. She began to gather a store of food – dried fruit and stale bread, and skins of water – and stored them in the hollow of an old tree outside the camp. She sharpened the knife Gweledydd had given her for skinning hares, and the short spear with which he had taught her to fish. And she watched Oriog as he worked on the flat bottomed boat. Watched, and waited for him to finish, praying to the marsh goddesses that he would before their wedding night arrived.

On the evening before the ceremony was to take place he looked up from his work and saw her sitting nearby, quietly singing to herself. For a moment he allowed himself to think, *she does have a beautiful voice.* But then he remembered his displeasure, and spat on the ground. "Well that's done," he said, and walked off to get drunk. It was beginning to get dark. Quietly, deep in the ancient marshes, the *Ellylldan* began to stir.

The young woman ran to her father's hut for her knife and spear, and a warm woolen cloak. Good, he was not there. He would be with the other men celebrating with Oriog, and would not return until late. By then she would be gone. She gathered her skins of food and water from the hollow tree and returned to the boat. It was harder to drag the flat bottomed dugout to the water than she thought, so she had to stop and rest several times. By the time she had it afloat and loaded with her provisions, darkness had settled upon the marsh.

Tresglen had no plan except to get away as quickly and quietly as possible. To avoid being missed soon enough to be successfully followed. To not get caught. *To never be found.*

Her marsh lay to the north of Ynys Calchfaen. It was in the days before the lake villages, so there was only open water beyond that. Tresglen shivered at the thought of the wide water with its vast openness in every direction and the unbroken sky stretching above. She was a daughter of the marshes, preferring the close covering of reeds, the gathering of shadows above the dark waters. In the end she chose a path through the marshes because, she told herself, it would be easier to hide and make good an escape. Still, the marshes at night could be as frightening as the wide waters. There were things in the marshes at night, she knew, and she looked cautiously about her as she paddled away from the bank. Somewhere in the huts of her people the men were drinking with Oriog, making crude jokes about the coming adventures of his wedding night. Somewhere, out in the marshes, the *Ellylldan* were beginning to stir.

There was no moon that night. Black clouds covered the stars. With no light by which to see, Tresglen decided to head east from Calchfaen, staying just inside the edge of the marsh reeds. That would take her counter-sunwise in a sweeping circle to the northeast, past the darkness of Ynys y Niwl and then on into the dark shadows of the north marshes. Folk who went in there often did not come out. It would be a good place to hide. So Tresglen paddled along the narrow channels, softly humming marsh tunes to herself in the dark.

She need not have worried about being missed. Far into the night Oriog, Gweledydd, and most of the other men sat around a blazing fire, drank untold skins of well-aged mead, and sang vulgar songs of conquests of every sort. Indeed her father never returned to their hut that night, nor Oriog to his. Blind drunk, they collapsed together beside a pathway and sang themselves to sleep on the ground. Neither Tresglen's absence, nor the boat's, would be noticed until they were both long gone. No, she would not be followed. But there were other things than men stirring in the shadows of the night.

All round her the night sounds of the marsh filled her imagination with visions of what she could not see. The humming and chirping of countless insects was deafening in the darkness. The deep croaking of a frog nearby in the rushes sounded as though it were with her in the boat. In the water there were things that glowed with a pale, eerie light. Things she could not see with her eyes she began to see in her mind. Her skin crawled as she felt things she had not touched; long, curling eels, and sucking leeches. She prayed there would be no tangling webs of spiders spun across the channel, as she felt her way forward between the reeds.

All of this is better than a life with Oriog, she told herself over and over. *All of this!* And she told herself the morning would come, though the night grew ever deeper. In the darkest part of the marsh, near unseen Ynys y Niwl, the *Ellylldan* were waiting, dancing among the reed tussocks where noisome marsh gasses hovered over black waters.

At first Tresglen thought the darkness was playing tricks with her eyes. Soft white lights appeared before her, indistinct, uncertain. They flickered and danced, then disappeared, only to appear again some distance away. She heard soft, taunting voices in her mind:

Come! Come, dance with us. Come and follow the lights, Tresglen. She shook her head to clear her vision and her mind. But the lights remained. *Follow the lights, Tresglen. Come with us.* The voices were like sweet songs. *No need to fear the dark. Come! Follow our lights!* The *Ellylldan* danced before her in the dark, and she knew not what it was.

"Come," she repeated, in a quiet voice. "Come." And she was entranced. Dipping the narrow blade of her paddle into the shallow water on her right, she began to turn her boat toward the beckoning lights. "Yes, I am coming," she breathed into the night air, and the lights danced away before her farther into the dark.

Something tugged at her awareness. What was it? A sense of unease that seemed to call for caution. *Beware!* The word was clear in her mind. But why? The lights were so beautiful, dancing slowly in the utter darkness. Then a tune emerged from deep within her memory, and the voice of her mother singing, the scent of her mother's body as she cradled the young child Tresglen in her arms. Finally, she remembered the words of the old marsh rhyme:

> *On darkest nights*
> *within the marshes deep,*
> *beware the lights*
> *that soft before you creep!*

Beware the ghostly dancing lights
before you in the dark:
they will not guide your steps aright,
nor safest pathways mark!

On darkest nights
when creatures in the marshes creep,
beware the glowing lights
that lure the mind to sleep

and trick the feet to wander from the way;
for there within the darkness will they keep
you, evermore, from living light of day!

Beware the lights, marsh traveler, if you can!
Beware the enchantment of the Ellylldan!

Tresglen froze, her paddle held still in the water. A quiet trembling shook her as childhood fears gripped her mind. Ahead the lights softly retreated and continued their dance, bidding her deeper in a direction she had not chosen. The *Ellylldan*! She shut her eyes tightly for several moments, hoping the lights would go away. But when she looked again they were still there, slightly farther off among the reeds. They danced in a slow bobbing motion before her.

Come, they softly sang. *Come follow us, come dance with us. Follow the lights.*

Her thoughts raced even as her body remained frozen, her boat sitting motionless in the still water. Insects sang their night songs around her. What did she know about the *Ellylldan*? Her mother's warnings had always fed childhood imaginings of dark, ugly creatures, wet and dripping with marsh water, weeds and slime matted in their stringy hair, their long and boney limbs, and large, bulbous frog-eyes lit from within with an unholy light. And their teeth. Long, needle sharp teeth.

On darkest nights
when creatures in the marshes creep,
beware the glowing lights . . .

The paddle slipped from her hands and slid away into the darkness among the reeds. The lights encircled her boat, still calling to her in her mind. Were there black, wiry, moving shapes behind the lights? She narrowed her eyes to the merest slits, trying to focus in the dark, but she could not see. Then, slowly, her boat began to move, gliding soundlessly forward as if being drawn by some unseen force.

Now it is well known the *Ellylldan* are spirit lights of the swamps and fens. Some say they are anguished souls of the lost dead, unable to find their way to the lands of peace, who haunt the marshes at night, drawing unwary travelers to a dark and solitary death in the lost backwaters where no one ever goes. Some say they are corpse-lights, death omens, appearing in a place where some tragedy is about to occur. Most believe the *Ellylldan* to be unearthly fairy-lights, with evil intent toward human beings, luring travelers from trusted paths into treacherous waters where they are never seen again.

Perhaps it was Tresglen's desire never to be seen again by Oriog that preserved her from deathly fright. Perhaps also that she was a marsh daughter, familiar enough with eerie tales to find them intriguing as well as fearsome. *Do not follow the lights!* Everyone who traveled in the marshes knew that. But as her boat began to move forward a strange calm came over Tresglen, though her paddle was lost somewhere in the reeds behind her. She was not propelling the boat, yet it moved in the darkness, following the light in front of her as others continued to circle around.

Tresglen's voice was barely a whisper. "Who are you?" she asked. There was no answer, but the lights glowed brighter for a moment, as if in response.

Then, in her mind, *Follow us, Tresglen. Follow our*

lights.

Follow them! It seemed she had no choice. Tresglen took several slow breaths, trying to ease the tension that had been building within her. Reeds had closed in all around her boat, and they hissed along the side as she continued forward. The *Ellylldan* did not seem malevolent toward her, neither did they seem friendly. They just were. There. In the deep darkness.

"Who are you?" she asked again. Still no answer except the insistent, *Follow. Follow us*, in her mind. She had no idea how long she had been following, or where she was. She suspected the shores of Ynys y Niwl lay behind her, that she was heading north and west into the north marshes as she had planned. But really she did not know where she was, or where the *Ellylldan* were leading her.

While she was thinking this, a gentle breeze began blowing from the northwest. Suddenly the mists parted, and the dome of the starry heavens appeared above her! Without the moon, the stars themselves provided enough light to see by, especially after such deep darkness. The high reeds cast star-shadows across Tresglen's face. She looked about her with new sight, and saw the *Ellylldan* surrounding her boat.

The tales tell little of the appearance of the *Ellylldan*, for they are usually seen only by their lights in the dreary darkness. What Tresglen saw filled her with wonder, and perhaps you will not believe it yourself. Around her boat, drifting just above the waters of the marsh, Tresglen saw thirteen little children all dressed in delicate white robes that drifted and swirled in the night breeze. Their faces shone with elf-light, and each held high a silver lantern in which a white candle burned. Each was the height of a roe deer, though they seemed taller for their hovering above the tops of the reeds. They gazed upon her with purposeful intent, but seemingly without interest.

Tresglen looked at each, from one to the other, around the circle. "They're lovely," she said, under her breath. Again the lanterns seemed to glow brightly for a moment as if they had heard. This time she almost thought she heard the words, spoken, almost sung, like liquid silver: *Come, Tresglen, come and follow us!*

Then she remembered. The *Ellylldan* have no personality, no actual will or desires of their own. They cannot have a conversation, can only express the will of the purpose for which they have been sent. Their childlike eyes were gentle, but empty. The fine hair rose on Tresglen's arms and the back of her neck, for this realization was more frightening than an encounter with intentional evil. One can confront the most fearsome of night demons and goblins, for their expression of evil is human-like, therefore potentially controllable. But the idea of an impersonal spirituality existing in human form can be unnerving. To Tresglen the experience was fascinating as well as fearsome, and she yearned to be able to speak with them. She knew too well what it is like to be without a voice. Still, all they could say was, persistently, *Come, come, come.*

As quickly as the starlight had appeared, it vanished. The marsh mists rolled in from the west and the darkness was again complete, the *Ellylldan* once more invisible except for the eerie light of their lanterns dancing above the reeds. And Tresglen's boat continued onward into the marsh.

All the following day her boat glided on through darker and deeper marshes. The mists were so thick she could not see the prow of her small boat, nor was there any sign of the lights in the pearl gray fog.

They reappeared when darkness fell on the second night. Tresglen had slept through much of the featureless boredom of the afternoon, and she was strangely relieved to wake after dark to the familiar presence of the *Ellylldan*. By then she knew they would not speak to her except to bid her follow them, but she began to speak to them, hoping they might understand.

"I know not who you really are," she said aloud, "or what your business with me might be. But I trust you, for you seem to me fairer than my mother's tales once warned. If you have a purpose for me, and wish me well, I will follow you."

111

She smiled bleakly, remembering she had no choice in the matter. But of course she had decided on her own to flee into the marshes, so in some way following the ghostly lantern bearers did seem to be of own her choosing.

Near midnight, several things happened all at once. The mists lifted, revealing once again the bright array of stars. There must have been a thin sliver of new moon by then but, if so, it had set hours before. Lit by the starlight, the *Ellylldan* appeared again in their billowing white garments, elf-children bearing silver lanterns and circling the little boat. A moment later they all emerged from the marsh reeds into a wide lake. The water was black under the night sky, and still as glass, the stars reflecting so magically from its surface that it was impossible to tell the heavens from the lake. An island lay in the middle of the waters like a great, dark shadow. Tresglen had no way of knowing it was Ynys y Cysgodion, for no one in her clan had ever seen it. Had she known, she would have been truly frightened, for Cysgodion was rumored to be the home of a strange sorceress known as the Dark Lady.

As the boat drifted over the quiet waters of the Lake of Shadows, the *Ellylldan* unwound their circle into two lines, forming an avenue to the shore. It truly was an island of shadows. Gnarled and bent yews grew to the water's edge, dripping with ferns and mosses. In the ancient tangle of forest that stretched beyond the shore lay the barrow tombs of the ancestors of the marshes; Tresglen could not see them, but she could feel their presence. As the boat drew itself up onto the mossy bank, the Dark Lady emerged from the shadows of the forest. She was a slight figure, shorter than the tales suggested. Her olive skin blended so well with her dark robe it was not possible to tell whether one could actually see her face, or merely its suggestion. Long black hair fell about her shoulders to her waist, where it seemed simply to fade from view rather than come to an end. She held a hand out, palm turned upward, in greeting.

"Welcome, Tresglen," she said. Her voice was the

sound of rushing marsh currents. "I am Vivian, Lady of this island and of the marshes."

As Tresglen stepped from her boat the *Ellylldan* faded away into the night. She looked after them as they disappeared from view, across the lake and back into the marsh. The night was silent, lit by the burning stars overhead, filled with star-shadows. Finally Vivian spoke again.

"They do my bidding. They are an expression of the will of the marshes."

"In the tales they are dark and ugly," said Tresglen. "And they are evil. They hate the Dwyrtrygydd, and lure us to our death in the marshes."

"Do you believe this?" Vivian asked. "Now that you have seen them?"

"They are fair and bright, and they seem like children. I do not know what to think," said Tresglyn.

Vivian motioned to Tresglyn to sit beside her on a fallen tree by the water's edge. "Like all things of the spirit," she said, "They appear as they are expected to by those who see them. "To people with dark hearts the *Ellylldan* are frightening. Some folk can never see them at all. But to one such as you, their true nature is revealed. I suspected it would be so. I summoned you, Tresglen of the Dwyrtrygydd. The lights of the *Ellylldan* brought you to me."

Tresglyn moved away on the moss covered log. "The old tales also warn about women who live alone in the wilds." She looked into Vivian's dark eyes, which were filled with ancient knowledge.

"And do you still believe those ancient tales, marsh daughter, now that you have seen me?" She held Tresglen in her gaze.

"No. No, Lady, I do not. But why have you summoned me? For what purpose? And how did you find me?"

Vivian smiled. "So many questions! It shows you are regaining your wits after your strange journey. But first you will want shelter and refreshment. Come." She stood, and in her upturned palm there appeared a glow of marsh-wisp, much like the lights of the *Ellylldan*. She started down a path toward an opening in the old forest. Tresglen rose, and followed, not yet daring to wonder who this lady of the marshes might be.

The ancient forest soon gave way to a wide bog where mists hung and swirled in ghostly patches above the wet ground. Vivian followed the way in the darkness with the ease of long use, a darker shadow in the darkness just ahead of Tresglen. Suddenly, out in the bog on both sides of the path there were lights again.

Tresglen touched Vivian's shoulder. "It is the *Ellylldan*. They've returned," she whispered.

Vivian stopped. "No, daughter," she answered. "The *Ellylldan* have not been summoned again. This is a natural doing of the bogs."

"But they look so much alike!"

"And so do many confuse them. The bog plants die and return to the earth, as we do. Sometimes, at night, the spirits of these plants appear for a time before passing from our world."

Tresglen stared in wonder at the soft, shimmering lights. "It seems the world is stranger than ever I knew," she said.

Vivian smiled. "And it seems your training has already begun!"

"My training?" Tresglen asked.

"Come, daughter. Shelter and tea first." Vivian turned, and continued down the old path. Tresglen followed, finding her own voice in the many questionings of her mind.

Daylight had begun to filter through the mists by the time they reached Vivian's hut. It was small, not a dozen paces across, a roundhouse made of mud and wattle, and a thatched roof covered with marsh mosses. A light wisp of smoke came through the roof, telling of a cooking fire within. Inside, the hut was warm and dry, though the firelight did not fully dispel the shadows. A young girl of perhaps twelve summers was pouring tea from a small pot. She turned and smiled at them as they entered.

"This is the daughter of my blood," Vivian said. "She is called Bendith, but one day she, too, will be known as Vivian."

Vivian must be older than she seems, thought Tresglen, who was herself not much older than Bendith.

"Is that a title, then?" Tresglen asked, returning Bendith's smile.

"A title and a name both," Vivian answered. "from ancient times when the first Lady of Ynys y Cysgodion emerged from the marsh waters."

Tresglen turned toward Vivian, gasping in surprise. "This . . . This is Ynys y Cysgodion?" she asked.

"It is, daughter. It is the Isle of Shadows."

"Then the tales are true," said Tresglen with wonder in her voice, and not a little fear. "You are the Dark Lady."

Vivian laughed, a quiet, pleasant laugh. "So they say. But do not worry, daughter, I am human as you are."

"But the Dark Lady is immortal! She is the creator of the marshes!"

Again Vivian laughed. "There are many tales about me. Nearly all of them are untrue, coming from imagination built upon too much fear or too much love. No one is the creator of the marshes, for they have been here always. And I am as mortal as you. The first of my grandmothers emerged from these waters in ancient times, and witnessed the coming of the first marsh folk of fur and feather, leaf and stone. In the beginning she was called Llyf, for the marsh currents from which she came, and later she was known as Morwyn. In time those who loved her named her Vivian, giver of life. Ever after my grandmothers have been known by this name, as will Bendith, when it comes time for me to leave this world." Her eyes turned away, and she sipped her tea of soothing herbs. The three women sat in silence for a long while, listening to the cries of harriers and marsh hens.

"Why did you call me, my Lady?" Tresglen asked, finally.

It took a few moments for Vivian to answer, as if she

were returning from a far place in a dream. "I heard your spirit calling over the waters as you fled Ynys Calchfaen," she answered. "I knew you to be a daughter of the marshes, and that you would be the first priestess to join us here. Bendith and I are to be alone no longer. It is time to begin our community."

"Priestess?" asked Tresglen. "I am no priestess!" In her mind she added, *I do not even know what a priestess is!* But she did not say it aloud.

Vivian smiled. "When you do learn what a priestess is, daughter, you will know that you are one."

Again the three women sat silently around the small fire, feeding it a bit of wood now and then, and refreshing their tea. They bothered not about the slow passage of time. When darkness returned they shared a bit of barley porridge, spread out their sleeping furs, and lay down together, side by side, near the fire. It seemed to Tresglen that Vivian and Bendith fell instantly into a deep sleep. But she lay awake in the shadows, wondering many things. What did the Dark Lady see in her to think she could be a priestess? And there seemed to be no male on the island, so where did Bendith come from? For that matter, where did the barley come from? Cysgodion was filled with mysteries, and they swirled about her in the darkness as did the mists outside.

Vivian spoke a strange word in her sleep, and far out in the marshes the *Ellylldan* began again to stir, for there were other priestesses to call. Tresglyn sighed and drifted off to sleep. The realm of Affalon had begun.

Chapter Twelve
VI. The Visit of the Bendith y Mamau

Once, a very long time ago in the far reaches of the western marshes, a daughter was born to a young woman who lived with her husband's clan of fisherfolk. The woman's name was Llefrith and she called her daughter Teg, for the child was truly fair. This frightened the clan members, for they knew too well the ways of *y Tylwyth Teg*, whom the marsh folk also called Bendith y Mamau.

"'Tis a dangerous thing to be mocking the subjects of Gwyn ap Nudd," said her husband's mother to Llefrith. "Sure they be called Bendith y Mamau, but they be not ones for young mothers to trifle with." She spat in the four directions. "Only the fairies may be called Teg. Ye'll have them comin' for yourself and the bairn both, if you're not more respectful." She spit again, a charm of protection, at Llefrith's feet. "They're a true Mother's Blessing is what they are," she said, hoping such flattery might avert disaster.

"Tush, Ma," answered Llefrith. "Be savin' your spittle for more important things. Gwyn may be lord of *y Tylwyth Teg*, but he'll be havin' no power over me or mine. And indeed my own little Teg is fair as they." Llefrith held little Teg at arm's length and danced with her around the hearth fire. "Yours is the only mother's blessing we'll be havin' around here," she said. "If you'll give it, that is."

"We've had enough bad luck already," said the old woman. It's not right ye be askin' fairies for more."

Llefrith's husband, Dubhydd, had been out fishing in the open waters just before the child came, and was lost in a storm, disappearing without a trace of him or his boat. Three full moons had passed, with Llefrith living in the huts of her husband's clan. She found solace in the daughter that was born to her, taking heart from the bairn's fair face, which reminded her of her lost love. Every day when the weather was fair she would take little Teg to the mooring that looked out upon the western waters.

"Look away out there, little Teg," she would say to her daughter as she stared into the setting sun. "Your Da's out there somewhere. He's out there beyond the sea, but he'll be comin' back for us one day. I swear it to ye, my little one. I swear it." Even so, Llefrith's words were not in her heart, and in her heart she wept. When there was a storm on the sea, she went not near the water.

It was mostly late at night, alone with Teg in the small hut Dubhydd had built for them just before he left, that fear would grip Llefrith's heart and crush further her dying hope. While her daughter slept she lay awake, hearing over and again the old tales her own Ma had told her, the warnings and reproaches hurled at her each day by Dubhydd's grieving mother.

She cried out into the dark, "Oh, Genwair, I know ye miss your son as I do, and there is a pain in your heart. But why must ye be so hard? The old tales left me when my husband did. If Gwyn could not send him back safe from the storm, neither can the old god send *y Tylwyth Teg*, frightful or fair, to cause me more grief." She stood up in defiance, and challenged the darkness:

"There will be no Bendith y Mamau come to this home while I am in it," she swore, her quiet voice firm with determination.

After that, Llefrith slept only fitfully until the first light of day.

In the morning, when marsh fowl greeted the rising sun, Llefrith took her daughter to the hut of Genwair and Curyll to share in their morning meal. Unlike Genwair, whose words multiplied with her grief, the death of his son drove Curyll to a bitter silence. He sat voiceless and uncaring while his wife scolded Llefrith.

"Do not try to hand me the bairn!" she shouted.

Llefrith withdrew the child and clutched her to her breast, turning away to shield her from her grandmother.

"I will not hold such a child," Genwair said in anger. "Nor will I hold with such an affront to *y Tylwyth Teg*." She made a sign of protection upon her own forehead and retreated to the far side of the hut. Curyll closed his eyes, retreating into himself. Llefrith, seeing his sorrow, went to him and placed Teg in his lap. His eyes, when they opened in surprise, were soft. He held the child gently, but spoke not. Genwair stood across the hut, her face to the wattle wall. Llefrith went to her, touched her shoulder.

"I know ye hold to the old tales, Ma," she said, "and ye know that since we lost Dubhydd I have not. But we canna let this come between us. Not when we are all we have left to each other."

Genwair turned slowly to face her. "I do not fault ye, and ye know it," she said quietly, her voice trembling. "But I fear for the bairn. Believing or not, ye canna call the child Teg and risk bringing the wrath of the Fair Folk upon her. She's Dubhydd's child as well as yours, as well ye know." She took both of Llefrith's hands in hers, her face suddenly softening.

Llefrith nodded. her eyes filled with tears, as did Genwair's. The women embraced for long moments, then sat together beside the hearth fire, watching Curyll hold the little bairn upon his knees.

After some minutes of silence, Genwair sighed and said, very quietly, "But, daughter, why must it be *Teg*? Why do ye take the risk?" She was truly concerned but, as truly, was trying not to offend.

With a determined smile Llefrith reached for Genwair's hand. "Now, Ma, don't ye be startin' that all over again. She's a fair young bairn, and she'll always be my Teg."

Genwair sighed and went to Curyll. Kissing him softly on his forehead, she took the child in her own arms and held her close. "If ye don't mind, daughter," she said, "I'll be callin' her Berthog, the name her Da gave her, for 'tis true she is a beautiful bairn. But I'll not myself be temptin' the *Teg*."

"It'll do, Ma." And, to herself she thought, *Yes, that will have to do*. Llefrith wiped the tears from her eyes, and in that moment she truly became Genwair's own daughter.

"I suppose you'll be movin' in with Curyll and me, then?" asked the older woman. Llefrith looked about the tiny hut and laughed softly to herself. Never would she leave the shelter Dubhydd had built with his own hands. No matter how sincere Genwair's offer of protection from the kithain of Gwyn ap Nudd.

"We'll see, Ma," was all she said.

~

Late that night Llefrith rose in the dark and went outside to relieve herself in the bushes beside her hut. The night was beautiful, warm and clear, with stars ablaze in the heavens and insects singing in the reeds. She breathed deeply, drawing in the scents of the marsh night that had always reminded her of childhood. She felt more lighthearted than she had since her last night with Dubhydd, in the warmth of their bed. A song came to her heart and found its way to her lips, so she decided to stay up a bit longer and watch the stars. It was unlike her to leave Teg alone in the hut, but she thought nothing of it. The other clan huts were nearby, it seemed so safe there on Ynys Bragwair, below the Polden Ridge. Surely it would be all right to stroll for a bit along the water's edge.

She left the shoreline and climbed the small knoll at the center of the island. From there, in the faint light of the setting crescent moon, she could just make out the high tor of Ynys y Niwl in the east.

As she gazed at the dark hill, a shiver went through Llefrith's body. She told herself it was merely the chill of the night breezes, but she knew better. Ynys y Niwl, the Isle of Mists, was uninhabited, but the marsh folk told tales of a cavern deep within the tor, the Great Hall of Gwyn ap Nudd, king of the Bendith y Mamau. She thought she could hear on the wind snatches of their beautiful songs. She tarried in the beauty of it longer than she had intended, knowing well the fairy hall was far away across the marshes and no danger to her. All the while Teg slept quietly in her cradle, alone and unguarded in the night.

Marsh mists finally obscured the distant tor, but the bright stars still burned overhead. Llefrith lay back in the grass, enchanted by the stars and by the unearthly music that seemed suddenly to be all around her. She did not notice that the chirping of the crickets had ceased, that bats and snipes had left the night sky, that the breeze off the marshes had died and the night air was dead still. The stars spun before her eyes as the music danced in her ears, and she lost awareness of all else.

Spiraling down the slope of Bragwair Knoll, drifting toward the sleeping huts near the shore, the haunting notes of the fairy song began to search, to seek the fair bairn whose name had drawn them to the small isle at the edge of the west.

Lying beside Curyll in their hut, Genwair stirred in restless dreaming. She heard the most beautiful singing, but when she looked for its source she saw sunken eyes, twisted limbs, and cold gray flesh. Large tufts of ginger red hair stood out from bulbous heads. From hideous, wide mouths filled with sharp and broken teeth came the words of the song, a song as fair and beautiful as ever had been heard in the marshes.

What child is there
who is so fair
within her cradle sleeping?
'Tis she we seek,
so small and meek
within her mother's keeping!

Even within her dream Genwair began to understand the peril. She thrashed about on her sleeping furs, trying desperately to wake up, while all the while the vile creatures danced and sang.

What child is there
who though so fair
alone at night is sleeping,
while mother lies
'neath starry skies
enchantment o'er her sweeping?

Ugly creatures with eerily beautiful songs. *Y Tylwyth Teg*! The Bendith y Mamau! Genwair sat bolt upright, suddenly wide awake, great drops of sweat glistening on her brow and wild fear shining in her eyes. She threw off her covering and ran from the hut. Outside there was a strange chill in the air. The stars shone brighter than ever they ought, and the strains of unearthly music swirled about her. Off to her left, up on Bragwair Knoll, she saw Llefrith lying still in the grass, clad in her white shift. Ahead, the music seemed to fill the hut where the bairn lay alone, a cold white light shining from the open doorway. Genwair screamed and ran toward it.

"Berthog!" she shouted. Then, "Teg! Teg, I'm comin' for ye!"

Genwair was only steps from the hut when suddenly all went dark, and the night was silent. In the marsh, crickets resumed their own songs. From Llefrith's hut came the piercing wail of an infant's cry. Genwair raced inside, over to the child's cradle. A small body bundled in the soft cradle blanket was moving restlessly, and crying out for her mother.

"Ah, Teg," Genwair said with relief, "Ye be all right!" She pulled back an edge of the blanket to kiss her granddaughter, and screamed for the second time that night; a blood chilling scream of one who watches as a loved one is taken from her, and is powerless to do anything about it. She dropped the ghastly bundle into the cradle and made a sign of protection in the air all about her.

"'Tis a crimble!" she breathed, "A changeling of the Bendith y Mamau!"

There was a stirring behind her. Genwair turned to look,

and saw Llefrith standing in the doorway, stricken.

"They've taken her, haven't they, Ma?"

The old woman nodded, in silence. From the cradle, the little changeling looked up at her and smiled, quietly humming a beautiful tune of the *Gwlad y Tylwyth Teg* . . .

A second shadow appeared in the doorway, just behind Llefrith, and quietly put an arm around her shoulder. Genwair watched in wonder as a deep, kindly voice said,

"Come, Daughter; come Gennie, let's be goin' home."

Genwair sobbed. "Curyll," she said, "bless ye." And she went to his arms.

~

The crimble lay peacefully in the cradle, quietly humming to itself and playing with its left foot as if trying to understand its toes.

"'Tis a shame changelings are so ugly," said Curyll. "They sing beautifully, like their elders."

"'Tis a shame crimbles are traded by the *Teg* for human bairns," sneered Genwair.

Y Tylwyth Teg when in the underworld were thought to be wonderous fair with long golden hair. But 'twas in the light of this world they appeared misshapen and ugly. For that reason they were jealous of beauty in human bairns, kidnapping them and placing their own bairns in the robbed cradle.

"Vile, evil creatures," said Llefrith. Her face was white with worry.

Again Curyll put a reassuring arm around her shoulder. "'Tis not so much that they be evil, Llefrith. It's only that they're terrible selfish, and care not for the pain they cause to others." At the look of reproach in her eyes he went on quickly, "I only mean to say they wilna hurt the bairn. They'll be teachin' her the beauty of their music, for they love to see the rapture that comes to a human face, not bein' able to feel it themselves."

"I care not whether they be evil or good," said Llefrith, and she began to cry once again. "I only want my Teg back.

123

Safe and sound. And soon."

"Aye, it best be soon," said Genwair. "It best be soon or she'll be trapped for good. Time works different in their land."

Llefrith began to cry uncontrollably. Curyll was at a loss to decide whose shoulder to comfort, so he stood above them both with a hand on each.

"I don't believe that was a help, Gennie," he said.

Genwair took her sobbing daughter in her arms and rocked her gently. "What is it 'twill help, husband? What can we do?"

Curyll went to the door of the hut and looked out at the sunlight glinting off the marsh waters. It was near mid-day. A good thing, for it was best to talk of such things when the sun was high. He hesitated a moment. "There is a way, perhaps," he began slowly. "Ye know it as well as I, Gennie."

She looked up from where she sat holding Llefrith. 'Twas true, she agreed. She knew the direction of his thoughts. "Cysgodion," she answered.

"Aye, Gennie, and the Dark Lady. 'Tis only a witch can treat with *y Tylwyth Teg* for the return of a kidnapped bairn."

Genwair held her daughter's face in both her hands. "We will go this very night, Daughter, though it be we know not the way!"

~

It would have been safer in the small boat to travel east along the line of marshes, and follow that line as it curved northward and back toward the west. But that way would have taken them past Ynys y Niwl, with another danger all its own. So they set out north by east across the open waters, following the night stars and hoping for peaceful weather. By sunrise the next day they were entering the dark waters of the north marshes. 'Twas a seeking meant for women only, so Curyll remained to worry at home, while Genwair and Llefrith had set out with the crimble to find Ynys y Cysgodion.

Cysgodion found them first. For they had become lost among the many channels when an old woman appeared, in a

124

small marsh boat being paddled by a young girl just past her entrance into womanhood.

"Greetings, travelers," she said. "What is it you seek?"

We seek the Dark Lady of Ynys y Cysgodion," answered Llefrith, "upon a matter of some urgency."

"Then you have found what you seek. Come, and bring the changeling you hide among those blankets." She led them to the shore of an island overhung with ancient yews, dripping with mosses and ferns, where there was a wattle hut and a warm hearth fire. "Gwennyth will make us some tea and barley broth," she said. "Sit by the hearth and tell me what you desire. Though I can guess at that with some confidence." Her eyes were upon the small bundle Llefrith carried uneasily in her arms. When Llefrith looked up to meet her gaze, the two women looked deeply into one another's eyes. "You are from the west marshes," the old woman said, "It was no small task finding me."

"How do you know this about us?" Genwair interrupted.

The old woman smiled warmly. "I am Vivian, Lady of Cysgodion. But once I was called Tresglen, after my great grandmother, who came to this place three generations ago at the bidding of she who was Lady then. That Tresglen, my great ancestress, became a priestess here in the new realm of Affalon. In her turn she became the Lady. I, in my turn, have followed her."

"Affalon," breathed Llifrith. "I have heard rumors of the name, but thought it only one of the tales of the marshes, a place imagined in the heart."

"It is all those things, child. But it is also real, as you can see. Affalon is this isle of Cysgodion, and the marshes and fens all about us. It is the many isles of these marshes, most especially Ynys y Niwl, though none live there yet save Gwyn, son of Nudd, under the tor. Affalon is the community of priestesses, who serve the Goddess of these marshes, and the folk who live among the endless reeds." Vivian turned to Genwair. "You knew this, Genwair, which is why you have

125

brought Llifrith to me, and her small, troublesome bundle."

Genwair answered, "It is true I have heard the tales, my Lady, but I had never fully hoped in them until you found us today."

Her eyes turning serious, Vivian took the little bundle from Llefrith. "Let me see this troublesome little crimble you would have me return to Old Gwyn," she said, and she pulled back a corner of the blanket. "Well, well. You are not so ugly as some of your kin," she laughed. "But your place is not here, young crimble."

~

Some time later, when Llefrith had finished her tale, Vivian sighed with concern. "Your Ma spoke truly," she said. "That was a dangerous name you gave to your little bairn."

Llefrith started to protest, but Vivian held up a hand to stop her.

"I will not chastise you, Daughter, for you have had more than your share of that. And you have learned a hard lesson. But what lies ahead is harder still. It is not as easy a task as the stories tell to bring a bairn back from *Gwland y Tylwyth Teg*. The Fair Ones do not part with their gains so readily. Then, too, the halls of Gwyn ap Nudd are a charmed place, filled with sweet music and the food and drink of magic. Many who go there never have a desire to return."

"I know this," Llefrith answered. Her voice trembled. "But we can try, can we not? I'll go anywhere, do anything, if only I can bring my Teg back to this world!"

Vivian shook her head. "You cannot go, Daughter, for you would not have the strength to return." She looked down again at the crimble, who had fallen asleep. "It is I who must go. I must make the exchange."

"You?" asked Llefrith. "I canna ask you to do such a task. I only meant to receive your guidance . . ."

"Hush, child." it was Genwair, who placed a steadying hand on her arm. "The Lady be right. Remember what Curyll said. Only a wi . . ." she paused suddenly.

"Only a witch?" asked Vivian. Your Curyll is wiser than you think, but not so wise as he imagines!" She sighed once again. "Yet among us four," nodding toward Gwennyth, who had been so quiet Llefrith had forgotten her, "among us four it is I who must go. The perils of this journey you can only guess at. It is better for someone older to make the journey. Someone who has already outlived those she has known on earth. Come little crimble," she said to the fairy child, "we must prepare to travel."

~

The next day Llefrith and Genwair stood with several priestesses on the shore of Ynys y Cysgodion as Vivian placed the crimble into a basket in the bow of a small marsh boat, and stepped in herself. As she took her paddle, she looked up at Llefrith, looked deeply into her eyes. "This is a perilous journey, Llefrith," she said. "Reality is not the same in *Gwland y Tylwyth Teg* as it is here. Even time is different. Even if I am successful, make no assumptions about the time or nature of my return." She looked at Gwennyth. "You know what you must do, Gwen, if need be." Silently, Gwennyth nodded. And with three strokes of her alderwood paddle, Vivian disappeared into the reeds of the dark marsh.

~

A full cycle of the moon later, Vivian had not yet returned from Ynys y Niwl. On the night of the full moon, Gwennyth took on the responsibilities of the Lady. "Do not fear," she assured Llefrith. "It is only until Vivian returns."

At the next full moon, Genwair desired to return home, lest Curyll fear some evil had befallen her. Two of the priestesses of Affalon were chosen by Gwennyth to accompany her, to guide her through the marshes and do the work of paddling the boat.

"I canna go with ye, Ma. Ye know that," Llefrith told her, with tears in her eyes.

"Aye, that I know Daughter. You stay here until the Lady comes home with the little bairn." Genwair kissed her

127

daughter and stepped into the marsh boat. They never saw one another again in this world.

At midwinter the small band of priestesses held a quiet ritual in which they bade farewell to Vivian, and named Gwennyth as Lady of Affalon. The ache in Llefrith's heart was nearly more than she could bear. At the following midwinter celebration Llefrith made her vows as a priestess, and Gwennyth reluctantly took the name Vivian. After that, the times and the seasons rolled slowly on in their endless cycles. Summers and winters came and went so that Llefrith ceased to count them. In her heart she still longed for Teg, but hope had long since given way to despair, and then to resignation.

One morning, early in the new growth of a springtime when gray had begun to appear in Llefrith's hair and her bones welcomed with relief the coming warmth, three elder priestesses came to her hut.

"Our Lady is unwell," they told her. "She calls for you."

By the next full moon, Llefrith was Lady of Affalon. Sometime after in the turning of the seasons she felt Curyll leave this world and, shortly after that, Genwair. *I am alone now in all the world,* she thought.

No, my Lady. It was young Fia next to her, preparing their evening meal. *We are all with you, always.* And Llefrith smiled.

~

For some reason she never took the name of Vivian. "It doesn't fit me," she would say. But the priestesses knew she still grieved in her heart. For her little Teg, and for the Lady of Affalon who set out to search for her so long ago. Every spring when the air turned warmer and the stars of a new season shone in the sky, she remembered that night of horrid enchantment on Bragwair Knoll, and the visit of the Bendith y Mamau, and Teg, her bairn.

One day Llefrith was walking by herself along the shore of Ynys y Cysgodion, where the marsh grasses grew

128

particularly close to land. The mists were especially heavy, and Fia had implored her, as always, not to go walking alone. As always, Llefrith had brushed aside Fia's concerns.

"It does not trouble me to be alone," she said. "That is something I got used to long ago."

Fia knew when it was useless to protest, and watched the Lady as she disappeared into the mist. *I will have tea waiting for her when she returns*, Fia thought.

And so Llefrith found herself walking along the shore of Cysgodion, alone with her old memories, when she thought she heard the sound of a paddle out in the mist.

You're an old woman, she told herself. *Old women are always hearing what isn't there. Or not hearing what is.*

But Llefrith had lived on Cysgodion long enough to know the sound of a marsh paddle. She stepped back from the shore several paces, peered into the mist, and waited as the sound became closer and more distinct. As often happens in the heavy Affalon mists, the boat appeared all at once, along with the soft scraping sound of its hull as it beached on the shore. A dark lady, somewhat younger, it seemed, than Llefrith, lay down her paddle and stepped from the boat. Her skin was olive, her eyes dark, and hair black as midnight fell about her shoulders. But about her were the airs of maturity, and she bore herself as one who was used to being obeyed. At first Llefrith could not believe her eyes. the two women stood facing each other, perhaps twenty paces apart, as the gentle marsh current washed upon the shore and tatters of mist swirled between them. Llefrith was the first to speak.

"Vivian," she whispered.

The woman from the boat was clearly exhausted. "Yes, it is Vivian," she said. "Who are you? I don't remember a priestess your age. Take me to Gwennyth immediately!"

"My Lady," Llefrith answered, "Gwennyth lives not in this world. She has been gone from us these many cycles." She wished to move to Vivian, to hold her, to rejoice in her presence. But she was rooted to the spot where she stood.

There was too much to fear, to much at stake.

"Then who now takes her place?" Vivian asked. "Who cares for Affalon in my stead?"

Llefrith dared a step forward. "Gwennyth was made Lady of Affalon long ago, Vivian, at the same time I was made a priestess. She died, also long ago. You never came back to us, my Lady. Then, when Gwennyth passed from this world I was asked to take her place. I am Lady of Affalon, and have been so for many cycles of the sun. Until this very moment, at least." She fell to her knees, but Vivian knelt beside her.

"Then you are now Vivian, in my place," she said.

"No, my Lady. The name is yours, I could not take it."

Vivian gazed intently into the face of the strange woman before her, trying to see something familiar, some clue to her identity. But she could not. At last, she must ask the fateful question.

"Then who are you, who claim to take my place in Affalon?"

With a flood of tears the answer came. "My Lady, you do not know me! I am Llefrith, of the west marshes. I am she whose bairn ye left to seek those ages ago."

A terrible wail escaped Vivian's lips. "Aye, it is true then! I am too late! The Goddess forgive me, I have fulfilled my task, but I have return too late!" She fell over in a swoon, caught in Llefrith's arms, and the two sat together in joy and anguished sorrow on the shore of Ynys y Cysgodion.

Llefrith, now the older of the two, rocked Vivian and wiped tears from her eyes. "My Lady, you have been gone a long, long time. Much has changed, many have grown old and left this world. But you seem no older than when I saw you last."

The details of conversation helped Vivian to compose herself. "I told you once," she reminded Llefrith, "that time can be different in the halls of Gwyn. By my reckoning, I have been gone a few days only. Forgive me, Llefrith! You were young and hopeful when I left, and I have come back too late."

Silence again between the two, until finally Vivian spoke. "Llefrith . . ." a hesitation, then, "Forgive me, my Lady. I have brought something you will want to see, but I know not how you will receive this now." She went to the boat, and lifted a tiny bundle, wrapped in a soft cradle blanket. Llefrith heard the quiet cry, and her heart broke at the same time that it leapt for joy. She ran to Vivian, her eyes blinded by tears, and took the small bundle into her arms. Inside the folds of the blanket, softly crying from fatigue but with eyes wide in wonder, was a fair, beautiful bairn – her bairn, no older than when she had last seen her, a lifetime ago!

"Teg! Oh Teg, me own fair bairn! Teg, it's you, you've come back to me at last!" She kissed the face of the little bairn and hugged her to her breast, before the world turned and swirled around her, and she fell to the ground in a faint. But even as she lost consciousness her heart was filled with joy, for little Teg had come home.

~

Some time later Llefrith awoke in the warmth of her own bed, a fire going on the hearth, and many of the priestesses gathered around her. Beside her, snug in the crook of her arm, lay Teg, fast asleep.

"I'm old enough now to be your great grandma, little one," said Llefrith, wiping away new tears. "We'll have to get one of these young priestesses to care for ye."

"She's your own bairn, and your own responsibility, and that's that," said Fia in mock reproof, handing her some hot tea. "You'll get some help from us, but that's all you'll get." They all had a good laugh at Fia's well meant insolence.

"That is no way to address the Lady of Affalon," Vivian remonstrated from beside the bed. Llefrith frowned at her. "It must be so," Vivian said to her. "It has passed from me to you already. My time is over."

A strange look remained on Vivian's face. "Lady?" Llefrith asked, holding Teg even more closely, if that were possible. "What is it?"

131

"I have something else for you, Llefrith. Something else that I found, quite unexpectedly in the land of fairy. It will be hard for you to accept, I fear. I was reluctant to reveal this to you yesterday at the boat."

Llefrith sat up in bed, puzzled. She took Vivian's hand. "What is it, Lady? I am so filled with joy at the wonder of Teg's return in my old age. What can be stranger than that?

It was hard to tell whether joy or pain filled Vivian's eyes as she looked to the door of the hut. "Now," she said quietly to the young priestess standing there who, in response, drew back the hide that covered the door. Sunlight streamed through the opening, crossing the center of the hut and falling upon the bed where Llefrith sat with Teg in her arms. Outside there was the soft music of the song of birds. For a moment a shadow stood in the doorway, and it seemed as though all the world paused in disbelief. He entered as though walking on the path of sunlight. A young man, with the powerful muscles and bronze skin of a fisherman. He stood before the bed where Teg slept and Llefrith sat in shock.

"Hello, Dear One," he said, tears of disbelief in his eyes. "I'm back."

For Dubhydd, too, had come home, as she had once sworn he would.

Chapter Thirteen
VII. The Old Frog of Bryn Llyffaint

Targh was a young boy of no more than five summers, which is to say he was very much like young boys had ever been before him, or are likely ever to be again while the ages continue to turn. One fine morning, at the time of the year when the breezes shift from northwest to southwest and begin to warm, he was playing in the shallows on the south coast of Ynys Mawr, where there has ever been open water rather than marsh. His father, Caddoc, was repairing a fishing net in the bright sun, so Targh was left to his own explorations, as long as he did not wade out above his knees, or wander from his father's sight. So it was that in a small inlet, among a very small stand of cattails, young Targh found something quite big, and very green.

It was the loud, deep *croak* he heard first. *A frog!* he thought. And a big one, by the sound of it. He turned his head this way and that to discover the direction in which the prize lay. One more loud *croak*, and he had it! Just off to his right, out in the cattails. Perhaps ten paces into the black mud. And surely no more than two paces out of Tada's sight! He looked back to where his father was working on the net, waving to him to establish his presence in the allowed range of wandering. Caddoc returned his concentration to mending the net just as the third loud *c-r-o-a-k* came to Targh's young ears. For a young boy of five summers there can never be any debate in such matters, and Targh knew at once exactly what he must do.

It was sitting on a fallen log just past the cattails, enjoying the warm sun. Targh became absolutely still and made himself as small as possible on the ground. He had seen his father and uncles hunt before, and was copying them, but what was about to happen owed as much to instinct as anything else. Targh watch, and waited. A black fly landed on his neck and it was agony to ignore it, but he kept still, proud of his hunting skills. The big frog showed no signs of moving in his direction, or anywhere else for that matter. *Croak*. Targh watched the frog's throat grow bigger and smaller as it breathed. He matched his own breathing rhythm to that to that of the frog's. Every so often the frog blinked its big, bulging eyes. Every so often Targh blinked his own gray eyes, which he had narrowed to tiny slits of concentration. The frog's tongue shot out to catch a passing fly. Targh licked his lips. The moments slid slowly by. One of them was going to have to move. The boy risked a glance over his shoulder to where his father was working, head bent over the net, hands carefully retying knots. And then Targh began to creep to his right. Slowly. On his stomach. With his arms and legs splayed out. Over the soft, damp, black earth. Either he was very good at creeping, or the frog was too busy with its own meditations to take notice, but it was working! Slowly, ever so slowly, he moved away from the frog's line of vision. *C-r-o-a-k.*

Targh's sideways maneuver put the stand of cattails between him and the frog, so he could no longer quite see his prey. So much the better! It felt deliciously stealthy to be hidden from view, preparing to pounce out of the reeds. He eased himself forward and met a new obstacle: the mud. Like the earth he had been creeping on, it was moist and black. But it was not at all soft. It was sticky. In truth, it was much more than moist. It was wet. Very wet. And it oozed. About a young boy's body length into the cattails, the black muck sucked at Targh's arms and legs until he could no longer creep. He got up on his hands and knees, water dripping from his belly, covered in the sticky, oozing, sucking mud from his chin to his toes. His nose itched. He raised a hand to scratch it, looked warily at the muck on his fingers, and rubbed the tip of his nose up and down on a cattail stalk instead. He hoped the frog was still there. *Croak. Yes!*

Just a bit further. He could see the frog! Still sitting on the old fallen tree and looking away from the young hunter.

Targh parted the last of the cattails just a bit and was ready to spring, when he realized just how big the old frog was. Not that he was suddenly afraid. His hunting instincts were far too engaged for that! But he sat back on his haunches and looked at his hands which, like the rest of him, were not quite five summers old. *Croak . . . Croak.* They were too small for the job. He slipped his mud-soaked tunic over his head and held it out in front of him. Fortunately for Targh he had no idea how silly he then looked: white as the winter snow from shoulder to loins, with five appendages sticking out in different directions, as black as midnight. But his eyes were fixed upon the green creature in front of him, for he was a hunter.

Long moments passed as Targh quietly flexed, tightened, and relaxed each muscle in preparation for the leap. It was the moment in which a wildcat's tail twitches nervously from side to side, its rump swaying back and forth as it shifts its weight from foot to foot, finding the best balance point for the pounce. Targh had no tail, of course, but his rump did sway, just a bit.

Croak.

Croak.

He leaped! It was not a graceful arc, but it was effective. Targh's arms extended out ahead of him spreading the tunic, his feet somehow found traction in the mud and launched him into the air. As he came down upon the log he folded the tunic around the old frog, and clutched it to his breast. *Got you!* he thought, triumphantly!

The one problem with his plan was that he was now in mid-air with nothing below him but black swamp muck. He landed on his right side, did a full roll, and came to a rest face down, with his precious bundle struggling and kicking beneath him. It was his first catch ever. He spit out a mouthful of swamp, and laughed out loud.

Caddoc was still working on the net when his naked, muddy son suddenly appeared, holding his equally muddy and squirming tunic out before him.

"Tada! Look what I got!"

Fortunately for Targh, Caddoc was also a hunter and saw immediately what his son had been up to. Had they been back in the village, Caddoc might have chastised him for getting so dirty. But out in the wilds, on a fishing expedition, there develops a special relationship between father and son. Caddoc smiled and put down the net, sitting back on the ground.

"Well, Targh," he said, "You've had a fine morning's hunting I see!"

Targh beamed, and ran to his father, jumping up and down with delight.

"I caught him! I caught him!" He sat down beside his father and recounted every moment of the hunt, while Caddoc listened with genuine interest. He waited until Targh ran out of breath before speaking.

"Aren't you forgetting something?" he asked.

Targh looked up at him, wide eyes puzzled.

"Aren't you going to show me?" his father asked with a smile.

A look of solemn importance came over Targh's face. He sat up straighter, and arranged the bundle carefully in his lap. He took a deep breath, holding the right side of his lower lip between his teeth, and slowly pulled back an edge of the tunic. A large green head with a wide mouth and bulging, black eyes peered up at him, its throat quietly pulsing in and out. There were several long, silent moments as father and son experienced together the awe of the situation.

"Well," said Caddoc finally, "that's truly a big old frog."

Targh gave a serious nod of agreement. It was. And he had caught it.

"I'm gonna take him home and keep him right by my bed," he announced.

Caddoc pursed his lips and cocked his head as if in serious thought. "Think you should?" he asked.

Targh was fully attuned to the onset of parental disapproval. He quickly went on the defensive, folding the old

136

frog back into his tunic. "He's mine!" he demanded. "I caught him, and I'm takin' him home!"

"Now hold on," Caddoc said, raising both hands in protest. "I didn't say you couldn't keep him."

Targh breathed a bit easier.

"It's just that, well, look at the size of him. He must be an important frog!"

Targh carefully felt the bulging outlines of the frog inside the tunic. He nodded again. It truly was a big frog. *But he's mine, and I'm keepin' him!* he thought to himself.

"He sure is big," his father said again. Then he looked straight at Targh, and in his best conspiratorial voice he said, "How do we know he's not the Old Frog of Bryn Llyffaint?"

"Who?" Targh whispered.

"Shhhh." Caddoc looked carefully all round them. Targh nervously followed his father's gaze. "We'd better be careful," Caddoc said. "He might already have his warriors out looking for him." Targh's eyebrows scrunched together as his careful gaze scanned the reed banks.

Caddoc helped his son to his feet. For a moment he considered Targh's muddy nakedness, then decided fixing that could wait until later. "Come on," he said, taking the young hunter by the hand, I want to show you something."

Together they climbed the low rise that ran the length of Ynys Mawr. It was Targh's favorite spot. From there he could see the slopes of the Mendydd hills above the north marshes or, in the other direction, far across, the shallow waters of the south marshes and the highlands of Crib Polborfa.

"Over there," Caddoc said, pointing westward.

On the horizon, at the boundary between the shallow waters and the great sea, rose the high cone of Ynys Bryn Llyffaint. Targh had seen the high hill often, of course, but he had never been there. It had always seemed a mysterious place to his child's imagination. They sat down together and gazed at the hill. Caddoc had brought a dry tarp with him from the boat. He draped it around his son's shoulders, though it was now nearly mid-day and the sun was warm.

"Have you never heard the tale of the Old Frog of Bryn Llyffaint?" Caddoc asked quietly.

Targh loved stories, but he had never heard this one. "No, Tada," he whispered.

Caddoc smiled. He knew his son had never heard the tale, for he was about to make it up then and there. "Hold him carefully, Targh," (Targh held the precious bundle carefully in his two hands, hunching his shoulders over it in protection.) "And I'll tell you the tale."

"It was a long, long time ago," Caddoc began.

Targh loved tales that started that way. He snuggled closer so his father could put an arm around his shoulder. "Is there a boy in it?" he asked.

"Not this time," said Caddoc. "It was too long ago."

"Tad-cu's long ago?"

"Longer than that. Before your grandtad's grandtad. Even before our people had come to Ynys Mawr."

Targh was silent with wonder. He hadn't known there *was* a time so long ago. He lay back against his father's broad chest, carefully holding the prize frog, and listened.

And this is the tale Caddoc told that day . . .

~

It was a long, long time ago, before ever anyone had come to the great isle on the edge of the northern marshes. Ynys Mawr was the last big island before the waves of the never ending sea, and no animals ventured beyond it except those that flew, or made their home in the water. It was a much larger island then, running in a long line nearly from the open sea to the bogs and fens around Ynys y Niwl, the isle of shadows. Chief among the animal clans who made the big island their home were those of the Cyfeillion y Llyffaint, the frog friends (for *llyffaint* means *frogs* in the Old Tongue.) They raised their young in the warm shallows that surrounded the island. Some grew dry, brown skins and moved inland among the central hills.

For many generations the Llyffaint clans lived and prospered on Ynys Mawr. All the animals spoke the Old Tongue of the marshes in those days, and the Llyffaint of Ynys Mawr, in their own dialect, had a rich body of folk tales, of their own heritage, and about the beginnings of all things.

One day the Cewri came to Ynys Mawr, a towering race of giants who were the ancestors of men, and whom they resembled closely except for their great size. The Cewri loved metals, especially those that shone like the stars, which they collected in great hoards. The Llyffaint held councils to decide what might be done about the Cewri, and how to live on the island with them, but the giants seemed not at all interested in matters concerning the Llyffaint, so the two races remained apart as much as possible.

Trouble began when the Cewri began delving in the earth of Ynys Mawr with shovels made of wood and iron, digging great clods of earth the size of mountains from the body of Ynys Mawr and tossing them into piles on the land across the north marshes. The Cewri were building the Bryniau'r Mendydd as a place to store their treasure hoards of lead and silver.

The Llyffaint were more troubled than ever, fearing that Ynys Mawr might disappear altogether, so they called a Great Council, known throughout their history as the Council of the Cyfeillion y Llyffaint, to decide what to do. Their deliberations went on for many days without a decision. Meanwhile the Cewri continued to dig. Ynys Mawr grew smaller and smaller, and the Bryniau'r Mendydd continued to rise above the northern shore.

Finally the Llyffaint settled upon a plan. They elected the biggest and oldest among them, a great old frog named Hynafgwr, to seek an audience with the Cewri chief. At first Hynafgwr was not pleased with this solution, but the Llyffaint enthusiastically told him of the honours and privileges that would go with his election, making up greater and greater rewards as they went along. Finally, armed with the title of

King of the Llyffaint for all the Ages, the promise of great wealth, and a bodyguard of trained warriors, Hynafgwr agreed to try.

The next day found him racing in and about the large, booted feet of the Cewri, and their massive tools, as they continued to shovel mountains of Ynys Mawr onto the rising Mendydds. Hynafgwr was at a loss for what to do. He did not stand as tall as the ankle bone of the shortest Cawr. Jump up and down and shout as he might, he could not make himself heard above the din of the shoveling and the work songs the Cewri were so fond of singing. Indeed, he was almost stepped upon several times, and once nearly cut in two by the blade of a shovel. Hynafgwr truly wanted to give up and hop quickly out of danger. But he had already accepted the title of King, and, once obtained, that is an honour hard to let go of.

When Hynafgwr finally hit upon an idea, he was more unhappy than ever. For the idea, though it possibly might work, was filled with danger. Still, to be "King for all the Ages . . ." Well, he decided to try it. Very carefully he crept near to where one of the Giants was lifting great shovels-full of earth and tossing them onto the Mendydds. He waited until, *tschunk*! The Giant's shovel was buried to the handle in the dirt of Ynys Mawr. Without waiting to be overcome with common sense, Hynafgwr leapt upon the shovelful of dirt as it came out of the earth. The old frog was immediately aware of his danger. If he could not make himself known to the Giant in the next moment, he would be hurtling through the air to the tops of the Mendydds with enough dirt to bury him for, though King, all the Ages. As the shovel rose within the Giant's line of vision, Hynafgwr hopped up and down with all his might. He tried repeatedly to shout "STOP!" at the top of his lungs, but he was so frightened, and so breathless, the only sound that came out of his mouth was a loud "CROAK!"

Now the Giant had never heard such a sound before. Truth be told, nor had anyone else in the marshes. He froze, with his shovel stopped in mid-swing. Great clods of earth the size of boulders fell out of it, hurtling down to the ground far below, so that Hynafgwr had to hold on for dear life to stay perched where he was. The Giant lifted his shovel blade and lowered his face to it, to peer more closely at his strange discovery.

The Llyffaint did not wear boots. If they had, Hynafgwr would have begun shaking in his. This close up, the Giant was far uglier than Hynafgwr had imagined. And his breath was far fouler. This was even worse because of the heavy breathing made necessary by the exertion of creating the Bryniau'r Mendydd! The Giant picked him up in his left hand, being quite gentle so as not to break any of Hynafgwr's delicate bones.

"Bagat es ganoch?" the Giant asked in the Old Tongue of the Cewri. "Bagot ant es blachen?"

Hynafgwr looked hopelessly puzzled, suggesting to the Giant he ought to rephrase the question.

"Who are you?" the Giant asked again. "And what do you want?" Hynafgwr remained puzzled, for he had not really expected the Giant to know the Common Tongue of the marshes. But he kept his wits about him, cleared his throat, and began.

"Ahem! Uh, take me to your Chief, please, sir, if you will."

"Cheef?" Now it was the Giant's turn to be puzzled. "What is Cheef?"

"Uh, *CROAK*." The frog was nervous, "You know, the one who is in charge."

"Charj? Where is Charj? Is on Ynys Mawr?"

Puzzled fear was quickly turning to aggravated frustration for the old frog. "Not a place!" he said. "Look, who makes your decisions?"

The Giant still looked puzzled. He was getting tired of holding a shovel in one hand and a frog in the other, and the strain was beginning to show.

"Dee-sid juns?" He asked.

141

Clearly this was not the path forward. Hynafgwr was beginning to understand the Cewri did not have such things as chiefs, or decisions. He decided to try another approach.

"O fine, great Giant," he began. The Giant grinned. "I have been sent by the Cyfeillion y Llyffaint on this island to ask a favor of the wisest and strongest of the Cewri." The grin turned to a smile. "We agreed . . ."

"What's a gree?" interrupted the Giant.

"We all talked together and thought you seemed to be the bravest and smartest of all the Cewri, and so they sent me directly to you."

The Giant did not quite understand all of that, but it sounded like a high compliment, so his smile widened even further.

"What do you want?" he asked. "I am a great Giant. I am *greatest* Giant, and can do anything!"

"Uh, first, could you please put me down?" Hynafgwr asked. He was getting quite nervous being held at such a height, and was worried he would begin croaking again at any moment. The Giant set him down on the top of a high precipice, then sat himself at its foot. so their faces, if not the same size, were at least at the same height.

"My name is Hynafgwr," began the old frog, remembering diplomatic manners. "What is yours?"

"I am Offrwm," offered the Giant.

"Fine, Offrwm, I need your help."

"Go on," said Offrwm. He was getting the hang of diplomacy.

Hynafgwr gestured to all the Giants who were still shoveling. "You see," he said, "Ynys Mawr is getting smaller and smaller."

"Yes!" agreed Offrwm. "And the Treasure Mountains are getting bigger and bigger." He looked up and surveyed his work with pride. "Soon there will be room for all Cewri silver and lead."

"But Ynys Mawr is our *home!*" Hynafgwr protested.

Soon there will not be any room here for *us*!

Offrwm was silent for a long moment. He scratched his head.

"Oh," he said, and paused a moment. His eyes swept over the diminished island. "I see."

Hynafgwr nearly stamped his foot. "What can be done about it?" he asked.

Offrwm scratched his head again. His race of Giants was not particularly unfriendly. And, strange to tell, they were somewhat smarter than Giants in other lands. It wasn't that they had wanted to displace the Llyffaint. Nor that they were insensitive to the frogs' needs. But the dirt was so nice. And it was in the right place. And they really needed those Treasure Hills.

"Wait here," he said, finally. He got up and walked over to where the other Giants were still working at hurling huge clods of Ynys Mawr onto the Bryniau'r Mendydd. He waved to them, and they all huddled in a great circle, where they conversed privately for some time.

Finally Offrwm left the circle, picked up his shovel, and stepped across the north marsh to the foot of the Bryniau'r Mendydd. He thrust his shovel into the side of the hills, lifted out a great mass of earth, turned, and flung it out westward across the open waters. With a loud roaring splash the earth landed in the water just where the shallows meet the deep never ending sea, and the mound of dirt stood in a cone like a high hill over the surface of the water. Offrwm thrust his shovel back into the earth and stepped back over the marshes to where Hynafgwr was looking on in amazement. He pointed to the new island.

"There is home for Cyfeillion y Llyffaint for ever," he said. "Cewri will never disturb it." Then pointing to the scar in the Mendydds, he said, "We leave gap in Treasure Hills to remind us not again to make others' land smaller." Indeed, that scar in Byniau'r Mendydd became known always as Ceunant y Gawr, the Giant's Gorge, which some call Ceodor.

Hynafgwr bowed low in thanks. From that moment the Llyffaint and the Cewri became great friends. Hynafgwr in triumph convened another council of the Cyfeillion y Llyffaint, in which he received great honours, including the title of "King of the Llyffaint for all the Ages." But he had been humbled by the experience, and never used the title himself. He oversaw the moving of all the frogs to the new island where the marshes meet the sea. When they were settled, he proclaimed,

"We shall call this place Ynys Bryn Llyffaint. But do not call me King, for I am only an Old Frog."

That is how Bryn Llyffaint got its name, and how there comes to be such a treasure of lead and silver in the mines of the Bryniau'r Mendydd. And, by the way, how the greatest of heroes can also be the most humble.

~

When the tale was finished Targh sat for a long time in silence. He opened the folds of his tunic and looked at the great green frog he had caught. It looked, curiously, back at him.

"*Croak*," it said.

"He's not *really* the Old Frog, Tada, is he?"

Caddoc smiled. "Well, I suppose not, son," he said. "That story happened a long time ago."

Targh put on his serious face again. "But he could be his great great grandson, couldn't he, Tada? Couldn't he?"

"Well, yes, I suppose he could."

Targh lapsed in to the deepest thought a boy of less than five summers can find. He was silent for a long time. Finally he looked up at his father.

"I think we should put him back," he said.

"Put him back? But I thought . . ."

Targh shook his head. "We should put him back, in case he wants to swim out to Bryn Llyffaint." He carefully wrapped up the frog, stood, and headed off for the cattails, with Caddoc following. When they set the great great grandson of Hynafgwr free, they could have sworn he gave them a deep bow, and almost understood what he meant when he said "*C-r-o-a-k*."

Finally the Old Frog turned and swam slowly off, into the west.

Caddoc tugged gently on Targh's ear. "C'mon, Pal," he said, "Let's get you cleaned up!" Together they walked back to the boat, ready to go home.

Chapter Fourteen
VIII. The Tinner and the Coblynau

Not so very long ago as time is measured in the marshes, Azariah of Beth-Shemesh came from the farthest east to settle in the Brythonic lands. He was of the race of the Iudde, those who say there is only one god, and that he lives at the top of a mountain in the midst of a dry and dusty desert in their own faraway land. Azariah's journey began with the scattering of his people by the warrior king Nebadd-kinesser. With his wife, Rebekkah, and seven children, he set out by boat from the coast of Iuddea to cross the wide sea that lies at the middle of the earth. After years of perilous travel through many lands Azariah came to the Brythonic shores and settled in the hills of Cornualle, which rise above the marshes that lie south of Crib Pwlborfa. Now Azariah was a delver in stone.

It is said that Azariah was the first to discover the rich veins of alcam that lay hidden in the Cornualle hills. Traders in the east called it "tin," and used it to carry water for great houses made of stones. Azariah dug deep into the earth to bring out this tin for sale, so the hills of Cornualle became known for the many mines of Aazariah the Tinner. He prospered, and his children grew and married young men and women of the land. In time, Azariah of Beth-Shemesh became known as Asaryedd of Cornualle. Though he remained faithful to his Iuddic god all his days, he learned the local ways of the Cernyw.

Never again did Asaryedd see the mountains of his home. His children came to consider themselves to be as Brythonic as they were Iuddic. His grandchildren and their grandchildren after them would carry on the business of the tin trade, knowing themselves to be in some way different from their neighbors, but living the life of the Cernyw peoples.

One day, when Asaryedd had grown rich from the sale of tin, he longed to explore more of his adopted land. Rebekkah had died, leaving him alone in their home, for their children were grown. So he left his mines in the care of his eldest son, and traveled north across the marshes into the hills of Crib Pwlborfa to see what he might find at the edge of the world.

But Crib Pwlborfa is not the edge of the world. When Asaryedd pulled his boat up on the southern shore and climbed to the top of the ridge, he looked out upon the wide sweep of fenland and open waters that is the ancient home of the Marsh Folk. In the distance, far to the north across the marshes, he saw the misty hills of the Bryniau'r Mendydd, for the edge of the world is always farther off than one can imagine. It was a good and pleasant land that Asaryedd saw spread out before him: cattle grazed, and sheep, on the northern slopes of Bryniau'r Pwlborfa. A long, straight line that appeared to be some sort of trackway led across the marshes to a small island. On the northern edge of the island, Asaryedd could make out the palisades and thatched roofs of a village, the home of the Lake People. *I will go and see this place*, he thought to himself, *and learn what sort of people live there.*

It was not easy to understand the tongue of the Lake People, but it was close enough to the language of Cornualle that they could, with some effort, speak together. They told him tales of the marshes, and marveled at his stories of the far-off Iuddean wilderness. But Asaryedd was most intrigued by their legends of the Bryniau'r Mendydd, the ancient Treasure Hills, so they said, of a race of Giants from ages past. Rumor told of deposits of a precious metal that shone like the moon. *Arian*, it was called in the marsh, for the moon goddess.

"Of what use is this arian"? Asaryedd asked of the lake elders as they sat one night around a campfire on the shore of the island, for he had never heard the name. An elder reached into the opening of his tunic and pulled out a leather cord. Attached to the end was a glittering crescent shaped like the waxing moon and traced with lines worked into twisted and tangled knots. It glowed and glittered in the firelight.

"Silver!" breathed Asaryedd as he reached out a hand to

touch it. But the elder quickly withdrew the sacred amulet and hid it once more under his tunic.

"The tales tell of great veins of silver deep within the mountains,' said the elder. "We use only what we find nearer the surface, for we are fishers of the marsh and know nothing of delving into the earth. It was hidden there long ago by the Cewri, a race of giants who made the Mendydd hills, and lived there before our people came to these marshes."

Though Asaryedd had started out in the Cornualle hills as a miner, he had grown rich as a skilled and cunning merchant. At once he understood the wealth that lay beneath the Bryniau'r Mendydd, and he determined to find it. With some bargaining, chiefly a hastily drawn map to the general location of his family tin mines and a note of introduction to his sons, Asaryedd obtained from the elders of the lake village a small boat to replace the one he had left behind on the south shore of Crib Pwlborfa, and a few digging tools. In the morning light he set out across the open water in the direction of the north marshes, as the slopes of the Mendydds rose through the mists before him . . .

~

It was dark and wet at the bottom of the long shaft. Rainwater soaked through cracks in the limestone rock and dripped in puddles around him, turning the dirt and rock dust of the mine floor into a thick slurry. Asaryedd sat in the darkness near three companions from a local tribe who he had hired on the promise of immanent riches. They kept a small fire going to see by when they were digging, but let it go out when they stopped for a meal, to save fuel. Somewhere near the mouth of the shaft the three were sleeping. He could hear the snores. But Asaryedd sat alone in the dark, pulling a scarf around him to keep the dripping water off his neck. Words of the bards of his people came to him . . .

Thou hast laid me in the lowest pit,
in the darkness, in the deeps . . .

Shall thy wonders be known in the dark?
Lover and friend thou hast put far from me,
and acquaintances into darkness . . .

Adonai, his god, was a god who dwelt upon the mountaintops. Could Adonai's help also be found deep within the bowels of the ancient Brythonic hills? It wasn't so much the dark of the mine that Asaryedd feared. He had seen such darkness often before. But alone, at the bottom of the shaft, he was aware of a growing darkness in his heart. A darkness of the loss of Rebekkah, and the separation from his children.

To you, Adonai, I cry for help,
for you are my rock,
and my sure foundation.

He sighed, and reached for his shovel. It was time to wake the others and get back to work.

Suddenly the earth groaned and shook, like the awakening of one of the giants of the old tales. The roof of the shaft opened above him and a river of water came crashing through. He leapt back to avoid the torrent, which saved him from being buried alive by the collapse of the tunnel. Still, a falling rock glanced off his left shoulder, throwing him to the ground near the back of the shaft. The fallen roof turned the flow of water toward the opening of the mine, where, unknown to Asaryedd, the raging current swept away his three companions. There were a few moans from the surrounding rock, and a shuddering of the earth, then all was silent again, as though the old giant had rolled over and gone back to sleep. There was a choking smell of damp earth. The darkness was complete.

Asaryedd was no stranger to cave-ins. Though lying, hurt, in utter darkness, he did not immediately begin to worry. But as he tried to stand, rubbing his sore shoulder, the worry suddenly came. He was not halfway to his feet when his head struck hard rock. He dropped to his knees and raised his hands to feel overhead. For several arm spans all around him the tunnel roof was just barely above his head as he knelt on the floor. Further probing led to walls of rubble in each direction. He was trapped in a small pocket perhaps not more than ten paces across, half again his own height. His thoughts immediately began to search a miner's knowledge of escape. But the cold fist of the dark earth gripped his heart, for it was in his heart he feared the worst. He shifted his legs so he could sit and lean back against the rubble. He listened for sounds, hoping to hear his companions digging through the collapse. But his companions were no longer in this world, and there would be no digging, no sounds. No help. Asaryedd knew his peril. The size of his small prison meant he would run out of air long before he missed either food or water. Death was not far away. The Death whose presence every man who delves in the earth sees ever over his shoulder, and hopes never to meet. Asaryedd began to pray.

Adonai, thou art my shepherd . . .
Thou I walk through the valley
of the shadow of death,
thou art with me.

His shoulder ached. There was a dizziness in his head. Hoping to save air, he closed his unseeing eyes and lay still.

He had been asleep for some time when a soft tapping entered his troubled dreams. The others were coming to save him. They were digging through the rubble. "Hinani!" he cried out in his own tongue, "I am here!" Only when he leapt up to go to them, crashing his head again upon the collapsed roof, did he realize he had been asleep. He sat heavily in the middle of his cell, the new ache in his head as bad as the ache in his shoulder, while flashing lights of pain seemed to appear before his sightless eyes. He held his breath and listened. No sound. It had been a dream.

Then it came again. Louder. *Tap. Tap. Tap.*

He crawled gingerly toward what he supposed was the source of the sound, though it was difficult to tell, surrounded by darkness and rock. Several times he thought he had found it, then, *tap, tap*, it was coming from somewhere else. He could already sense the foulness in the air. Dizziness was growing in his head. *Tap. . .*

When at last he was certain the sound was in the wall directly in front of him, he knew instantly that he was imagining it. For as he reached out to touch the wall he found it was not the fresh rubble of the cave-in, but the hard, smooth wall of the end of the tunnel. Yet there it was again. *Tap. Tap. Tap.* Asaryedd drew his knife from its sheath at his rope girdle, and frantically pounded the handle against a large rock in the wall. Inside the wall the tapping ceased. He leaned forward and put his ear to the packed earth.

KNOCK.

In the total silence of his prison the sound rang in his ears. He fell back from the wall, sitting upon his heels. His eyes fought to focus, to see the wall that stood before him in total darkness. And then the sound began in earnest, as if it had found him and was determined to communicate. *Knock, Knock, Knock.*

The part of Asaryedd's awareness where mining legends were stored knew what he was hearing, though there was no place for it in his Iuddic understanding of the world. In the tin mines of Cornualle they were named for the sound they made in the rock walls. *Bwbachod.* But surely they were not real? What name had the Mendydd miners used?

"*Coblynau,*" he whispered, under his breath. Knockers in the mines. Immediately there came to his mind the vision of an ugly little goblin, not as tall as a man's knee, wearing a bright red cloak, a red kerchief spotted with yellow tied about its head. In Cornualle the Knockers were feared, for they were able to cause rockslides. But in the Mendydds it was believed they knew where lay the rich veins of silver, and could guide a miner to great wealth.

Knock. Knock.

Asaryedd picked up the knife he had dropped by his side. With both hands grasping the hilt, he began using the long blade to dig into the earth before him, avoiding the larger rocks, prying loose the smaller stones. After what seemed like ages he had dug perhaps an arm's length into the earth. The knocking seemed to retreat before him, as if leading him on. Beads of sweat stood out upon his face. His breathing came in ragged gasps. The air was nearly gone.

Knock. Knock, Knock.

Suddenly there was no resistance under the blade of his knife, and a blinding light filled the small chamber. Fresh air rushed in with nearly the force of the water earlier. Asaryedd blinked, trying to adjust his eyes to the light. When finally he did, it was not a blinding light at all, but the soft glow of a tiny lantern. It contained a single candle, and was held by a tiny, hairy hand about half a man's arm-length from the floor. Behind it was the open expanse of a new mine tunnel; beside it the gnarled, misshapen, and grinning face of the first Coblyn that Asaryedd had ever seen. Its white teeth sparkled in the candle's light, in the midst of a deeply lined and copper colored face. It stood there, blinking, and smiling up at him.

Asaryedd's lungs burned with the joy of clean air. For long moments he could not speak. The Coblyn seemed content to stand there before him in the lamplight. But finally it was the Coblyn who broke the silence.

"Asaryedd," he said with a voice that sounded like the grinding of pebbles, "Where have ye been? We've been waitin' for ye."

The Coblyn stepped through the hole to sit down beside the Tinner, who was still gathering his wits. He set down the lantern and offered his hand in greeting. "Creigiog," he said, "at your service." Asarayedd fell into a dead faint.

When he awoke, Asaryedd found himself in the comparative expanse of the new shaft, lying on his back with a cobly cloak folded under his head for a pillow. The light from several lanterns flooded the tunnel with a warm glow, and several Coblynau were sitting in a circle around him. They were all smiling, having cheered loudly when he opened his eyes. Creigiog gently lifted his head and gave him a long drink of water, followed by a few sips of rich, red wine.

"Just a bit for now," he said. "More later, after you've eaten."

Asaryedd sat up slowly, feeling his shoulder and head for injury. He seemed to be in good shape, though his left arm was in a sling. He looked questioningly at Creigiog, who gave him another smile. Though Coblynau are immensely ugly, they are good tempered and friendly, and smile often.

"Nothing broken," said the little goblin. "Just rest it a bit." His voice had softened some, but he looked even worse in the brighter candlelight. His long nose and chin curved toward one another, nearly meeting in front of a huge mouth with thick lips that covered large, crooked teeth. On his chin, just to the right of center, was a huge, hairy mole. Tufts of ginger colored hair grew from his ears like witches' brooms in a hackberry tree. He had a great round belly that made him nearly as wide as he was tall. It peeked out from under his short cloak. A Coblyn does not smell very good. Several of them sitting together in the tunnel very nearly caused Asaryedd to yearn for the stale air of his cave-in. There was a long silence.

"Well that's that," said one of the Coblynau at last. "Time to get back to work." He stood up and slung a pick over his shoulder. The others followed, singing a mining tune and disappearing in single file down the tunnel. Creigiog sized up his patient.

"Can you walk? We really ought to follow them."

Asaryedd got to his feet. The dizziness was nearly gone, and he thought he could walk for a bit. Creigiog picked up his lantern and a small shovel and hurried off after the others, with Asaryedd shuffling along at his heels, managing to keep up only because of the great difference in their sizes.

They had not gotten far when thin, spidery lines appeared in the tunnel walls, sparkling faintly in the light of the lantern. The tin miner, curious, stopped to look, and Creigiog went on for several paces until he realized he had left his charge behind in the shadows.

"Arian," he called out. "Come on, we're falling behind!"

Asaryedd reluctantly turned and struggled to catch up. They could just see the lanterns of the other Coblynau off in the distance. The deeper they went into the belly of the mountain, the wider and brighter were the veins of silver. Presently they approached a tunnel that turned off on their right, with a sign over it that read "OUT" in the cobly tongue. Asaryedd could not read it.

"That way to the surface," said Creigiog in explanation, and he hurried on further down the main tunnel. Just as Asaryedd reached the mouth of the exit tunnel a Coblyn came rumbling out of it pushing an empty mine cart, nearly running him down. Making a quick right turn, the Coblyn raced his cart down the tunnel, just missing Creigiog in passing. A second and a third cart followed quickly after, turning Asaryedd round and round several times. When he finally got his bearings, Creigiog was standing before him.

"Lots of work to do, and so little time to do it! We never get it all done." He turned and hurried on again, with Asaryedd close in his tracks. "Watch out for the carts," the goblin said, as an afterthought.

The passageway began to get brighter and brighter, not because of Creigiog's lantern, but because the veins of silver had grown pure and wide. Occasionally they would meet a Coblyn coming toward them with a loaded cart which shone like the moon. Pushing his cart slowly and struggling with the weight, the Coblyn would nevertheless greet them cheerfully before continuing on his way to the surface. After a bit, Asaryedd could hear voices ahead of him, and the sounds of delving so familiar to a miner's ears. A glow at the end of the tunnel became brighter as they approached, until it completely outshone the goblin's lantern and nearly blinded the Tinner's eyes, so that he bumped into Creigiog when the little Coblyn stopped.

"We'll wait here a bit," said Creigiog. "Let yer eyes get used to it." They shared a biscuit and some wine before moving on to the end of the tunnel, which opened onto a dizzying precipice at the edge of a wide cavern. To their left a pathway as wide as two Coblynau descended in a twisting spiral around the walls of the cavern and down into its depths. Everywhere he looked, Asaryedd could see Coblynau miners at work on the walls with picks and carts, and the sound was like the crashing breakers of the sea upon a rocky shore. Up from the depths of the cavern came Coblynau in their dusty boots and red cloaks, struggling with silver-laden carts, singing their mining songs.

> *Deep we delve in halls of stone*
> *through tunnels long and caverns wide!*
> *Found by Coblynau alone*
> *the arian that the Cewry hide!*

The Coblynau were hard at work throughout the great cavern. Some carved chunks of silver the size of a man's fist out of the rock. Some carried it in sacks to where little wooden carts waited. Some pushed silver laden carts slowly up the spiral track to the top of the cavern, while others returned empty carts to the site of the digging, barely able to hold them back from careening down the steep slopes.

Asaryedd rubbed his eyes and blinked several times, but the amazing sight remained.

"There ye be!" beamed Creigiog. "We'll be a-goin' now!"

Suddenly all was silent. No singing, though Coblynau mouths continued to open and shut. No clanging of iron tools upon rocks, though Coblynau arms continued to swing their picks. And then the Coblynau left. They did not lay down their tools and walk out of the mine. They simply, well, faded away. In mid-swing and mid-verse. They faded until Asaryedd could see the shining veins of silver through their bodies. And then he could see them no longer. The Coblynau were simply gone, along with their tools and carts. All that was left were the tiny lanterns hanging from the walls, lighting the cavern, and the tunnel which led to the surface. For that, indeed, is what Coblynau do. Asaryedd stared in wonder for a very long time at the wealth that now was his, before he turned and slowly climbed the long path to the fresh air that lay under a starlit sky.

~

In the days that followed Asaryedd sent word to his sons in the Cornualle mines, by means of the Lake People. Two of his sons, Jaredd and Eosaidh, came to him with their wives and children, and they founded a small village there at the Coblynau mine head. Prydde they named the place, which means earth, for it was from the earth that Asaryedd had received his wealth. And it was not far from the Giant's Gorge of the old tales.

Men of the Mendydd tribes came to work with them in the mines, and the wealth of Asaryedd, the old Iuddic tinner, increased until no one could count it. For generations they worked the mines around Prydde, and oversight was passed down in Asaryedd's family from father to son. In time, oversight became ownership. They traded the tin of Cornualle and the lead and silver of the Mendydds in ever growing regions of the world. And sometimes, in a dark and quiet stretch of an unused mine shaft, a miner walking alone would swear he heard a soft knocking in the rock walls. But no one ever saw the Coblynau, in those mines, again.

Chapter Fifteen
IX. Hiraeth's Tears

Far to the north of the marshes, off the rocky coast of a storm-swept land, the isle of Ynys y Ywen lay on the edge of an endless sea. Wild winds howled across the rocks, raising a great salt spray that joined with flying rain to lash alike sea and skerry and stony strand. Gray were the rocks, gray the heaving waves, and gray the whirling dark clouds of the lowering sky, where lightning flashed and the loud thunder roared without pause.

Far from shore and yet within the circling cliffs of the bay there was a small skerry which at the turning of the tide yet stood above the crashing waves. And upon that skerry a maiden sat, with long golden locks of hair that curled about her shoulders and fell in wild waves over her young breasts. Her pale white hips blended into the long, curving, silvery sheen of a scale covered tail, the fins in which it ended dipping into the churning gray green sea. A mor-forwyn was Hiraeth, a seamaiden of the lineage of Llyr. She was brushing her long, golden hair, all the while singing to herself in her silver mirror a song of maidens and the sea. For the mor-forwynedd are at home in the element of water, be it peaceful lake or raging sea, and the wild rain is naught to them but akin to the realm in which they live. The heart of Hiraeth was attuned to magic, and in her heart she knew there was fate hovering about her that day.

Not so accustomed to the violent wind and wave were the twelve men, sea-hardened though they were, who fought to flee the angry sea and make landfall among the rending rocks. Their coracle, fashioned of alder and sealskin, spun and heaved upon the waves, at each crest threatening to capsize, and drop them into the depths. Twelve men they were, warriors of a clan that dwelt beyond the isles, lost upon the sea and seeking haven where it might be found.

Hiraeth spied the tiny craft as it entered the bay. She lay her mirror in her lap, gazing into the very teeth of the gale to see the faces of the desperate and determined men, for it was their fate, she knew, which suddenly was bound with hers. Between the men and the safety of land lay many a rock and reef that surely would tear apart a better ship than theirs. Her eyes moved from rock to rock, seeking a safe path through the mortal danger. From rocks to coracle she looked, back and forth in the storm, and the song was gone from her lips.

The man who must be captain she saw leaning to the fore, searching into the gloom as she for a way through the rocks. A look of forceful will there was upon his face. But his eyes were hard with a practiced hardness that dwelt there before ever they peered through the storm that day. In the hardness of those eyes she saw not any trace of one who, in his living, did ever love or laugh. She thought it sad that he faced the moment of his death without the consoling memory either of laughter or of love.

With desperate oars the men the currents fought, calling courage or direction to one another over the din of crashing breakers, crying out at a blow from a hidden rock, or loss of an oar to the violent sea. All day the craft had been filling with sea water and dusk was fast approaching. With wooden buckets they gave as much as they could back to the sea between turns at the oars.

From her skerry seat Hiraeth searched the faces of the struggling men, seeking any face that would in look of eyes or set of jaw reveal an inner heart that burned with a love honest and true. At last, in the midst of the coracle she saw him, and knew it in her own heart. Other faces either strained in fear or even fright at the wild sea, or rage that such a fate had overtaken them. Or, like the captain's, not calm but stolid, as hard and unfeeling as the rocks around them. But the one. . . She strained to see more closely in the rain swept gale. Bare to the waist he was, with muscles in his arms and shoulders that tensed and strained upon his oar. Yet in his face there was a peace. The peace that comes when great danger is known and accepted, but not feared. The calm that comes when a man understands he is one with the sea, that his fate is his whether he succeeds in surviving or no. The gentle strength borne by a heart that is able truly and deeply to love. And when she saw this, Hiraeth sang in her own heart, and the song escaped her lips and rose above the gale.

To the others her song was only the wild wind, but Adolwyn heard her voice and understood. As he pulled on the oar he raised his head and lifted up his eyes to hers, and in a moment of time they saw one another and each fell deeply into the other's gaze. For the two, for that brief moment, the wind no longer howled and the sea no longer crashed upon the rocks. Adolwyn lifted up his eyes to hers, and kissed with his eyes her heart, across the churning, heaving sea.

Without a word, Hiraeth lifted one long, pale white arm, and pointed toward the shore. As she traced the air with her finger, a silver thread appeared upon the storm waves, turning and twisting its way between and past the threatening rocks, showing him the pathway that would surely save the little coracle and bring the men safely to the island's shore.

Of another and far off place these men were, and of a faith that knew not the tales of the mor-forwynedd except as deamons of the sea who oft would lure lost mariners to their deaths upon the rocks, and take their very souls along with their lives. Nothing did they know of all the ancient and mysterious lore that gleamed still within the heart of Hiraeth. But the one. . . Adolwyn, she knew yet not his name, he whose eyes had touched her soul and sent a kindred spirit's kiss above the waves, he alone did seem to understand her old and ancient faith. He in his heart her song returned, and they sang together in the sea and storm.

Through the peril of the rocks and waves the men rode their coracle along Hiraeth's silver pathway, coming at last to the safety of the stony beach. Harsh was the grating of stones

159

upon the bottom of the craft, but greatly welcomed after the time at sea. For long moments they sat in silence, each thanking his own gods for the gift of his life, while the surging waves continued to lift the rear of the little boat and push them further onshore. One by one they dropped their oars, and with reverence for the solid ground stepped out onto the stones. Once they had dragged the coracle out of the reach of the sea, they set about searching the rocky crags and overhangs for wood that had escaped the weather and was still dry. Near the mouth of small tidal cave they kindled a fire for drying and for warmth.

But Adolwyn forsook the fire, and found his way to the water's edge, not minding the breakers or the storm. He lifted his eyes against the wind and looked out to the skerry where Hiraeth still sat, combing again her golden hair and singing to him over the gale. Adolwyn felt a warmth in his heart that spread outward to cheer his body and his mind. When he stepped into the waves, the water was warm where he trod, and the breakers parted before his feet. In perfect love and perfect trust Adolwyn waded into a gentle surf. Never taking his eyes off the mor-forwyn, he walked out to her seat. There in the waters of the bay off the shore of Ynys y Ywen, upon the rocky skerry, did they meet. As he stepped upon the rock the storm quiet did become, the winds died to a soft breeze, and the waters calmed around them. Hiraeth dropped her brush and looked deeply into his gray eyes as he stood before her. Indeed, their eyes and hearts together did embrace before ever their bodies touched, before he knelt at her side and took her in his arms as she sang, before she clung to him and held him to her breast. Their kiss began as gently as the song of a lark, then deepened and deepened until finally it was like a wild whirlpool in the sea, spinning and turning and drawing all into itself. In the sky above the sea birds wheeled and cried, and in the sea around dolphins circled and leapt and blew fountains of spray into the air, as together Adolwyn and Hiraeth embraced. At that one instant in the turning ages high heaven rang with the sound of joyful song to think that humankind, despite its fears, would cease to judge which faiths were right, or wrong.

"This love is blessed by Llyr," said she, as in her face he saw the wild reflection of the wild sea. "Now to your chief and captain let us go, that he may call upon the gods you bring to these shores, so old and new alike may blessed be, and from each other learn to love and grow."

The captain was a hard and willful man who would not hear of anything so bold as the man and mermaid's tender hearted plan to join in one the myths of new and old. His face grew red, and anger filled his eyes, as he glared upon Hiraeth beside her Adolwyn in the shallow waters of the bay. But anger soon gave way to freezing hate. With a cold and judging heart he cast her out, cast her back unto the skerry rock that sat off shore. As she in sadness left she heard him shout,

"Mor-forwyn thou art accursed! Be gone, thou deamon spawn and return here nevermore!" Adolwyn a warrior was, bound unto the service of his chief and captain, so powerless was he to change what happened on the shore or to follow his beloved as she left. Behind them, around the fire all the rest played at games of chance and drank their ration of mead and sang, unaware of the sadness on the shore. Nor would they have cared had they known.

With a grunt Grym, the captain, turned back toward the fire. Then stopped and over his left shoulder to the man who stood alone upon the shore, "Come, lad," he said. "There are wenches plenty to be found in this new land. Thou needest not the company of fish." He spat upon the stones, then turned again and to the fire strode, Adolwyn a broken man but faithful warrior at his heels. They lifted their provisions on their backs and soon were headed for the hills, all but Adolwyn already beginning to forget to whom they owed their lives that day when they in peril were upon the waves.

But love cannot be banished by the whim of hatred and of cruel heart, so Hiraeth once more did on the skerry sit and long for him who up the far hill climbed and left the sea.

As darkest night descended on that holy place, the morwyn's mournful song like haunted seal-song filled the sea. Tears of deepest sadness marred the face where only laughter's love was meant to be. Each one, a great green sea-drop, left her eyes to mingle salt seawater with salt tears. But they ne'er did dissolve, as did her cries of sorrow, with the passing years. Ever after, on Ywen's rocky southern shore, Hiraeth's deep green tears of love may still be found by those whose hearts are filled with her love-longing for what could never be.

This tale is true, I swear upon my heart.
Gods, grant that all true lovers never part.

Chapter Sixteen
Summer of the Silures

"This peace cannot last."

Cethin and Fianna were in front of her roundhouse beside the sheep meadow. During the quiet summer the human inhabitants of Llan y gelli had little need of a healer, so the herbalist and the priestess were helping with the wool gathering, checking each animal for illness as it lost its thick coat. Silure sheep were small, less than an arm span high at the withers. Their coarse brown wool, in full molt at midsummer, was gathered by rooing with a large wooden comb.

Cethin finished inspecting the skin and hooves of another sheep and gave it a gentle smack on the rump. It trotted off to the edge of the meadow where it began with delight to strip a blackberry bramble of its large summer leaves.

"Brambles, thistles, and nettles!" Fianna said. "All the things we will not eat, but the sheep know them to be the healthiest food in the meadow."

Yet if she was intending to distract Cethin from his dark mood, he did not hear.

"This peace cannot last," he said again, grabbing another sheep as it was brought over by one of the rooers.

"Why do you say that?" Fianna asked. "Seutonius is still far to the east, and the II Augusta sits without a commander on the Mendydds. Rome is not interested in the Silure forest, where patrols must travel single file and risk ambush in every ravine."

"What you say sounds reasonable enough, but look at him." Cethin gestured to the young man who had just delivered another sheep, and was returning to the flock. "He gathers wool, but carries a sword on his belt. It is not the Romans I worry about, but the young men of the tribe. They grow tired of being prisoners in their own lands. They are ready to take the fight to Seutonius, and every day Cadael grows more willing to lead them."

It was more than bravado, Cethin knew. As Boudicca's defeat faded into the past, it became ever more likely the Romans would turn their attention once again to the Silures. This tribe alone, out of fierce independence and sheer unruliness, was the last holdout among the Brythons. It seemed every day there was rumor of a new Roman camp not far off. Rather than invade the bogs and ravines of the Silure forests, Seutonius had decided to build a line of outposts in villages just across the Wye and the Hafren. For a time he was content simply to contain the troublesome tribe, while the legions consolidated Roman rule everywhere else. It did mean peace of a sort for the Silures, but it was a tense, wary peace. Young warriors bridled at being prisoners in their own land.

"Patience, lads," the old men were saying. "Enjoy your wives and children while you can."

"The elders speak true," Cethin would say. "I have no desire to be patching up bleeding Silures anytime soon."

But the young men bristled with anger, and wore sharpened swords to work in the fields. Although Cadael was trying to hold them back, his heart also was longing for an honest fight.

Fianna looked up at Cethin, still holding a sheep's hoof in her hands. "Cadael has led the Silures for a long time," she said. "He will not lightly take them to slaughter."

~

Hard after wool gathering season, when the sun was hot and high in the sky, came time for the barley harvest. It was as though nature contrived to keep men busy at domestic tasks who would rather be working with swords. Occasionally Roman patrols would be seen in the area, but they never came close enough, or stayed long enough, for a fight. Yet more and more often, Cethin noticed, Cadael could be seen in close consultation with seasoned warriors, men who would be his commanders in a fight.

"Cadael is preparing for battle," he told Fianna one day while they were gathering sunwort at the edge of the sheep meadow.

"Perhaps they are only making sure of their plans should a patrol come too close," she suggested.

"I think not. I think he is growing tired of living inside a ring of Roman forts. I think he is planning an attack across the Wye."

"Then we must gather quite a bit more sunwort," Fianna said. "And begin making bandages. For when fools go to war, it is the lot of the wise to bind their wounds."

"What tale is that from?" Cethin asked.

"Some truths, Healer, need no tale to be understood." And she dropped a final bunch of sunwort into her basket. "Do you remember the Old Frog?" she asked.

"Of Bryn Llyffaint?" Cethin smiled. It was the one tale that made him smile. He liked to think that as a boy he had been, himself, very much like young Targh.

"It is a lesson in courage," Fianna said. "But it is also a lesson in humility. And in the wide world things do not go well for frogs who wrestle with giants."

~

The summons Cethin feared came a day later. He watched them arrive along the forest road in their chariots, their robes and tunics a blaze of red and yellow, polished swords and spear points flashing in the sun. Leaving horses and equipment at the paddock in the care of aides, each strode purposefully along the pathway to the chieftain's roundhouse. When at last Cethin entered, Cadael was already surrounded by his war council; clan leaders from several villages in the forest: Cai, Meilyg, Penllyn, Gwyr, Caddoc. At the appearance of the Healer the conversation stopped, and all faces turned to him in silence.

"Why him?" asked Gwyr. "He is not Silure."

Cadael was grim in his response. "His father came to us when the Dubh-bunadh capitulated, long ago. When he was a young fighter of twenty summers he saw his father fall, fighting side by side with Caradoc, and he has been our Healer ever since. He is part of this council." The Silure chief was not yet ready to be convinced by that council. He valued Cethin's steady judgment, welcomed his presence. He sat in the chieftain's chair, part of a circle of benches around the hearth fire, and bid the others sit after him, studying each face carefully, as tribal chieftains learn to do, before he spoke.

"You have asked me to call a council meeting. Here I am." His words did not seem to invite reply. The circle remained silent, while the hearth flames crackled and sent oak and maple scented smoke into the thatch above.

"Here I am," Cadael said again. This time he added, "What do you want of me?" He knew, but they had to be made to say it.

He is hunting them like Targh hunted the frog, Cethin thought. *He wants war as much as they do, but he wants to make them take the responsibility for the decision.*

"Every day Seutonius brings elements of the XIVth closer to our lands," said Gwyr finally. He was not the eldest of the clan chiefs, but they recognized him as the strongest, so he spoke for them all.

"But he is not yet here?" Cadael asked in a carefully measured tone.

"No, he is not," admitted Gwyr.

Cadael looked around the circle, waiting long moments before he spoke again, weighing what he saw in men's eyes. Ready to take action as he was, he would not go to war with a council bullied by Gwyr.

"It is not possible to maneuver a full legion in pitched battle in our forests," Cadael reminded them, "and they dare not expose smaller units to our raids and ambushes." Again he watched their responses. Cai and Penllyn seemed to agree with this line of reasoning.

But Gwyr was not dissuaded.

"True, we can easily defeat one of their centuries at a

time, especially if they are under staffed. But if they were to send several cohorts at once from different directions, it would be trouble."

"Can they do that without us seeing the preparations?" Cadael asked, momentarily off balance.

"They are already preparing." It was Caddoc joining the argument. Seutonius is reinforcing all the major outposts around us. Already troop strength is growing at Viriconon, Gray Woods, Glevum, Corinium of the Dubh-bunaidh" – he glanced at Cethin – "and Dyfroedd Sulis. We are surrounded on three sides and cut off from the rest of the tribes." This time Gwyr and Meilyg nodded their agreement. There it was. Dwyr, Meilyg and Caddoc for fighting, Cai and Penllyn against. If Cadael agreed with the majority, they would attack, probably at Glevum or the Gray Woods. If he disagreed, the council would obey, but it was always a bad plan to alienate the majority.

It was then Cethin spoke.

"It is now past high summer," he said. Seutonius may soon begin sending out raiding parties, but he will not risk multiple cohorts in the field during the winter, especially if that field is the Silure forests. Perhaps we might maintain our own patrols in the passes, where we can harass or defeat their raiding parties. Make the winter as uncomfortable as we can for Seutonius in this way and he may think twice about invading, even when the weather improves"

Cadael's eyes swept around the circle. Meilyg nodded. Then Caddoc. The decision was made. Cadael would have sided with Gwyr in favor of battle, but not outnumbered in council four to two.

"We wait," he said, and hoped to all the gods that Cethin was right.

~

Later, in the healer's hut, Cethin recounted the news to Fianna.

"If a frog is to wrestle with giants," she laughed, "it pays to choose the right giants. You fared better against the clan chiefs than they would have done against the Romans."

Cethin sighed. "Gwyr is right about one thing, though. The noose is tightening. Even now the way to Affalon leads through occupied lands. You should not stay here much longer."

"We have three more tales, Cethin," she said. "And perhaps two more cycles of the moon before the frosts. When I am done, I shall be done. And then I will leave.

"Now let me hear again, Hiraeth's Tears, from 'The captain was a hard and willful man . . .'"

~

"It is the saddest of the tales," said Cethin after he had finished reciting. "I cannot see what it teaches, or why it is included with the rest. Indeed, it does not even take place in the marshes, but on the coast of far off Alva."

Fianna sat on her old cot and poured cool tea for them both from a stone crock. When Cethin too had sat, she said,

"You tell me why it is included in the Marsh Tales."

Cethin was silent for a long time. Fianna's mind wandered, almost drifting to Ynys y Niwl, when finally he spoke.

"It seems there is another world," he ventured, "an otherworld of the spirit. One may lose something in this world, yet hold it still in that otherworld." Again he was quiet, as though he were watching thoughts form inside his head.

"Go on," said Fianna.

"Perhaps it is possible to lose something precious in the real world, but lose it not at all in the spirit."

"Real world?" asked Fianna. "And which is the real world?"

Cethin looked confused. "Is it not the real world that contains sea spray, and rending rocks, and tears?"

"Cethin, think for a moment. Where was Hiraeth's love born? In the spray? Amid the rocks?"

Again Cethin was silent for a long while. But Fianna stayed with him, holding his spirit gently while he searched.

168

"It was born in her heart," he said quietly.

"And what lives in the heart," Fianna answered, "cannot be taken from you by anyone in the wide world. It is in the heart that truth is found, and that which is truly real."

"The captain took her lover from her, but he could not take her love," Cethin said. It seemed to him hollow recompense, yet an aura of profound truth hung about it.

"The tribes cannot stand against the power of Rome," said Fianna. "In the end they will take our lands. Even if we all die in the fight we will not prevent that. But all the Roman legions cannot take our Brythonic soul."

~

The moon waxed and waned in the gray autumn skies. As the feast of Summer's End neared, the cellars of Llan y gelli filled with the harvest. New woolen coats began to grow upon the backs of sheep who would, with the cattle, soon be returned to the winter paddock. And as the frosts came ever nearer, Fianna taught Cethin the last of the Marsh Tales. The story of how fair Edain of the Gwragedd came to Ynys y Cysgodion and played a role in the changing of Morwyn, the Dark Lady. The story of how the Lady first came to Ynys y Niwl, and the birth of the community of priestesses there. And the tale of a strange cup of blue glass that would one day bring about the changing of the world.

Chapter Seventeen
X. The Gwraig Annwn

Beyond the misty shores of Ynys y Niwl, along the marshways that lead to the place of the holy wells, lie the quiet waters of Llyn Hydd. There roams the white hart of legend, and there live the most ancient of the Old Kindred. There is a glamour upon that lake, hiding the island on which they dwell in the midst of the waters. No living mortal has seen this isle, but tales say the sun shines there always, that its gardens abound in fragrant flowers and summer fruit. There the air is filled with haunting music and other magical wonders. The way to Ynys Gwragedd now is hidden; none may enter evermore, save for the fair women of y Tylwyth Teg, the women of faerie. This is the tale of one such faerie woman, and the role she played in the coming of the Lady of Affalon.

~

Alawen of the Gwragedd stepped from the waters of Llyn Hydd at first light. It was at the balance of the turning seasons, when light overcomes darkness and a new cycle begins. The air was colder and, despite the surrounding mists, drier than on the isle. It burned her lungs, so she sat for a moment on the cool mosses and looked out across the lake. From where she rested, no island nor sign of the dwellings of the Gwragedd could be seen. The gray mists and barren branches surrounding the lake were reflected in its still, gray waters. White herons circled in the glamour, the enchanted banners of the home she was leaving. A tear grew silently in her eye.

The Gwragedd do not measure age as mortals do. Alawen had the appearance of a woman who, yet in her youth, possessed the bearing that comes only with the wisdom of age. Fair and pale was her skin, with the blush of summer sun not seen in the marshes, and her eyes were bright with the blue-green color of mosses growing on wet rocks along the shore. She seemed at once lithe as a maiden, yet full and rounded as a mother, so one might not guess with ease her height or the weight of her presence upon the soft ground. Her hair was streaked with silver and white, as long as the ages through which she had lived. It stirred with the breeze, as if carried by currents flowing deep beneath the surface of the lake. She wore a white gown which, though fully dry, glistened with the sheen of lake water and left tiny droplets on the ground. Her feet were bare.

All the Gwragedd are in the form and aspect of women. For mortal women and their children they have great affection, caring not for the company of men except, on occasion, when they desire children of their own. Such a desire filled the heart of Alawen that day, as she rose to her feet and set out eastward across the bogs toward the solid earth of the broad and high plains, where lay the dwellings of mortal men.

It was early on the third morning when she came to the tiny village of Pwysi that lay at the foot of the chalk downs which rose on the northern edge of the Salis Plain. A few wattle and thatch huts were clustered upon the green grass in the bend of a small river. Early flowers of pink and red grew 'round about, giving the settlement its name. Smoke from hearth fires rose through the thatched roofs. The scent of morning meals was in the air, reminding Alawen of her hunger. Though she had not eaten since leaving Ynys Gwragedd, she did not wish to enter the village of humans, choosing instead to wait and watch for those who were about to disperse to the surrounding fields. Perhaps she would see a young man to her liking before she might reveal her presence, for it is easier to win over one lad in the fields with beauty than to sway an entire village.

One by one men emerged from their huts, carrying their daily needs upon their backs. They slung rakes or hoes over their shoulders and left the village in all directions to prepare the spring planting. For long moments Alawen watched from a bramble thicket overlooking the village.

171

Finally she saw him. Young and broad shouldered he was, kindly of face, with ruddy curls that hung to his shoulders and danced with his bright blue eyes. He sang as he approached her on the path. When he drew near, Alawen rose and stepped from her thicket. Muddied with travel, pale with hunger, she was yet fair to the eye. The young farmer stopped in mid stride and beheld her with wonder.

"Have you something to offer a hungry traveler?" she asked. The sound of her voice was like the song of living waters. He knew at once that a woman of the Old Kindred stood before him. He dropped his hoe on the path, could not find his voice, his eyes locked in her gaze. There was silence around them save for birdsong on the morning breeze. Then she spoke again.

"I hunger," she said. "Have you something in your sack for me?"

"You are of y Tylwyth Teg," he answered, still transfixed.

"This does not mean I have no need of food," she said with a smile. "Again I ask, have you aught to share with me?" She stepped aside and sat upon the trunk of a fallen tree. Placing a hand beside her upon the old wood, she looked up at him and said once more, "Come, sit beside me. I am hungry and you have food for the day in your sack."

He sat beside her, his eyes never leaving hers. Taking his worn, woven sack from his shoulders, he reached inside and found a dried apple that had been carefully stored over the winter. When he held it out to her she took it slowly, not wishing to betray the extent of her need. She took a small bite and ate it carefully, relishing the sweet-sour taste, feeling the renewal of her body as she swallowed. After a time, she spoke again.

"I am Alawen, of the marshes," she said. "What is your name?"

In his wonder he heard her first words, but not her question.

"You are of the Gwragedd?" he asked. "You are a Gwraig Annwn?"

She laughed. "That I am," she answered. "And you are a man, I suppose?" He nodded, though it was hardly necessary. "And your name?" she asked again.

He cleared his throat. "Arddwr," he said. "I am called Arddwr."

"A noble name," said Alawen. "It is an honour to be called Plowman." She rose from her seat on the log, leaving a patch of dampness behind. "Come," she said, "I will go with you to the fields." And he followed, not thinking to wonder how she knew which plot of dark earth was his.

As the sun rose in the sky Arddwr went about the preparation of his fields. Alawen stood by, singing to him songs of the marshes, and his work seemed light. As darkness approached and Arddwr collected his tools, Alawen came near to him, her face close so he could feel her breath on his cheek, her eyes again holding his.

"You live alone," she said. "Yet you are young."

His countenance fell. "I was married," he answered. "She died of an illness this winter past, before she could bear a child. Yes, I am alone." They were still, quiet in the evening breezes. Alawen was aware of eagles that circled overhead, aware that from their height they might well be able to see the marshes from whence she had come. Slowly, she leaned forward. Almost without moving, she kissed him gently on his mouth. She tasted of marsh mallow, and her lips were like cool, clear waters. "I would be gwraig to you," she whispered. "I would be your bride." With her kiss a glamour came upon her. A brighter color came to her face, a warmth to her skin, and the dampness of lake water left her clothing and hair. Standing before Arddwr, she took upon herself the appearance of a mortal woman, and he marveled at her beauty.

Alawen took his hands in her own, and pledged herself to him. "I will truly be your bride," she said, "in all the joys and trials of life. I will bring you passion and comfort in our life together, and I will bear our children. To all of this I swear, but you must promise me two things." She paused.

Arddwr felt the warmth growing stronger moment by moment in the flesh of her hands, changing from cool detachment to passionate ardor. And he could feel the heat of love rising in his own body. "I will promise you anything, if you offer me your love," he said.

"I will truly love you," she answered, "If you swear to these things. First, you must always remember that although in seeming I shall be as a mortal woman to you and all others, I shall surely ever be of the Gwragedd Annwn. So shall my feelings always be, and my ways of being in the world. You shall not begrudge me this."

Arddwr raised both her hands to his lips and kissed them. Never had he felt a woman so warm. "That is an easy vow," he said. "I swear to it."

Her soft eyes became for a moment hard and determined. "Next, you must never strike me if I have given you no cause. This is a strong *anogaeth* with me as with all Gwragedd, a vow that cannot be broken." With this she held his hand tightly. "If you strike me three times without cause, I must leave you forever."

A shadow crossed his face, then his eyes sparkled. "Easily do you hold me *yn gaeth* with this vow as well," he said. "And I am enslaved." Alawen kissed him again, but was troubled in her heart for she knew he did not understand what he had promised.

So in the new furrows of a spring field were Alawen and Arddwr pledged one to another. She came to his hearth and his bed, desiring quickly to realize the treasure she had sought, the conceiving of her own children.

The people of Pwysi welcomed her into their midst, marveling at her wisdom and beauty. If any wondered that she had never before been seen in the villages, they did not say. As the seasons turned from planting to harvest, so Alawen's fertility was displayed. Her belly grew large with the child it carried. Midway through the longest night, with the flying of snow, Eira, their first daughter, was born.

~

So did Alawen live together with Arrdwr in the little village. Arrdwr was a farmer during the growing season, a skilled hunter when the ground was hard. Alawen became known as a healer and herbalist, caring for the women and children in the villages and countryside around Pwsyi. But she cared not for the company of men, and shunned them all except for her husband. The following year, in the midst of a long rain that ruined much of the harvest, Alawen gave birth to a second daughter and gave her the name Alaeth. Often would she be seen walking from village to village with Eira and Alaeth playing or sleeping upon sacks of herbs, or garden produce, in her small handcart.

So the years passed, and Alawen's reputation as a healer grew. The women called upon her for help in childbirth or relief from sore feet. Some of the men resented her skill and the honour it brought to her and her family. It was not rare to hear the word *gwrach* whispered as she passed two men on the path. Out in the woods, as they drank around a fire after the hunt, they would utter it aloud: *gwrach*, witch. But she cared for their little ones, and healed their animals, so what they condemned in one breath they accepted with another.

When at last the way of women came upon Eira, so did Alawen's belly swell once more. Though nearly past the time of motherhood, with the last flowering of her fertility she conceived her third daughter and brought her forth into the world. Resting upon a dry blanket spread out on fresh, soft straw, Alawen nursed her newest daughter with tears in her eyes.

"You have brought me new life," she said to the child, "I shall call you Enaid." The child paused for a moment to look toward her mother's voice, then hungrily returned to her full breast.

That winter Eira was promised to Calad, a young farmer

175

from a neighboring village, and with the spring planting they said their vows. Though it was a time of joy for Eira, for Alawen it was the beginning of sorrows. For she was, though Arddwr had nearly forgotten, of the Gwragedd Annwn. And the Gwragedd do not feel as mortals do. For as mortals express their joy with laughter and song, so the Gwragedd are wont to show their happiness with tears and lamentations. As the young couple completed their vows and kissed with passion, a shout went up from the gathered villagers, with laughter and singing, and good-natured cries of encouragement for the events of the marriage bed to come. But as Alawen looked on, tears came to her eyes. Slowly at first, unnoticed by those around her. But they came faster and faster, and her body shook, and she threw her head back and uttered a loud, piercing wail as of one in deepest grief. The crowd became silent, staring. A look of bewilderment came over Calad. Eira and Arddwr, suspecting, trembled with fear. Then another shriek from Alawen, and a bursting of uncontrollable, hysterical sobs. Arddwr, finally realizing what was happening and fearing his wife would be discovered for what she was, took her by the shoulders and shook her. There were gasps and mumbling in the crowd. It seemed Alawen would not be consoled, though in truth it was great joy she was expressing. In desperation Arddwr swung his open hand and slapped her face. Instantly she was silent. For a moment Alawen looked at her husband in shocked disbelief. Then, without a word, she turned and walked back to their hut. The crowd, no longer in a mood for celebration, dispersed each to their own homes leaving the young couple standing alone and wondering what had taken place. It started to rain.

Alone in their hut, Arddwr was truly repentant and Alawen forgave him. "But it cannot be forgotten," she told him. "It is a most solemn *anogaeth* of the Gwragedd, and it cannot be forgotten. You must not strike me again, my love." She came into his arms and he held her close, stroking her long silver hair.

~

When next the snow came again it came with a wrathful vengeance, freezing the earth like iron, the water as if it were hardest stone, and deep it lay upon the ground. The cold crept into each hut and the clothing people wore, threatening, if it were possible, to overcome the flames of their hearths. Many in Pwysi fell ill, and many of those lay wrapped in blankets upon the straw, near to death.

So it was with Alaeth. In the dark of the night her life spirit fought with the illness. A fire raged within her, and she was hot to the touch. Delirious, she thrashed about, throwing the blanket off her, exposing herself to the night chill that worsened her illness. Alawen sat with her all night, bathing her hot flesh with cool water and laughing quietly, under her breath, hoping no one would hear.

Arddwr slept an uneasy sleep nearby. In the stillness just before dawn he was awakened by fits of hysterical laughter. Every candle had been lit, and the oil lamp which hung in the corner. Alawen's eyes sparkled, the wattle walls shook with her roars of joy. But it was not joy, and Arddwr knew it. Quietly he went to the corner where his daughter lay, as his wife danced around him. Alaeth had lost the struggle with her illness. Her skin was no longer warm. She was dead. Arddwr knelt beside her, bowing his head to kiss her brow. His eyes closed, flooding with tears, he withdrew into his grief and ceased to hear his laughing wife.

But those in the neighboring huts heard. Awakened by cries of laughter they came out in the early morning light to stand before Arddwr's door in wonder. There sat Arddwr in silence, holding his lifeless daughter in his arms. And there sat the mother, back against the center pole of the hut shaking with tears of laughter. Arddwr looked from his wife to the people at the doorway, and back to her. Gently he lay Alaeth upon her blanket, and went to Alawen, kneeling before her.

"Dearest," he said, feeling her grief as well as his own. "Dear Alawen, I know it is the deep grief of the Gwragedd you show, but," he looked over his shoulder at the scandalized villagers, then back to her, "but can you not be silent if you cannot cry?"

Silent she was, for a moment, looking into her husband's eyes. Then she suppressed a bubble of laughter, cutting off most of it in her throat though some made it past her clenched lips to spray his face. And then she could hold back no longer, letting herself go and laughing wildly.

"Alawen, don't!" he shouted. "For the sake of all that is holy, don't!" And he slapped her face. At once her laughter stopped.

"How could you?" she asked slowly, coldly, in disbelief. She rose and went to sit with her daughter, turning her back on her husband and the people at the door.

Arddwr uttered a dark curse, turned to the crowd and shouted, "Go home, all of you! There is nothing more here to see!" As they left, he fell to the floor weeping in agony.

~

Arddwr would not allow Alawen to be present for the burial of their daughter. He would not trust her strange emotions. So she stayed in the hut, the fire gone out, wrapped in several blankets against the cold. The Gwragedd have strong emotions, and they are easily offended. As the chill deepened in her body, the fire of anger rose in her heart. She rocked back and forth on the floor, nursing her rage as it grew. *How could he?* she said to herself over and over again. *How could he!*

When at last he returned to the hut, weakened with his own grief, she was ready for him. She sprang at him with the rage of a wildcat, spitting and clawing at his face, pounding her fists upon his chest and shoulders. For a time he held her off as best he could, trying not to hit back, trying to see her rage as understandable, not deserving of retaliation. He tried to hold her wrists, to wrap his arms around her and pin her own flailing arms to her side. But her anger grew and she fought with increasing strength, at last breaking free. She slashed the nails of her right hand across his face, drawing blood in dark, red lines. And then her left hand swung to do the same.

Unthinking, he raised his right arm in self defense to ward off the blow. His arm glanced off hers, and his closed fist hit her hard in the jaw. She swayed for a moment on uncertain feet, then her legs gave way and she collapsed on the floor.

Instantly and badly afraid, Arddwr dropped beside her, trying to take her into his arms. "I'm sorry," he breathed, as he begin to cry. "Oh, Alawen, I'm so sorry. Forgive me, please." She looked at him from a growing distance, life seemingly gone from her eyes. "Alawen, I didn't mean . . . can't you forgive me?"

Alawen stood. Her flesh, grown cool, turning pale. There was the seeming of water in her hair and her clothes, and a smell of ancient lakes in the room. Quietly she turned and walked through the door, into the gathering dusk. Arddwr stood staring at the doorway. He knew he would not see her again. Behind him, in the dark shadows, stood young Enaid, her tears falling like droplets of lake water about her.

~

Alawen walked alone through the darkness on the eastern borders of the bogs. Beyond the bogs the marshes would begin. And beyond the marshes, the quiet waters of Llyn Hydd and Ynys y Gwragedd. She would not have left, she knew, if it depended upon her own will. But the *anogaeth* of her people was more than a vow, more than a taboo. It was the nature of who they were, who she was. Had she remained, she would have stopped living. But the ache in her heart was worse than the ache in her tender jaw. Guiltily, angry with herself, she suppressed a quiet laugh. And the heartache deepened.

With the mists of another morning the soft earth of the bogs became damp, and the damp became wet with marsh water. When finally her feet entered the waters of Llyn Hydd, the glamour on the lake lifted and she saw again the shores of Ynys y Gwragedd, her home.

~

Often in the years that followed Alawen returned to the heights overlooking Pwysi. Arddwr never did see her again, but she saw him often, watching as he worked in the fields. It seemed he would not find another wife, and she felt sorrow for him, but she would not return to him. Her journeys to Pwysi were for her daughters. Enaid had gone to live with her sister Eira, and Calad, for they now had children of their own and welcomed the help. Alawen would meet Enaid, Eira, and her three new granddaughters on the hillside. She would look after their health, and teach them the magic of the Gwragedd.

In time, at the gathering in of the harvest, Enaid took a husband of her own from the next village. She needed no glamour to seem a true mortal woman to him, for her father's blood ran through her veins. But though her body was that of a mortal, the magic of the Gwragedd was in her spirit. The joining of her father and mother had produced in her a woman of great wisdom and surpassing beauty. She stood a head taller than all others in the village. Her skin was the color of starlight. Curling silver hair fell across her shoulders and over her breasts. Her eyes were blue and piercing. Her voice was swift and light, like the waters that fell along the slopes of the Mendydds which towered over the faraway marshes. She gave herself willingly and passionately to her young husband in the soft darkness of their bed, and in time gave birth to daughters of her own. Human descendants of the Gwragedd they were, who spread their ancient magic throughout the reaches of the Brythonic lands.

In time, Alawen's visits to Pwysi ceased. But Enaid visited her often on Ynys y Gwragedd in the midst of Llyn Hydd, learning more of healing, and of the ways of women, and other wonders as well. Indeed, it is said that Enaid once visited the marshes of dark Cysgodion before ever the realm of Affalon came to be, a white spirit in the ancient darkness of those marsh waters, and so came to be called by some *Gwen-hwyfar*, the ancestress of a new myth that had not yet come into the world.

Chapter Eighteen
XI. The Coming of the Lady

Before ever there were priestesses on Ynys y Niwl, the tiny island of Ynys Bol Forla was a sacred place, wrapped in the old tales of the women of the marshes. Morla's Belly, it was called, for the softly rounded hill at its center resembled the full belly of a woman rich with child. Morla's Tale is the oldest of tales, its origins hidden in the mists of the turning ages. And always, from time out of mind, Bol Forla has been the hope and refuge of those whose hope was lost, or whose sorrow was great. It was upon Morla's hilltop that priestesses of Cysgodion stood and first looked across the channel to the shores of Ynys y Niwl, where lies Glyn y Ffynhonnau, the deep valley of healing springs between Bryn y Afalau and Bryn Ddraig.

In the oldest of days, women came alone to Bol Forla to seek the aid of the goddess. But across open waters, in the marshes of the north, a community of priestesses had gathered around the Dark Lady of Ynys y Cysgodion. For many generations they had kept to themselves, for most had fled there from fearsome men; husbands, chieftains, warriors. Some arrived carrying children, either in their arms or their bellies. In time the small community grew, and rumors of their existence drifted in the marsh currents. But their time had not yet come. The Dark Lady, as her ancestors and her descendents, wove spells of shadows that kept them hidden from the wide world. Their time had not yet come, but they knew they would be needed one day, so they studied the ways of women and of goddesses, and learned the lore of healing and the magic of the marshes.

~

Three women from the hill country of Crib Pwlborfa slowly wove their way through the southern marshes. The old walkway had not yet been built, so they traveled in a flat bottomed marsh boat. Braith, youngest of the three, poled or paddled as the waterways demanded. Owena sat near the front watching for landmarks in the marsh, and cradling Llwyfren, who was with child, in her lap. The way to Bol Forla was well known. Owena had made the trip before with other women who faced danger in childbirth. But always there was the fear of a wrong turn, of being lost in the marsh as the time of birthing drew near. Owena was a skilled midwife, but the danger Llwyfen faced required the magic of the sacred isle.

The day was already waning when at last Owena found the marker for the final channel leading to the shore of Ynys Bol Forla. In her lap Llwyfen moaned softly, drifting in and out of consciousness. As the water grew more shallow, Braith leaned upon her alder pole and pushed the little boat ever forward.

It was a familiar problem. Llwyfen had given birth seven times before, and three of her children had survived infancy. Now she was beyond the age of safe childbirth, but her husband was not beyond the age of his pride and virility. She had carried the child safely nearly to its birthing time, but in the past several days things had begun to go wrong. The bleeding had begun as little more than spotting, which she washed away in the cold stream near her hut. It was not uncommon among her people when an older woman approached her delivery. But the flow grew until she had to fold a piece of woven cloth and bind it between her legs. When even that did no good, her daughters lay her upon her sleeping furs and sent for Owena, the midwife.

The sun was rising upon a fateful day when Owena arrived at the hut.

"The bleeding is getting worse," said Braith, Llwyfen's eldest daughter. "I fear for her life." Her own face was somber as she bathed her mother's with cool water. Llwyfen had already begun to drift into unconsciousness.

Owena removed the blood soaked cloth, looking, then feeling into the birth canal. She washed her hands in a bowl of warm water beside the cot, then felt the hard round surface of Llwyfen's belly, tracing the ridges and outlines of the child within. When she was at last finished, she turned to Braith.

"Where is your father, child?" she asked.

"He left at the full moon and has not returned," said Braith. "Fishing," he told us when he left. "But clearly he is gone." There was contempt in Braith's quiet words, and a hardened coldness beyond her thirteen summers.

Owena sighed. This problem, too, was familiar. She took Braith's hand and led her from the hut.

"She is in grave danger," Owena said. She is too old to be giving birth. Her womb is tired and damaged. It has grown too small. The child has not turned. Its feet are nearest the birth canal. All this has caused the placenta to be low, and it covers the birth opening."

"Will she live?" Braith asked. "Will the child live?"

Owena was silent for long moments. "I do not know. The flow of blood is from the damaged placenta, and it will get worse. If we cannot turn the child and it comes forth feet first, there is grave danger of compressing the cord. We may lose the child from suffocation before we lose your mother from loss of blood."

Tears welled in Braith's eyes. But her voice was calm with the strength of sudden womanhood. "Then what shall we do?" she asked.

"We will go to Bol Forla for the birth," said Owena. Perhaps the goddess will help us."

~

And so it was that as the dusk of evening gathered, the bottom of their small boat came to rest upon the mud of Ynys Bol Forla, among the tangle of willows that grew along the shore. Gently as possible, daughter and midwife moved the unconscious form of Llwyfen and lay her upon furs arranged over the soft carpet of moss below the willow branches. Llwyfen moaned in her delirium, the air about them filled with the silver metallic scent of blood. Again Owena felt the hard belly, inspected the birth canal that was wet and slick with the bleeding. Braith held her mother's hand, placed her own hand upon Llwyfen's brow and found it hot. Silently, she prayed to the goddess. *Lady of the marshes, save my mother from danger as you once saved Morla.*

"Now there is a fever," said Owena, sensing the reason for Braith's new concern. "She is beyond my skill, and I have not seen the goddess come to help in troubles such as this."

"Then she shall surely die here," said Braith, tears in her eyes once again. And they sat in silence. After a time Owena spoke again.

"Child, you have heard the tales of Ynys y Cysgodion?" It was not really a question. All who lived in the marshes or on the surrounding ridges knew the tale of the mysterious Dark Lady. It was rumored that she had lived from time out of mind in the shadows of the north marshes. Some said she was a sorceress, others that her seeming magic was only great wisdom, and skill in the healing arts. Some said she was not mortal, but the very spirit of the marshes, perhaps the goddess herself. Tales of recent memory told of women who had found their way to the Dark Lady's realm, forming a community of priestesses.

"I have heard of the Lady," Braith whispered. "And of Cysgodion. But I know not where it is."

"Not far," said Owena. "Across the open water to the north, in the dark marshes that lie in the shadows of Bryniau'r Mendydd."

"You have been there?" Braith asked.

"Not myself. But I think I might find it. I know not whether the Dark Lady ever leaves that place, but it is rumored that sometimes her priestesses travel through the marsh to aid those in distress. Perhaps I can find them, find help."

Braith protested. "But you cannot leave us here alone, without the aid of a midwife. What if the child comes in the night?"

Owena hugged her to her breast, and kissed her brow.

"Child, you have every woman's knowledge of birthing. I have told you my skills cannot add enough to yours to save Llwyfen now. And your presence as daughter carries more magic for her than my presence as midwife. Keep her comfortable as you can. With the help of the goddess, I will return by the sunrise."

And, with her words, darkness fell upon Ynys Bol Forla.

~

Some time later Owena paddled alone across the open water to the northwest. Keeping the pole star, the tail of the Little Bear, before her over the bow she sought the border of the northern marshes. To her right, in the starlight, rose the dark tor of Ynys y Niwl. The mist shrouded isle was uninhabited, had always been, as far as anyone knew. It was wrapped in mystery as in mist. The tales told of great power that lay in the dark belly of the tor, and of healing springs that flowed from its side. But no one had ever dared brave the unknown magic of its shores. Owena shuddered, though the night was not cold, and turned her eyes once again to the north, happy to leave the shadow of Niwl behind. Not long after, in the full darkness of the night, her boat slipped through the first reeds of the northern marshes.

She had no skill for finding her way through the twisting channels. Nor did she know where Ynys y Cysgodion lay. *Guide me,* she said, more to the marsh itself than to any goddess. *Guide me to the isle of priestesses. Keep Llwyfen alive until I return. Strengthen Braith's heart.*

Suddenly her boat broke free from the reeds and drifted out into open water again. Owena could sense the broad expanse of a lake, but the darkness was deeper than ever it had been. The cry of an owl told her that solid land was nearby. An island?

"It is Cysgodion," she breathed aloud to her own spirit. "It must be Cysgodion. I must have found it."

The island emerged slowly out of the darkness, old and twisted yews along its shore rising into the star filled night. Then, under the branches, the light of a small lantern appeared.

185

And then another. *Thank you, Lady*, Owena said within, and this time to the goddess. And she paddled harder, driving the little boat up onto Cysgodion's shore. She stepped from the boat, and two women clad in dark robes held their lanterns high before her face.

"Why are you here?" asked the older one, in a level voice, gentle, but bold with authority.

"I am Owena, midwife on Crib Pwlborfa across the marshes. I have charge of a woman who lies near death on Ynys Bol Forla." Owena looked over her shoulder, as though searching for Llwyfen in the darkness across the marshes.

"What is that to us? Why are you here?"

Owena dared not ask for the Dark Lady. "It said there are priestesses on this isle who are skilled in the healing arts and the magic of the marshes. My skills alone can no longer save the woman. I have come seeking compassion, and help.

"I am Glynys," said the older priestess, holding her lantern nearer her own face. "And this," indicating the other, "is Gwenyn. Come."

The two priestesses of Ynys y Cysgodion turned into the shadows of the yew forest, and Owena followed closely behind. They walked quickly, but without sound, along the dark pathways. The paths twisted and turned like the marsh channels, Owena noted, branching out here and there to one side or another. She wondered how anyone could find their way through such darkness, lanterns or no. Finally they emerged into a small clearing, where several round huts circled about a central fire. The priestesses led her to a hut on her left, pulling aside a woven door curtain to enter. It was empty of anything, save a few hides on the floor. Glynys hung her lantern on a crossbeam under the thatch.

"Wait here," she said, and the two priestesses left.

The small lantern was no more than a rushlight. Owena sat on a hide in the near darkness and waited. Outside there was silence, except for the music of the night insects, and the calling of an owl.

Finally Gwenyn returned with a bowl of hot barley soup and a wineskin. "You will be hungry," she said, "This will help."

"There is urgency in this matter," Owena protested.

"This I know," answered Gwenyn in a voice that was suddenly softness and compassion. "The Lady will come soon."

Owena had no answer for this revelation. She took the offered bowl and wineskin and began to eat as Gwenyn went back out into the night.

~

Owena knew not how far spent the night had become. Inside the hut she could not see the stars, but feared they had turned far in their nightly course. Silently she prayed for Llwyfen and Braith on Bol Forla. She reached out in her mind to find them, but had not that gift. *Grant that they both are still safe*, she thought.

Owena knew the Lady the moment she entered the hut, followed closely by Glynys and Gwenyn. She rose, and bowed in silence. The Lady took her hand in a gentle clasp, and looked into her eyes.

"Sit," she said, and the four women sat together on the floor hides. Gwenyn and Glynys had each brought rushlights with them, brightening the inside of the hut.

"I am Vivian," the lady said. "You have come for our help?"

"Vivian," Owena breathed. The Lady who sat before her seemed younger than she should be, though an air of the ages hung about her. Her eyes were dark and deep, her skin a warm olive in color, showing no lines of age that could be seen by rushlight. Her hair was long and black, reaching the floor where she sat. She had given Owena the impression of height when she entered, but, sitting on the floor, she seemed smaller than the priestesses. Smaller, yet wiser and more powerful.

"The tales tell of Vivian from generations past," Owena said. "The tales say you are immortal."

187

The Lady smiled. "Tales say many things," she answered. "Some helpful, some not. My mother bore the name Vivian, as her mother before her and many grandmothers before that. One day I will have a daughter who will outlast me, and doubtless people will call her Vivian when I have gone."

A cloud came across Owena's face.

"Do not fear, my sister," Vivian assured her. "Power is not dependent upon immortality. Mere humans may do magic if need be. You have brought need to Bol Forla?"

Quickly, Owena told the tale. The night was long gone, and she feared Llwyfen would not last until dawn. Feared for young Braith, who held her mother, alone, in the darkness.

"People of the marshes often bring us children who are born and abandoned on Bol Forla," said Vivian. "Wild and dark children, who they believe to be part sprite as well as human. Children born with too much marsh power in them, or children who are alone, their parents lost to the waters. They are, all of them, brought up here as beautiful beings, blessed by the goddess, children of love. Most of the girls stay, joining the community of priestesses. Boys are eventually fostered out to the tribes, where they find new families. Many children come to us from Bol Forla. But rarely do we leave Cysgodion to travel across the marshes."

Vivian's words were a picture of the way things were, not meant as words of rejection. But Owena's heart sank. When she spoke, her words were barely more than silence.

"If you do not come, my Lady, the woman will die."

"I will not leave Cysgodion," said Vivian. "For I am Cysgiodion." She paused, and hope drained slowly from Owena's eyes.

"But do not fear. I will send help. Gwenyn and Glynys will go with you this night." Only then did Owena see the two priestesses wore traveling cloaks, and bore packs slung over their shoulders. She turned again to Vivian, who was still speaking.

"Glynys and Gwenyn will go with you. They are skilled

in the healing of women and wise in the ways of childbirth. May it be they can help you." She did not say also the priestesses were wise in the ways of the goddesses, skilled in marsh magic. Owena hoped this was so. Llwyfen was in much need.

Glynys rose, and Gwenyn after her. "Come," she said, and they went out into the late night, leaving Vivian alone in the rushlight.

~

First light was appearing in the east, behind the tor of Ynys y Niwl, as Bol Forla came into sight. But darkness and a deep foreboding hung over the tiny island. The night creatures had fallen silent, the folk of the day had not yet arisen. Only the sound of Owena's ashen paddle in the water broke the deathly stillness around them. And when, as they neared, they saw the solitary figure of Braith standing on the shore, Owena knew they had come too late.

Together in silence they washed Llwyfen's body, and that of the daughter who had come dead into the world. They wrapped them both in clean cloths brought by the priestesses, and put them in the boat, to take out to the deep, open waters. As they rested beside a small fire, it was Owena who finally spoke. She put her arm around Briath's shoulders, pulling the younger woman close.

"I am so sorry I did not travel faster," she said, "Nor return sooner."

Braith turned and looked into Owena's face. "Do not fear," she said. "It was no delay of yours that brought this end." And Braith told them the sorrowful tale.

"It was not long after you left, Owena," she began. "Mother stirred, and tried to speak, but I could not understand her words. I thought if she were warmer she might rally, so I gathered wood for a small fire. But before I could kindle the flame her body was wracked with convulsions, and I knew the child was coming.

"I covered her with her own cloak and knelt between her

legs, spreading them wide, and removed the breech cloth, which was soaked in blood. Her body shook and trembled again, and a great rush of red blood came forth over the cloth with which I had hoped to receive the child." Braith broke into shuddering sobs. Owena held her close. The priestesses looked on in silence, no expression upon their faces. At last Braith began to calm. She went on, in words so quiet she could scarcely be heard.

"The blood kept coming and coming. I knew I could not save her. And then she lay still, and I could feel her spirit leave. The child thrust a foot out into the world, and then was still itself. I pulled a blade from our pack, cut the bottom of the birth opening to make it wider." Braith's body began rocking back and forth where she sat. "I reached inside, found the other foot, and drew it out. Then slowly, there was so much blood, slowly I drew the child forth. I saw she was a girl. She squirmed in my arms, and her little arms and legs thrashed about, but she was blue. The cord was twisted about her neck, flattened with the press of her head in the birth channel. She was suffocating, and in a moment, she was gone." Braith lay back upon Owenas's breast, crying quietly. No one spoke.

"So I lay the child on her breast," Braith said, finally. "I covered them both with my blanket, and stood on the shore to watch for you. How long, I know not, but the stars traveled far across the sky before I saw your boat in the morning light." At last Braith was silent in Owena's arms. In a few moments, she fell asleep, exhausted.

The priestesses took the bodies in the little boat out into the open waters, where they gave mother and daughter to the marsh. Later, as Braith and Owena both slept, they walked silently together around the island until Ynys y Niwl came into view. They watched as the light from the rising sun made its way slowly down the flank of the tor. Between them and Niwl lay a narrow marsh channel that sometimes, in the midst of a dry summer, became passable land. To the left of the tor rose a rounded hill not half as high. Even from a distance the priestesses could see the wild apple trees growing on its sides.

"The apples of Ynys y Niwl," said Glynys. "Some call the island Affalon, the place of apples."

"Some say that between that hill of apples and the high tor lies a valley with healing springs," answered Gwenyn. "I should like to see for myself it is so."

~

When the sun was high in the sky and Owena and Braith were rested, the priestesses sent them home.

"If we take the boat," Braith protested, "how will you return to Cysgodion?"

"That is a way of the world over which we have some power," said Glynys. "The Lady will send a boat to take us back."

So the four women parted, who had found a bonding in the sorrows of death. Braith and Owena, in their small marsh boat, disappeared into the reeds in the direction of Crib Pwlborfa. When they had gone, Glynys said, simply, "Come." Gwenyn followed her over the crest of Bol Forla, down to the shore that faced Ynys y Niwl. Together they waded the shallows between the two islands, and became the first humans, as far as it is known, to set foot on the Isle of Mists.

They walked across a long open field which priestesses would one day call Dolgwyl Waun, the festival meadow. Above them, to their right, rose the long spine of Bryn Fyrtwyddon, which some now call Wirrheal. And then, for the first time, priestesses of Affalon entered Glyn y Ffynhonnau, the valley of the sacred springs. There they set eyes upon y Ffynnon wen, the spring whose calcium laden waters deposited white faerie-land forms upon all they touched. And then the iron filled waters of y Ffynnon goch, the Red Spring. This they followed uphill to where it emerged from the ground, in a small valley shaded by ancient yews, between the tor and the hill of apples.

"There is healing here," said Glynys. And, Gwenyn answered simply,

"There is healing in this place."

~

Nights later, Glynys and Gwenyn sat with the priestesses of Affalon around the hearth fire of the council hut. Vivian sat as one of them in the circle.

"Had we been found on Niwl," Glynys was saying, "We might have arrived in time to save the woman.

"But you heard the daughter's tale," said another priestess. "She likely had died before the midwife reached Cysgodion. Even if you had been on Ynys y Niwl you could have done nothing.

"But, sisters, this happened not in isolation," Glynys urged. More and more often the folk of the marshes seek our help. Many cannot find us here in the shadows. And for those who do, we often come too late."

"Do not blame the shadows, they have for all these years kept our community safe from the world." There was power in Vivian's words, and all were silent for a time.

"My Lady, I do not deny the shadows have protected us, and our mothers and grandmothers as well," Glynys said finally. "But we cannot wish to be protected for ever. Not when there are those in the marshes whom we might serve."

"Ever there is a battle between safety and service," said Vivian quietly. "I am called to keep and care for Cysgodion. What do I care for the wider marshes?"

"It is not the marshes, themselves, Lady, but the people who live there."

Vivian grew irritated. "Alright then, what care I for the people of the wider marshes? My community is here, on Ynys y Cysgodion. The people who swarm the other islands care not for us," she said. "They are not of our kind."

"But, my Lady, they are people, notwithstanding." Glynys' response was a dangerous one, but, for a long time, the Dark Lady was silenced. She seemed to wrestle with voices within, with unseen spirits, or ancestors who hovered about her. At last she spoke.

192

"Glynys speaks the truth, though this time it would not have saved the woman on Bol Forla. Some of you will go to Glyn y Ffynonnau on Ynys y Niwl, and form a community there. On Niwl people of the marshes may come for help and healing at y Ffynnon goch. But Cysgodion will remain here, inviolate, in the shadows. And I will remain on Ynys y Cysgodion."

~

So came the community of the priestesses of Affalon to Ynys y Niwl. For many seasons they served the people of the marshes, offering counsel in time of trouble, healing in illness, comfort in grief. Women came in great numbers to Bol Forla, for help in childbirth, or relief of orphan foundlings, or occasionally, for refuge from men whom they ought not to have loved. And often a priestess from Ynys y Niwl would return to Cysgodion, to relieve or replace one of the small number who remained there and cared for the Lady.

Then one day, in the spring of the turning year, when myrtles were in bloom upon Ffyrtwyddon, a dark woman robed in black came walking up the valley of y Ffynnon goch. She arrived at the springhead, where members of the community were bathing those with illness or injury. Priestesses and marsh folk alike turned and gazed at the solitary figure in wonderment, as the red waters tumbled downhill over blood colored rocks.

"So I have come," said Vivian. "But do not expect me to stay."

Chapter Nineteen
XII. The Dragon's Womb

"We have always known the gods are everywhere, Annwyl, but in the marshes there are places of mystery and power where they can more easily be found." The Lady of Cysgodion dipped her alder paddle in the dark waters as she spoke, easing their small marsh boat through the tall reeds. Annwyl, a young girl of six summers, sat in the bow, immersed in her mother's tale.

"Is it *really* a dragon's belly, Mam?" she asked. Her eyes were fixed upon a large blue and green dragonfly that had come to rest on the bow.

Vivian smiled. "We will be there soon, Little One, then you may see for yourself."

The marshes were young then. Not many women had yet carried the name of Vivian, nor borne the duties of the Lady. Yet some things were already ancient as we now reckon time, and Vivian was taking her young daughter that day to the most ancient of all. They had long since left Llyn y Cysgodion behind. Reeds hissed along the sides of the boat as Vivian found her way down the narrow channels that turned and twisted their way eastward. Annwyl reached for the dragonfly, but it escaped her grasp, hovered for a moment before her eyes, and then sped off down the channel ahead of them. Again Vivian smiled.

"It seems your dragon is leading us," she said.

They glided slowly along as the sun rose higher toward midday. Together they sang marsh songs, laughed at the clowning of an otter, watched in wonder as a covey of marsh hens was flushed before them and flew off into the reeds. At the sun's height, they shared a meal of barley bread and cool chamomile tea, while the boat rocked gently on a slow current, held fast by the closeness of the reeds.

"Tell me again, Mam, what is a womb?" Annwyl turned to face her mother as they resumed the journey. There were so many mysteries she did not yet understand. Her mother was full of them.

"It is a little sack in a mother's belly," Vivian told her, "where her babies grow until they are big enough to come into the world."

Try as she might, Annwyl could form no image of such a place. She screwed her face up into the most intense concentration she could, but it was no use. In her earliest memories she was always curled up on her mother's lap, already out in the wide world.

"Will we see the mother dragon?" she asked. Will she have a little one in her belly?"

"Such questions!" Vivian laughed. Wait and see, we are nearly there."

The boat passed into more open marsh where the channel was wider, the reed tussocks farther apart. Annwyl noticed the brackish smell of the marsh waters had lessened, and the currents had grown stronger. They were not far from the north shore. The Bryniau'r Mendydd loomed over them on their left.

"Look, Annwyl," Vivian said, pointing toward the hills. A silver brook was falling through a rough gorge in the high hills, tumbling over rocks and falling over ledges higher than the trees. "That is Ceunant y Gwar, made long ago by the giants who hid their treasures in the hills. They threw all the rocks from the gorge out into the open waters that flow into the neverending sea, to make Ynys Bryn Llyffaint."

Annwyl had never been that far west, beyond Ynys Mawr. She tried to imagine a great hill made of frogs, but the giants were easier.

"Look, down by the shore." Vivian pointed to the last waterfall, where the brook cascaded into the marsh. "That is why the water here is sweeter," she said. "We call this place y Gors Felys. We are nearly at Ynys Groth Ddraig."

~

They pulled the boat up onto a narrow beach of smooth, green pebbles. Annwyl looked overhead at the twining arches of three lush marsh willows, waving slowly in the gentle breezes.

"Blessings of the day, gentle spirits. Yes, the young one is my daughter," Vivian said. Then to Annwyl, "They are the guardians of the island, and they are delighted by your presence." There was a whispering in the green branches. "They welcome you," Vivian told her daughter.

Annwyl stared in wonder. "Can they really hear us?" she asked.

"Say something to them," Vivian answered.

Annwyl stepped forward into the midst of the willows and looked up to where their green branches crossed against the deep blue sky. "Hello, trees," she said. Boughs waved above her, and whispering grew in the leaves. Annwyl plopped down where she sat, wide eyes entranced. "Oh, my," she said, quietly.

Vivian held out a hand to lift her daughter from the ground. "Come, Little One," she said, "It's on the other side of the island." Together they climbed the narrow path that wound over the crest of Ynys Groth Ddraig.

As they came down the other side, the rays of the lowering sun slanted over their shoulders, lighting the way ahead. Several paces off to their left the underbrush on the dry hillside gave way to damp mosses and ferns, and the soft sounds of a gentle flow of water.

"Come and see where the ground bleeds," said Vivian. "It is woven about with protective spells, but you and I may enter." They crept quietly closer, Vivian aware of the sacredness of the place, Annwyl conscious only of a power she could not identify. At their feet, in a crescent perhaps an arm's span across, water, clear and cool, rose up and bubbled out of the earth. "Here rise the waters of life," Vivian said. She stooped to dip her fingers in the water, and with them traced a waving design across Annwyl's forehead. Immediately the young girl felt a tingling throughout her body. The light around her grew brighter and more clear. She looked at familiar trees and ferns as if she had never seen them before.

"I, I can feel it," she whispered to Vivian. "I can see!"

Vivian took her by the hand. "Come," she said, and led her downhill alongside the gathering stream. Ahead and just below them, a pool of crystal water sparkled in the sunlight. Vivian stopped, stood behind her daughter with her hands upon the young girl's shoulders. "Y Groth Ddraig," she murmured. "The Cauldron of Life."

~

The Dragon's Womb was a stone cauldron perched in the hillside, surrounded by the tall trunks of oak trees, their roots weaving a basket of sorts around the rock and holding it fast. The bowl of the cauldron was perhaps an arm's span deep, and yet more broad. It was worn smooth with the flow of the water, and its rim was covered with blue-green lichens that reveled in the water's touch. Opposite the flow, a dip in the bowl's rim allowed water to pour out onto the rocks below, and make their way downhill toward the marsh.

Vivian led her daughter around the cauldron to where the waters flowed out with a sparkle of silver. From there the wet lichens on the rim seemed to glow a deep blue, as if they were dragon's scales made of crystal. "Dragons are a way of talking about the power of life," she told her daughter. "The power is inside you, and you cannot see it. But it is bold and strong, like the wings and talons of a great dragon of the old tales. And sometimes as dangerous." She dipped a cupped hand into the water, and held it high, letting the water fall again into the stone bowl. "It is even more powerful here than up on the hillside," she said. "Come and see."

Annwyl stepped cautiously to the rim of y Groth Ddraig. Her chin was just above the edge, and her eyes could look on the level across the rippling surface of the water. Raising her arms, she placed her hands upon the lichen covered rim. Ice cold water welled between her finger, over the backs of her hands, and ran down her bare arms. She gasped out loud from the cold, and then again as she began to see what the waters held. Again, but stronger this time, the tingling sensation coursed through her body. And again she whispered,

"Oh, my."

Vivian came to her side. "What do you see, Dear One?" she asked.

"I see people," she said, "Shining people. And I hear singing!"

Vivian took both her hands and led her to a nearby patch of soft grass. "And you shall see even more in a moment," she said, looking deeply into her daughter's eyes. She stepped back a pace and took the hem of her summer shift in both hands. Lifting it up over her head and dropping it onto the grass, she stood naked in the rays of the lowering sun. And then she did the same for her daughter, and the two women stood facing each other.

"This is a gathering place of goddesses, Annwyl," Vivian said. And she showed her daughter each one, speaking their names in the old language as well as the common tongue. Raising both arms over her head, Vivian intoned,

"Awyr!"

and freshening breezes swirled through the trees, caressing mother and daughter and raising the hair on their skin.

"Pridd!"

Vivian called, and Annwyl's toes sank into the soft loam at her feet, the scent of humus rising about her.

"Dwr!"

A fine, cool mist rose from the marsh and floated over the hillside, covering Annwyl in droplets of water that ran down her body and dissolved again into the ground. She shivered with the coolness of it.

"Tan!"

and the rays of the blazing sun broke through the mist, warming the bare skin of the two as though it were a blazing bonfire.

Annwyl danced in the soft grass, rejoicing in the wonders she had beheld.

"The goddesses are that which bring us life, and death," Vivian explained. These are the ones that bless us the most, and there are some I must not name until you are older and stronger. Come now, and step with me into y Groth Ddraig."

Vivian eased herself up onto the rim of the cauldron and slowly lowered herself in. As the ice cold water enveloped her body, freezing her blood, her mind began to swim with images of living spirits. She longed to give in to their songs, but gently suppressed her awareness. This visit was for her daughter. Moving the swirling patterns to the back of her mind, she stretched out her arms towards the young girl.

"Come," she said. "Step into the water and let your soul come with me."

Annwyl sat at the edge of the cauldron and swung her feet into the water, as Vivian's hands held her by the waist, easing her in. Vivian sang to the water, warming it, calming the spirits, for her daughter's first experience. Annwyl stood before her mother, submerged nearly to her shoulders, and felt the living water swirl around her, while Vivian opened her own soul to her, and journeyed with her.

"Oh, Mam, it is so so beautiful," Annwyl said, her eyes glazed over as if she were looking at something far away, or deep within. Slowly, unafraid because of the nearness of her mother, Annwyl released herself to the songs of the spirits that sang and danced with her. They told her tales of their living, tales from the earth's dark womb, secrets of the ages. And among them she saw shining ones, like those she had felt while standing naked on the soft grass. Goddesses took her by the hand and sang to her the songs of life, and she felt in an instant the birthings of children across the wide marshes. She swayed and began to swoon, but Vivian saw and gently lifted her from the water and lay her beside the cauldron on the soft grass in the sunshine, drying the girl's skin with her own shift. Annwyl's eyes closed, a glow of deep peace in her young face.

"Sleep, my child, sleep. I will keep you warm." And Vivian lay down beside her daughter, covering them both with a blanket she had brought from the marsh boat. Slowly dusk gathered over Ynys Groth Ddraig. Night insects began to sing in the trees as though the trees themselves were singing, and ancestors of the marshes gathered around the sleeping women, as bright stars wheeled across the sky.

~

The sun had risen high above the horizon when Annwyl opened her eyes, rubbing them against the bright day. Vivian was sitting before her, holding out a piece of the barley bread, and some warm tea.

"Good morning, little sleeper," Vivian laughed. "I was afraid you had decided to join the spirits and dance away!"

Annwyl was hungry. She ate all the bread, and drank most of her tea, before she spoke.

"What happened, Mam? Well, I know what happened, but what did it mean?" She was still a child, but there was a wisdom in her face that had not been there the day before. Vivian reached out and drew her daughter close against her breast; kissed the top of her head.

"The Dragon's Womb is the cauldron of life, Little One," she said. "It is the gathering place of goddesses, and the birthing place of living things. In its waters you have learned not only what it feels like to live, but how it feels to give life, and what it means to be life itself. Such is my task as Lady of the marshes. Such will, one day, be your task as well."

Suddenly in Vivian's hands was a cup, made of gourd and highly polished so that it shone brightly in the sun. She rose and held the cup in the flow of water that emerged from the Dragon's Womb, then lifted it high and uttered a prayer in ancient words that Annwyl did not understand except for the last, y Groth Ddraig. Then Vivian came to her, and, knowing in her heart, she rose to her knees in the soft grass. Murmuring other ancient words, Vivian poured out the cool water over her daughter's head, and handed her the cup.

"It has been emptied, but it is not empty," the Lady said, "for such cups, when blessed and filled with power, are never empty again. This is your soul cup. It bears the power of your life even as you do in your own body, and its future is bound up with yours." She gave Annwyl a cloth of soft white wool. "Wrap it in this cloth and keep it safe, Child, for you will use it as Lady when at last I am gone."

Annwyl did as she was told. With every movement of her hands there appeared more wisdom in her eyes, more strength in her posture. When at last all was done, the two women walked hand and hand back to the marsh boat, and set out into the waters of Sweetwater Marsh.

The journey home was a strange one for Annwyl, for it seemed to her she had never seen the marshes before. A dragonfly lighted on the bow of the boat, shining brightly with iridescent blues and greens. She knew it to be the very one she had seen the day before, and she knew its name.

"Blessings of the day to you, Ddraig Athar," she said with a smile. The dragonfly circled once around her head, then landed on her shoulder. In a small voice, barely heard about the soft hiss of the reeds against the sides of the boat, it replied,

"Blessings of the marshes, my Lady." And off it flew, leaving Annwyl to wonder at what the world had become.

~

In time Vivian did leave this world, seeking the abode of her ancestors. Annwyl became Lady in her place, taking, in her turn, the name of Vivian. It was in the day of Annwyl's own great granddaughter that the Derwyddon came to the marshes of Affalon, bringing with them their own magic, and the skill of transforming sand and cobalt into the deep, glowing wonder of blue glass. In those days it was such glass that was used to craft the Lady's cup, ever after called the Cup of Enaid Las. With the same glass was the Dragon's Womb lined, casting its deep blue glow upon the surrounding oaks. But always the Derwyddon knew the magic of y Groth Ddraig Las was older and deeper than theirs, and they went there never. It was

Annwyl's great granddaughter who told her own granddaughter,

"We have always known the gods are everywhere, Child, and one day the Cup of Enaid Las will travel to far worlds, and work wonders that no one can imagine."

But that tale waits for another time, and another day.

Chapter Twenty
A Return to Affalon

Three nights of heavy frost passed before Fianna was ready to leave Llan y gelli. Need to wait for the dark of the moon required five nights more, for crossing the wide mouth of the Hafren without being seen by Roman patrols required complete darkness. Cadael had offered to send two of his warriors with her, but she had asked for Cethin, preferring an escort who would keep her out of a fight rather than get her into one. They left late in the afternoon on the first day of the moon's darkness, following the ravine of the Nantmeal creek downhill toward the coastal plain.

They were dressed in woolen cloaks of brown and forest green, protection against discovery as well as weather. Though he hoped dearly not to use it, Cethin carried his old sword, newly reworked after years of neglect. For the first time since her attack, Fianna bore the short, secret dagger of a priestess in the folds of her cloak. Such precautions were not taken lightly, for three real dangers lay ahead of them. If they were discovered leaving Silure lands, they could be taken for spies or, worse, assassins. As they neared the Mendydds, traveling alone, they risked being impressed as slave labor for the lead mines. Most troubling, Fianna had been in a fight where a Roman soldier had been killed. She remembered the terrible moment when, dropping her hood, she had looked directly into the face of one of the soldiers before she felt the bite of his sword. He would not likely have forgotten her face. True, she had been left for dead with the others, but Romans left little to chance. The incident was not that long ago, and she might be recognized. That would mean death for them both.

Except for spare clothing, they carried no provisions. This first part of the journey was through Silure territory, so they relaxed, enjoying the autumn scenery, before nightfall and their arrival at Porth-is-coedd, the tribal hillfort on the north bank of the Hafren estuary.

"I would like to have seen the place where they died one more time," said Fianna, "But we are already late. Sianed came to me in my mind last night. They have now closed the mists around Ynys y Niwl. I will have to call for a guide to enter."

"I fear you have waited this long on my account, Mother," Cethin answered.

Fianna smiled. "Yes, on your account, Healer," she said. "Is that such a bad thing? But we may charge the delay also to the wide world, for all will gain from your knowledge of the Marsh Tales." And so she eased his mind somewhat. It was past the season for birdsong, but wood thrushes and blackbirds called to them along their leaf covered path.

The fort at Porth-is-coedd had been advised of their approach, and sentries were watching for them. They were welcomed inside and given a hot meal, after which they sat at a wide table with one of the scouts, studying a cowhide map.

"Just down below the fort here," he indicated a spot on the north bank west of the hillfort, "there is a small skiff tied and waiting for you. When we get to the boat, I will show you how to find y Aberafon, here," and he pointed to the mouth of a small river entering the Hafren on its south bank. "There you will receive provisions for a three day journey, and enough, Cethin, to get you started back. It is a two day walk along the coast, around the flank of the Mendydds, to Llecychod. There you will be given a flatboat for the final part of the journey into the marshes. Here," he pointed to a star just north of Ynys Calchfaen, "is the lake village of Pentreflyn, where you will part company. We believe the village may now be deserted, but we are not sure."

Cethin was still studying the route around the west flank of Bryniau'r Mendydd. "The hills are garrisoned with Roman units, are they not?" he asked. "I have heard they now operate the mines."

"True," the scout said, "but their supply lines are

eastward. They are not interested in the western shores. Still, the most dangerous part of the route will be here," he pointed to western flank the Byniau'r Mendydd. "But with luck you will pass unseen, traveling at night."

Cethin rolled the map and slipped it into a woven bag slung over his left shoulder. He looked up at Fianna.

"Well, Mother, are you ready?" he asked.

"Yes, it is past time to go," Fianna answered.

~

It was pitch black on the wooded bank as the scout led them to their boat, hidden in the reeds on the river's edge. The south bank, far off, could just be seen against the night stars. They followed the pointing of his finger as he swept it westward to where a dip in the treeline indicated the location of a tributary.

"That notch is the marker for y Aberafon, where the Afon empties into the Hafren. Make straight for it, regardless of any lights that may appear. There will be Romans in the area, a Dubh-bunadh raiding party will be waiting nearby with your food and water. Luck and the gods be with you both."

Cethin and Fianna settled themselves in the small boat, he in back, she in the bow. They pushed off from the bank and, swinging the craft around, began to paddle southwesterly for the Afon mouth on the far shore. They encountered a light chop as they moved out into deeper waters, and a strong current. The crossing was not great in distance, something over three leagues, but though it might have been walked on land in a little over three hours, the journey by boat across the Hafren would take longer. Not only would they be fighting currents and rough water, but they had to move quietly as possible, so their paddles would not be heard, nor their wake seen in the starlight. For a long time they kept complete silence, both lost in their own thoughts about what lay ahead. Several times Cethin saw lights in the darkness, seeming to flicker through the trees as they paddled in on diagonal toward the shore. Whether the lights were tribal huts or Roman campfires he could not know.

Do not follow the lights, he thought, remembering the tale of the Ellylldan. Roman soldiers were likely more dangerous than marsh spirits, he supposed.

It was cold and damp out on the water. Though the sky above them was clear with the Hunter rising in the east, a wide fog bank hung off to the west, coming in from the sea. A heavy fog would be helpful once they were on land again, but if it arrived before they reached shore they would lose sight of the gap in the trees that marked y Aberafon.

To avoid thinking about what Romans might lay across their path ahead, Cethin turned the Marsh Tales over and over in his thoughts, the ancient wisdom of Affalon that Fianna had entrusted to his keeping. If all went well they would soon be in those marshes, would soon see places that as yet lived only in the corners of his mind.

"Will we see Bryn Llyffaint when we set out from Llecychod?" he asked quietly, breaking their silence.

Will we even get to Llecychod? Fianna wondered. "We will," she said, "If the night is quite clear. There will only be the first curve of the new moon, and that will already have set."

It took much of the night to cross the Hafren. But it was still dark, and the fog had not yet set in as they steered toward y Aberafon and swung in to shore. Immediately they were met by four silent men, dressed in tribal clothing. Cethin recognized them as Dubh-bunadh. Before he could greet them, the leader raised a finger to his lips, demanding silence. They were led some ways into the forest, and crowded into a small outcropping of rock that was nearly like a cave, before their new guide spoke.

"Welcome to Dubh-bunadh lands," he said, clasping both their hands in greeting. "Though now there are Romans everywhere, especially in the hills. I am Bryn"

"It is good to find you here," said Cethin. "I am Cethin, Healer to Cadael of the Silures at Llan y gelli. Also Dubh-bunadh," he emphasized. "This is Fianna, priestess of Affalon."

Bryn nodded his head in a simple bow. "Mother," he

said, "It is an honour to serve you." Fianna nodded in response, keeping silent, and the guide turned again to Cethin.

"You will stay the day here," he said. It is not comfortable, but it is reasonably safe. We will post sentries to watch for any Roman patrols, though they are not active here at the moment. The most dangerous time will come two nights from now as you pass the flank of the Medydds. There are furs here for sleeping, and food and water in backpacks for the journey." As silently as they had appeared, the men dissolved into the night, leaving Fianna and Cethin alone in the cave.

"I suppose the first thing is rest," Cethin said, handing Fianna a covering.

Wrapped in furs, and huddled together for warmth at the back of the cave, the two travelers drifted to sleep as a wall of thick fog covered the rising of the sun.

~

It was late afternoon when Fianna awoke. She rose, and stood at the opening of the cave, seeing for the first time it was indeed only a shallow outcropping in a low cliff. Remnants of the morning fog still drifted through the trees. She could smell the Hafren waters, though she was too far inland to see them. A quiet sound behind her was Cethin stirring, searching through their packs of provisions.

"Dried meat," he said. "Mutton, I think. Barley bread, and a few apples. Four water skins and, yes, some mead."

"You are welcome to keep the meat and mead to yourself," said Fianna. "But it looks as though we will have enough to see us through."

They shared a light meal, waiting in the outcropping for nightfall.

"The blue cup in the last tale," Cethin asked while they ate, "That is not the cup from the story of Vivian and Eosaidh, is it?"

"No, it is not," said Fianna. "There have been many such cups, and there will likely one day be more. But the cup in the tale was the first, made to represent the natural formation of the Dragon's Womb. They were made by the Druid Fferyllt, far to the north on the flanks of yr Wyddfa, but they were conceived, and filled with marsh magic on Ynys Groth Ddraig. They held the power of living and of dying, and were bound to those for whom they were made."

As the sun set and darkness settled over the Dubh-bunadh forest, Fianna told him the tale of Vivian and Eosaidh, and the last cup of Enaid Las. How it held the lives of her dead son, and his dead nephew, and how the latter, in a dry desert far away to the east, had held it high after a meal and changed the world.

"His followers did not understand him," she said. "They thought he was a god. It is men and women who change the world, Cethin, not gods. Remember that. They came to stay on Ynys y Niwl even before the Romans. And today, so I hear, near the place where Eosaidh's hut stood there is a temple to that new god, the dead nephew of a tinner from Cornualle."

"On Ynys y Niwl?" asked Cethin, in disbelief.

"Not so they can find the priestess community," said Fianna. "Glyn y Ffynhonnau and the sacred well are hidden from them forever by the mist. When at last we come upon it you will see the island and the temple they have built. But the island you will see is called now Ynys Witrin. Niwl you shall never see, nor shall I again, if I cannot draw the mists and call the boat."

Fianna's face turned from him, and her eyes journeyed far away. He dared not ask another question.

When it was fully dark they packed their things and set off to the southwest, staying just inside the eaves of the forest but keeping sight of the shore. It was not the straightest route to Llecychod, but it would keep them from wandering into the Roman held Mendydds. Aside from bogs, briars, and low hanging branches, all unseen in the blackness, it was an uneventful night. Near dawn they arrived at their halfway point, the mouth of the river Tyllwyll. Going inland a bit, upstream, they came to a thicket that would keep them hidden through the day while they slept. Cethin dreamed they were surrounded by Roman soldiers, shouting battle cries as they approached, running through the trees. He awoke with a start to the cries of ravens, and quickly fell back into a fitful sleep.

~

Travel on the second night was longer, nearly seven leagues. They decided to use the coastal road, out from under the cover of the forest, even though this increased the possibility of meeting a Roman patrol.

"Roman occupation has been settled here for some time," Cethin assured Fianna. Unlike the Silures, most of my tribe has made a reluctant peace with them. If we meet soldiers on the road, perhaps we may say we are Dubh-bunadh farmers on our way home to Llecychod."

"I think they would not believe I am your wife," said Fianna. "I am nearly old enough to be Mother to you in fact as well as in spirit."

"Fortunately a priestess of Affalon looks ageless," Cethin answered with a smile, "and a Dubh-bunadh who once fought Romans looks older than his time."

They walked on in silence for many paces before Fianna said,

"Perhaps. We shall see. And how will you explain that sword?"

Cethin fingered the sword hilt hanging at his waist. It might have been needed closer to Silure lands, but the farther south they went the more its possession was a danger in itself. A farmer and his wife walking home in the middle of the night would not be carrying a polished and honed sword. They stopped near a copse of alders while he took a spare tunic from his pack and used it to carefully wrap the weapon. Then he climbed one of the trees and fastened the bundle high in the upper branches.

"I shall likely come back this way," he said as they set off again, "and then it may be needful" It was a strange feeling that came over him, for though he preferred not to be armed, he found he missed the weight of the weapon hanging at his side.

As it turned out, they met no patrol on the road. Once, just before first light, they saw a campfire up in the hills to their left, but it was far off, at the west end of Bryniau'r Mendydd. Not long after, they saw the low rise of Bryn Gwaun, reaching out into the bay. The hill was actually a western outlier of the Mendydds, made of the same limestone and containing deposits of lead and, perhaps, silver. But its separation from the main body of hills by some four or five leagues put it in an isolated and exposed position. The Romans seemed not interested in it. As long as the local Dubh-bunadh remained peaceful, they were allowed to occupy the hillfort atop Bryn Gwaun. It no longer protected Llecychod on its southern slope, but it was at least a remnant of tribal autonomy. Circling Gwaun to the west, along the water, they came finally to Llecychod. "The place of boats," it was called, for it lay at the confluence of the Hafren estuary and the great marshes. There larger boats and smaller were exchanged, depending upon the direction in which one was traveling. Cethin and Fianna had come on foot, but word had arrived before them and a flat bottomed marshboat was waiting for them at a small mooring hidden in the reeds at the edge of the village. No one was there to meet them, but the boat was where the guide at y Aberafon had said it would be. In the boat lay the prearranged sign, a small sack of apples, the fruit of Affalon. They found a thicket of brambles nearby, and hid themselves for the day, getting what sleep they could.

~

When darkness had fallen on the fourth night of their journey, they quietly pushed off from the mooring and turned eastward into the open waters of the wide marshland. It was a sight Cethin had never seen before, but it touched Fianna's heart with awakened memories of home. The night was cold and clear, with a waxing crescent moon near to setting. A crisp wind blew out of the northwest, chilling the bone through layers of sleeping furs pressed into use as clothing. The tiny boat, made from the hollowed out trunk of an oak and flattened on the bottom, was difficult to handle at first. It was made for the shallow waters of the inner marshes. They carried a light load, so the boat sat high in the water. That, and the lack of a keel, made sails of their bodies, twisting and turning the boat with each gust of wind and passing wave. They sat as low as they could and still paddle, trying to stay out of the wind, to keep warm.

When the west end of Ynys Mawr loomed before them, they steered to the right, seeking the channel between the great island and Ynys Bryn Llyffaint. As the dark outline of a high hill rose against the stars on their right, Cethin broke their silence.

"Mother, is that Bryn Llyffaint?"

"It is," Fianna answered. "It was from there Eosaidh of Cornualle set out in a boat like this one for Ynys y Niwl, sixteen summers ago."

The open channel was narrow as they passed between reed ringed islands that were as myth to Cethin. He imagined the giant shovel of Offrwm, countless ages ago, hurling the great conical hill to where it rose in the water before him. And Hynafgwr, King of the Llyffaint for All the Ages, sitting in state upon its summit.

"At that time," Fianna said, following her own thoughts and not Cethin's, "the fort atop Bryn Llyffaint was held by the Dumnoni. I know not who, if anyone, is there now." Though they saw no lights they kept close to the reeds for cover, and glided by in silence.

Beyond Bryn Llyffaint the water opened wider again, with the shores of Ynys Mawr still on their left. Above the great island, and beyond, rose the dark outline of Bryniau'r Mendydd. There were campfires at several points along the ridges. These, they knew, indeed were the fires of Roman outposts, for the tribes had lost the Mendydd mines. They still worked them, but the wealth now belonged to Rome.

The moon set behind them and the Hunter rose higher in the east. As night wore on the wind eased, bringing a new sort of heavy chill that hung in the air and sat upon the lungs. They passed through another narrow channel, between Ynys Mawr and an island they did not know, and the waters opened out again. But not as wide as earlier, for they were entering the inner marshes, near to the realm of Affalon. As they passed the southwest cape of Ynys Mawr, they reached the last stretch of open water before the true marshes began. Ahead of them lay the isles of Llefrich and Bragwair, and Ynys Calchfaen, yet unseen, where Gobaith once hunted marsh deer with little Dyfrgi, and Doeth learned the secret of living upon the tides. On their left the Mendydds retreated farther off. The deep darkness at their base, Cethin knew, was the supposed location of Cysgodion, still home to the Lady whose priestesses lived on Ynys y Niwl. He wanted to ask Fianna about that. But when he turned to her she was sitting sideways in the boat, paddle across her lap, staring into the darkness.

She is with her even now, Cethin thought. *She is with Sianed on the isle of shadows.* And he remained quiet, respecting her silence.

The night's darkness was dissolving into early morning light when they saw Ynys Calchfaen before them and turned to the left along its north shore. The sky above them was clear, but a morning mist hung above the waters making it hard to see. Fianna strained to peer through the mist, knowing the lake village of Pentreflyn to be near, somewhere ahead. They paddled slowly along the edge of the Calchfaen reeds, watching for signs of the Pentreflyn huts rising on a great platform out of the waters. By now, Fianna thought, there must be smoke from cooking fires, sounds of the day beginning.

Suddenly the reeds fell away on their right, and open water led up to the shore of Calchfaen.

"Cethin, look!" said Fianna, pointing to the deserted beach. "That is where they say Doeth watched her husband's boat rise and fall, and learned the secret of building a lake village." As Cethin stared, hoping to see Gobaith's mythical mooring pole, Fianna's heart fell at what she saw ahead.

The outlines of Pentreflyn emerged out of the low mist, black outlines at first then in more detail as they neared. But all was silent save for the cries of curlews overhead. No smoke rose above the huts, for there were no cooking fires. They tied up at one of the pilings of the little village. Where once a ladder would have been climbed, they stepped out onto the wooden platform into water that covered their ankles. No one challenged or greeted them. No one was there. A pair of crested ducks splashed noisily around the corner of a hut and, encountering human intruders, took flight out over the reeds. They walked through the village in silence, looking into huts as they went, finding no one On the island side, a walkway led into the marsh toward the Calchfaen shoreline. But a few paces out there were broken and missing planks. And a few paces beyond that the ruined end of the walkway dropped off into the water. It was so quiet they could hear the gentle hiss of the light breeze in the surrounding reeds, the gentle lapping of waves against the outer pilings.

"What happened here?" Cethin asked.

"I cannot say," answered Fianna. "As in Doeth's time, the waters have been rising. It may be the village was finally overwhelmed by tides. Or it may be the Romans took their grazing pastures on Crib Pwlborfa. What is certain is that no one has lived here for several summers." An otter pulled herself up on the end of the walkway and began prying open the shell of a marsh clam. "No one, that is, except for the marsh folk who were here first."

"Good morning," she called to the otter. "Blessings of the day to you, Dyfrgi." The otter looked up at her for a moment, then went back to her morning meal. Fianna turned to Cethin,

"Come," she said, wading through the shallow water toward the east end of the village.

As they stood, looking eastward, the morning sun burned off the last of the marsh mist. There, perhaps three leagues away across the southeast point of Calchfaen, rose a

213

green island out of the marsh. Three hills stood upon it, one long and low, one softly rounded, and, between them, one that rose like a tower into the sky. Across the marsh came the faint sound of a tolling bell. Cethin knew what he saw before she spoke. But Fianna took his hand and said,

"That is Ynys y Niwl, Cethin," and there were tears in her eyes. "But what you see is Ynys Witrin, the isle of glass. And the bell you hear is from the temple of those who call themselves Christians. There!" she said, and pointed. Just below the long low ridge of Bryn Fyrtwyddon a small whitewashed building sat in the sunlight.

"That must be their temple," Fianna said. "It was there sat the round hut of Eosaidh when last I stood on the island. But by then he had already left this world, he and Vivian."

"If that now is Witrin, how will you find Ynys y Niwl?" Cethin asked.

"I hope I know, Healer," Fianna answered. "You saw me talking with Sianed last night in the boat as we passed the darkness of Cysgodion. She told me how to call the mists, how to summon the boat. But this I have never done before."

Fianna turned to Cethin and surprised him by taking him in her arms and drawing him close to her breast. He noticed for the first time that he was much taller than she, and it was rather her head that lay upon his chest.

"You have done well by me, Healer. You have saved me from death, and brought me home. And you have learned the Marsh Tales, the ancient wisdom of Affalon. Now I must leave this world, and where I am going, through the mists, you cannot come. Through you, alone, will Affalon continue to live in the wide world."

"Are you to be the Lady, at the passing of Sianed?" Cethin asked.

"That I do not know," Fianna answered. "Nor do I know aught of what lies ahead for Affalon. But Sianed has called me, and it is time for me to go." She drew his head down and kissed him on his forehead, then turned away toward the

214

isle in the east.

Cethin stood quietly behind her as she moved to the edge of the platform. For long minutes she stood still, silent, seeing with her eyes things he could not see. Then she raised her arms upward from her sides, holding them spread above her head. For long moments nothing happened, but Fianna did not move, nor did she speak. A white egret landed on the roof of a hut behind them, and perched there, watching. Then, from around both sides of Ynys y Niwl there appeared white banks of mist hanging over the marshes. Slowly they came together and met, so the shores of the isle were no longer visible. Slowly they rose into the sky, engulfing the high tor of Bryn Ddraig. Slowly they flowed toward Pentreflyn across the marsh, until they hung silently before Fianna, not many paces away. Still without speaking Fianna lowered her arms and stepped forward, as it seemed, on the waters. And out of the mists before her came a small boat, and a young priestess was at the paddle. The boat came up beside Fianna and she stepped in, standing in the middle.

"Tell the tales, Cethin," she said softly. "Tell them the Marsh Tales."

Then slowly and silently the boat turned, and vanished into the mists. Cethin stood alone on the submerged platform of Pentreflyn. Behind him his small boat, tethered to a piling, rocked gently upon the waters of the marsh.

Chapter Twenty-One
The Changing of the World

Ides Junius
IX Imperator Domitianus

It is the ninth year of Emperor Titus Flavius Domitianus, son of Vespasian who conquered the tribes. Often, now, I come here to this bluff below the Prydde mines in the Bryniau'r Mendydd, overlooking the wide marshes where thirty summers ago I watched Fianna disappear into the mists. Much has happened in that lifetime. Ynys Witrin, once called Ynys y Niwl, lies below, lit by the high summer sun. There are fewer mists about the isle now that Roman engineers have begun a vast project of water drainage. There now lay broad areas of raised bog where once there was marshland. And new marshes that were once open water. The bogs are crisscrossed with canals and ditches which year by year have produced many hectares of new farmland. I have been to Ynys Witrin a few times, but it pains me to go there. In the field below Wearyall Hill there is a stone church, which is what Christians call their temples. Beside it hang three bronze bells that toll throughout the day, marking times of prayer. Many Christians live on Witrin now, in a community nearly the size of a small village. *Glaston*, I think they call it. From there they send men out to every corner of the land, seeking converts to the new god they call *Christus*. Only the old folk remember this Christus to be the nephew of Eosaidh of Cornualle, who once lived where the church now stands.

After I was parted from Fianna I returned to Llan y gelli of the Silures where, for a time under Cadael, we held out against the Roman conquest. Under Cadael the Silures finally began attacking Roman settlements, taking Roman prisoners. But in the end they, too, fell like all the tribes. When the Silures won a victory over the famed II Augusta legion it was too much for the old commander Vespasian, who had become Emperor. He decided to tolerate the holdouts no longer. In the thirtieth year of the occupation, Sextus Julius Frontinus overran Llan y gelli, removing its people to the Roman settlement of Venta Silurum. With the defeat of the Silures the Brythonic lands became known as Britannia, and were no longer free. The II Augusta valued my skill as an herbalist, so they brought me here to the Mendydds, where they had taken control of the mines long before. Ever since have I cared for those Brythonic prisoners who have labored in these mines, and I have buried their dead. Now the soldiers, too, are gone. The IInd has moved north to Glevum and civilian officers control the mines. Indeed, Rome is so confident of its conquest it has already removed two legions from these shores. Men of the tribes still work the mines, but the wealth, as the silver and lead, all goes to Rome. Many Brythons have welcomed the new way of life, and it seems we are all Romans of a sort now.

Below, the hills of Witrin are surrounded on three sides by fields golden with barley and summer wheat. To the west there is marshland still, and open water not far beyond that. But Witrin is an island now for only a few months in the midst of winter, when the rains come and flood the fields. So it is deep winter I love the most, for it is that view of the surrounding marshes that reminds me of Ynys y Niwl. Fianna, I suppose has by now left this world. I never heard whether she became Lady, or took the name of Vivian. But I feel it in my being that Ynys y Niwl is there yet, unseen by our eyes, and that a Lady of Affalon still lives.

What difference does it make, that the ancient world still exists, somehow, in the midst of a new age?

Arius, a healer's apprentice, struggles down to the bluff and sits by my side, wiping the sweat of exertion from his brow. He is the son of a Roman administrator and a Dubh-bunadh woman, bearing in his flesh and heritage a sign of these times. He holds a leather gathering bag filled, I hope, with herbs for identification. If the gods had given me children, Arius would be the age of my grandson. Perhaps unfairly I sometimes treat him as such, but I do not think he minds. For a long while we sit in silence, his own eyes following mine as I search the levels below.

On the western edge of Ynys Witrin, no longer separated from it by marsh, is the gentle rise of Bol Forla, where the first of the Marsh Tales took place. Women go there still to seek the blessing of the goddess, whom they now call Bride. Though more and more often they also seek prayers of the male priests at Glaston. Still farther west I can see Bryn Calchfaen, no longer an island but a low rise surrounded by bog. I have not been there, but I am told that scattered ruins of Pentreflyn can still be seen at its edge, lying about. And out at the horizon stands Bryn Llyffaint, always my favorite. There is open water near it still, but it is mostly surrounded by marsh. If frogs live there yet, they must find it a habitable place.

My eyes drop to the levels just below, between the hill of Bryn Mawr and the old wells at Llw Fynnon where once the tribes gathered. Somewhere in those fens was Ynys y Cysgodion, home of the Lady who was mother of all living, home of the Lady still in the days of Fianna. Is it there yet, I wonder, hidden like the heart of Ynys y Niwl? At the memory of that name, my gaze completes its circuit, as always, by turning to the deep valley where y Fynnon Goch lies between Bryn yr Affalau and Bryn Ddraig. All this while, and for some time longer, Arius understands and respects my silence. He has no memory of Fianna, and knows the levels only as they appear now. Yet he knows them also through the Tales, and imagines them as once they were.

"It matters, Cethin," he says, surely reading my thoughts, or at least feeling the emotion that floods my heart. Again we sit in silence.

A light breeze from the south brings the sounds of sheep to our ears from the valley, and the scent of ripe grain. Large white clouds with the texture of lamb's wool drift slowly

218

towards us from Crib Pwlborfa, and the sky is more blue than usually seen over the levels. The bluff is a worn, rounded edge of Mendydd limestone, covered in high grasses, with small outcropped ledges here and there. The ledge on which we sit is barely wide enough for the two of us, with Arius' bag spread between. A strangely placed hawthorn hangs over us, giving a little shaded relief from the hot sun. Rock rose and wood sedge grow in the creviced outcrops, but mostly there is high grass waving in the breeze and harboring several kinds of butterflies. A downy emerald dragonfly hovers before us for a moment, then darts off, and grasshoppers buzz incessantly.

I try to change the subject by asking Arius what he has found, so he empties the contents of his bag onto the limestone. Birdsfoot, mouse ear, red clover, sunwort, lady's mantle. I ask him what each is for and he tells me, his lessons well learned. But he sees by the mist in my eyes that my heart is not in this lesson, so neither is his. He is learning herb lore, it is supposed, so that I may give up my duties in the Prydde mines and do more teaching, traveling the marshes and hills and spreading the Marsh Tales among people who have all but forgotten the old ways. And he will make a good herbalist, but he would rather learn the Tales and travel with me. Though my mind wanders he is still speaking, and gently raises his voice to call me back.

"Cethin, it does matter," he says.

"What?" I ask him. "The scarcity of mouse ear this summer?"

"You know well what I mean, old man," he answers, with a playful laugh that does not mask his concern. He lowers his voice. "It matters that the old is out there yet," his eyes turning to Bryn Ddraig where it rises on Witrin. "Whether we see it or not, it matters that the ancient places yet live under the surface, and that the old knowledge is, somewhere, taught still."

"There is more of Druid in you than it is healthy to admit," I chastise him.

"Even so," he says, "it matters."

There are other apprentices and other healers in the hills.

Perhaps, indeed, Arius should come with me. I have lived in this world more than sixty summers, I think, and always I have been alone. It would be good to have a companion. I gesture to Arius and he gathers the herbs, returning him to the leather bag.

"How much of the Tales do you know?" I ask. I have told them all to him many times, but we have never worked at memorizing.

"A small rounded hillock still rises out of the mists to the west of Bryn Fyrtwyddon . . ." he begins. Sometime later when he finishes, gently singing "*Daughter of chieftains, bride of the fens, come back to your home once more*," I am speechless with amazement.

"Do not be overly surprised if someone believes you when you tell him it does matter," he says quietly. And I realize it is at this moment that Arius' apprenticeship has turned from herbalist to bard.

"The world is changing," I tell him. There are some who will not listen to the Tales. Some who do will call them mere children's stories and mock you for it. Some will fear the old wisdom greatly, thinking it a threat to their new ways of understanding things. It will not be an easy life, being a teller of Marsh Tales."

He looks deep into my eyes, and I see in his a calling that will not be denied.

"True enough," he says, "but there are some who will know in their hearts the truth of what they hear, and that will change their world yet again. And some there are who will tell others."

I stand, and he with me.

"Come," I say, "you will eat with me this evening, and then your learning will begin. On the way I have a new story to tell you. I did not learn it from Fianna in the old days. It came to me one night, not long ago. Where it comes from, or who first told it, I know not. But it is the last of the Marsh Tales."

Together we reach the crest of the bluff, and head down to the village of Prydde, spread before us in the afternoon sun.

Chapter Twenty-Two
XIII. The Last Tale

Once, when first the tribes found their several ways into the wide marshes, a young girl of eleven summers sat looking into the darkness. She was Aelwyd, daughter of Broga of the Dumnoni, who was chief of the hillfort built on the crest of Bryn Llyffaint. Aelwyd sat on the eastern ramparts of the fort, high on the hill, in the warmth of a late summer night, looking east across the open waters, toward the dark marshes and the hills beyond. Bryn Llyffaint lay at the boundary where the open waters of the marshes met those of the endless sea, and it was surrounded by the dense sedge and reeds of a narrow salt marsh. So the night, though dark, was far from silent. Nightsongs rose to her ears from the reeds and wooded hillside below, from bog and bush crickets, and other insects she could not name. Now and then she thought she heard a frog, perhaps because of the full moon rising nearly overhead. Usually the frogs of the island sang only during the mating season of *gwanwyn*, but a bright moon and a warm night could encourage them at any time. That night, the moon sparkled upon the marsh waters, lighting a pathway to the shore of Llyffaint just below her, and bathing the far hills in a soft glow.

Her eyes rose to the long, low line of hills that began just across the narrows and trailed away eastward out of her sight, the Bryniau'r Mendydd. Along the crest of the hills she could see an array of lights, like a dotted line strung in the darkness. Brighter and seeming to sparkle they were, nearby; becoming dimmer as distance increased. They were fires, she knew, campfires of tribal settlements along the ridge. Though she could not see them in the distant dark, there were people around those lights, or perhaps sleeping in circling huts. Those nearer were Dumnoni, like herself. She had friends whose families had gone to live in the Mendydds, and cousins who came to visit occasionally from the hills. Farther along the ridgeline were the camps of people she did not know, the Dubh-bunadh, the dark people whose swarthy appearance spoke of distant origins. She had never met one, but her imagination caused her to shudder as she stared at the far lights.

The two tribes faced each other across a great gorge in the hills which split the Bryniau'r Mendydd into two territories, with Dumnoni in the west and Dubh-bunadh in the east. They were there, Aelwyd's father had told her, because of a strange bright metal in the earth called *arian* that shone like the face of the moon. She held up a small disc that hung by a cord from her neck, and it flashed in the moonlight. It was a beautiful metal, much treasured, that brought great wealth. Arian was taken with great skill and difficulty from a heavier metal her father called *plwm*, which was dug from the surface of the ground in long furrows. This heavier metal was of little use to the tribes, as she understood things, but traders from the east paid well for it. Aelwyd's eyes found the darkness on the ridge, in the middle of the line of campfires, that was the gorge. There, she knew, was the site of sporadic but bloody fighting as the Dumnoni sought to move eastward, and the Dubh-bunadh strove toward the west, each seeking a greater share of the Mendydd mines.

"Aelwyd, it is late, come to bed," came a voice behind her.

"In a moment, Mam," she answered, "the night is so beautiful!" She loved the night, and her mother had long since given up trying to get her to bed early.

Her eyes fell upon one of the nearer Dumnoni fires, and she wondered whether anyone known to her sat around it. Its twinkling, she knew, was the crackling and dancing of flames too far off to see. As she watched, her gaze became fixed and her eyes gradually lost their focus. Her sense of her own body faded, and her mind reached out over the marshes, across the dark rise of Ynys Mawr, to the campfire burning brightly on a Mendydd hilltop. From the high treetops she looked down upon the circle of the camp, a large bonfire with men and some women sitting around it, and a ring of small huts just at the edge of the trees. And then she was seated before the fire, feeling its warmth upon her face, watching sparks fly upward into the night sky. No one around the fire seemed to notice her, but she could see their faces clearly, and hear their speech.

They spoke of another hard day at the mine, of a birthday coming up, of a marriage feast just past. They spoke of children sleeping in the circling huts, of hopes for the future, and of fears. They talked of loving, as two or three couples rose and disappeared into the shadows. Aelwyd felt the warmth of the little community that was owed to something other than the bonfire, and she smiled, for these were her people, just like the gatherings of her own family within the palisades of Bryn Llyffaint. She sat for a long time, listening to tales and songs, until most around the fire had risen and gone to their huts. Finally the scene around her began to fade, and in the darkness she felt herself being pulled back across the marshes.

When her sight returned, she was sitting again on the ramparts of Bryn Llyffaint. The moon had begun to descend toward the west and the nightsong of the insects had grown quieter. She looked over her shoulder toward her family's roundhouse and saw that it was dark. She laughed softly, knowing her mother had finally given up on enticing her to bed. It was not strange, for she loved the night, and her mother left her to it. Just then a quiet voice spoke inside her.

"Aelwyd," it said, "there are other campfires." She had never heard the voice before, waking or sleeping. It was the voice of a woman, and it sounded like the flowing waters of the marsh. She looked around to see from whence it came, but no one stirred within the moonlit confines of the ramparts, save for herself.

"Aelwyd," came the soft voice again, "the Dubh-bunadh sit around fires as well."

Aelwyd looked down the ridge of the Mendydds to where the Dubh-bunadh fires burned, and again she shuddered,

223

a cold chill going down her back even in the warmth of the night. She had never met one, but she knew what they were like. She hated and feared them, for they were killers of her people. Who was this strange person whose voice spoke to her of the Dubh-bunadh?

"Who are you, my Lady?" she asked into the night. "Why can I not see you? What do you want of me?"

There was no answering sound but for the rustle of wind and the song of crickets. And then the silent voice inside that spoke again, saying,

"There are other campfires to visit, daughter. There are other people."

Aelwyd turned and looked toward the dim lights at the far end of the hills. Her eyes fell upon one and, dim as it was, she saw that it, too, sparkled with the crackle and dance of flame. Once again her eyes lost their focus, and her body seemed to fade. Her mind reached out over the eastern tip of Ynys Mawr, over the shadowy marshes that people called Cysgodion, to a hilltop in the eastern ridges of the Mendydds.

From the high treetops she looked down upon the circle of a camp, a large bonfire with men and women sitting around it, and a ring of small huts just at the edge of the trees. And then she was seated before the fire, feeling its warmth upon her face, watching sparks fly upward into the night sky. No one around the fire seemed to notice her, but she could see their faces, and hear their speech. Their faces were different, yet clearly they were people with feelings like hers.

They spoke of another hard day at the mine, of a birthday coming up, of a marriage feast just past. They spoke of children sleeping in the circling huts, of hopes for the future, and of fears. They talked of loving, as two or three couples rose and disappeared into the shadows. Aelwyd felt the warmth of the little community that was owed to something other than the bonfire, and she smiled, for these were, no, not her people, but it seemed just like the gatherings of her own family within the palisades of Bryn Llyffaint. She sat for a long time, listening to

224

tales and songs, until most around the fire had risen and gone to their huts. Finally the scene around her began to fade, and in the darkness she felt herself being pulled back across the marshes.

When at last the awareness of her body returned, Aelwyd sat again upon the ramparts of Bryn Llyffaint in the dark of the night before the coming of dawn.

"What have you learned, daughter?" the voice within her asked.

It was long moments before Aelwyd replied, for she was puzzled and amazed at what she had seen. Tribes that fought to the death over rights to the silvery arian were both made of people with the same hopes and dreams, the same loves, fears, wishes and joys.

"I have learned, Lady," she said at last, "that there are indeed many campfires. And that the folk who sit around them are more alike than they are different."

"You have learned well, daughter," the voice said. "When you have learned what that truly means, perhaps one day you will join us in Cysgodion." Then the sense of presence was gone, and Aelwyd sat alone under the stars.

She looked up, gazing at the lights twinkling across the night sky, picking out the pictures they formed in the dark expanse; Telyn, the harp; yr Haeddel fawr, the great plough; Llys Don, the palace of the ancient goddess; Alarch, the swan; Eryr, the eagle; Rhyfelwr, the warrior. And arching through them all, the broad, milky cow's path, Llwber Llaethog. As she looked, Aelwyd saw for the first time that they twinkled. Twinkled like the fires on Bryniau'r Mendydd.

"What if," she said into the deep sky, "what if they are all campfires, with people like me sitting around them, telling tales?"

She wished to send her mind out among them. But there were too many to let her gaze fall upon only one, and the gulf between was too great. Try as she might, she found her mind only floating in deep darkness, with the sky fires still tiny points in the great distance.

"So far," she breathed aloud, "so far away I cannot hope to go to them, or meet the tribes who sit around their glow." She sat in silence for long moments, as morning light crept into the sky, and the fires twinkled out, as above, so below.

Compared to the tribes who travel yr Llwyber Llaethog across the broad sky, she thought, *the people of the Dubh-bunadh are my neighbors.* She paused then in deep thought. *No, not neighbors*, she realized, *but kin, my sisters and my brothers.*

As she thought this, the morning sun rose slowly over the eastern marshes, and the world welcomed a new dawn.

~

Here end the thirteen Marsh Tales,
the ancient Wisdom of Affalon.

GLOSSARY and PRONUNCIATION

Many of the names in this book are based, sometimes only loosely, upon modern Welsh, to give a sense of the ancient while remaining accessible to modern readers. Proper names with mythological significance in the Tales are included in the glossary. Words or names in chapters nine and thirteen that are unknown to the protagonists are not included, and thus unknown also to the reader. Some place names (e.g. Pwysi) are puns on the names of modern places. Pronunciation notes are a guide only, and not intended to be a full explanation of Welsh pronunciation. Use your own intuition with confidence.

Consonants

c   Always as in "cow" (even before e, i and y)
ch   As in Scottish "loch" (guttural "kh"-type sound)
dd   Like "th" in English "the", never as in "think"
f   Like English "v"
ff   Like English "f"
ll   Put your tongue in the position for "L" and blow out.
mh   Like it looks; not as hard as it sounds, since it almost always occurs after a vowel. Split it between two syllables if you like.
ngh Sort of like "mh"; split it into ng-h.
nh   Similar to "mh".
r   Trilled with the tongue-tip.
rh   Like "r", followed by an aspiration of breath (h).
s   As in English, though "si" is pronounced as in English "sh",
th   Like "th" in English "thug", never as in "this".

Vowels

a	As in English "can" (short) or "father", (long)
e	As in "let" (short) or "late" (long) no "eee" sound at the end of the vowel.
i	As in "pit" (short) or "lean" (long).
o	As in "lot" (short) or "coat" (long) no "ooo" sound at the end of the vowel.
u	Completely equivalent to "i" (long or short)
w	As in "put" (short) or "soon" (long), can be either a vowel or consonant
y	like the vowel written "u", can be long or short. Long when standing alone.

Dipthongs

ae, ae, au	Long "a" followed by long "I" (ah-ee)
ei, eu, ei	"e" in Mother, followed by "ee" sound (eh-ee)
aw	like "ow" in "now"
ew	like "e" in "get" followed by "oo" (eh-oo)
iw, uw	like "ew" in "hew" but emphasis on first rather than last sound
ow	as in "home" including a trailing "oo" sound
oe, oy, oi	like "oy" in "boy"
wy	"oo-ee" if w is vowel and y is consonant; or "wee" if w is consonantal and y is a vowel (e.g. Gw+ydd, GOOH-eethe = Goose; or Gwy+dd, GWEETHE = Trees)

Glossary

Aberafon	Mouth of the Avon
Adolwyn	Wish
Aelwyd	From the Hearth
Affalon	Avalon, Land of Apples
Alaeth	Sorrow
Alawen	from White Water Lily
Alcam	Tin

Andraste	War Goddess
Annwyl	Beloved
Anogaeth	Oath, Taboo, Admonition
Anwtledd	Love
Arddwr	Plowman, Farmer
Arian	Silver (*metal and color*)
Awyr	Air, Goddess of Air
Bendith	Blessing
Bendith y Mamau	Mother's Blessings, fairy folk
Berthog	Fair, Beautiful
Bol Forla	Morla's Belly (*Modern: Bride's Mound*)
Borefwyd	Breakfast
Braith	Gray
Broga	Frog
Bryn y Affalau	Hill of Apples (*Modern: Chalice Hill*)
Bryn Ddraig	Dragon Hill, the Glastonbury Tor
Bryn Fyrtwyddon	Hill of Myrtles (*Modern: Wearyall Hill*)
Bryn Gwaun	Moor Hill
Bryn Llyffaint	Hill of Frogs (*Modern: Brent Knoll*)
Bryn Mawr	Big Hill
Bryniau'r Pennard	Pennard Hills
Bryniau'r Mendydd	Mendip Hills
Brythonic, Brythons	(*adj*) British - (*n*) British People
Bryw	River Brue
Bwbachod	Goblins
Cadael	From, a leader in battle
Cernyw	Cornish People
Cethin	Dark, or Ugly
Cewri	Giants
Ceunant y Gawr	The Giant's Gorge
Chweg	Sweet
Coblynau	Mine Goblins

Creigiog	Rocky
Crib Pwlborfa	Polden Ridge
Crika	Like "a sharp poker of red marsh reeds"
Crwban	Turtle
Curyll	Hawk, Falcon
Cyfaill, Cyfeillion (pl)	Friend
Cymru	Wales (*cf. Cymry: Welsh People*)
Draig Athar	Air Dragon (*e.g. Dragonfly*)
Dwrgi	Otter (*older usage*)
Dwrtrygydd	Water Peoples
Doeth	Wise
Dolgwyl Waun	Festival Meadow (*Beckery*)
Drwyd	Druid
Dubhydd	from Black Stag
Dwr	Water, Goddess of Water
Dyfrgi	Otter
Ellylldan	Marsh Goblins similar to Will O' the Wisp
Enaid	Soul, Life
Enaid Las	Soul Cup, Cup of Life
Eosaidh of Cornualle	Joseph of Arimathea
Eira	Snow
Eryri	Snowdonia (*in Wales*)
y Fynnon Goch	The Red Spring
Galan Gaeaf	First Day of Winter
Galan Haf	First Day of Summer
Genwair	Fishing Rod
Glaston	Place of Glass (*Glastonbury*)
Glyn y Ffynhonnau	Valley of the Springs
Gobaith	Hope
y Gors Felys	The Sweet Marsh
Groth Ddraig	Dragon's Womb
Grym	Power
Gwalch	Marsh Harrier
Gwanwyn	Spring (*the Season*)

Gwlad	Country, Land
Gweledydd	Seer, Shaman
Gwen-hwyfar	White Spirit
Gwrach	Wisewoman, Witch
Gwraig Annwn	Woman (Bride) of the Underworld (*pl. Gwragedd*)
Gwrol	Manly
Gwyn ap Nudd	King of the Fairies
Hafren	River Severn
Hiraeth	Deeply felt longing of homesickness
Huan	Sun, Sun God
Hynafgwr	Elder, Old Man
Iudde	Jew
Iuddic	Jewish
Iwerydd	Atlantic, the wide encircling ocean
Iwrch	Roebuck
Llan y gelli	Village in the Woods, Silure hillfort capital
Llecychod	Place of Boats
Llefrith	Milk, Sweet Milk
Llyf	Current (*in water*)
Llyffant	Frog (*pl. Llyffaint*)
Llyr	Sea God
Llyn y Aberthau	Lake of the Sacrifices (*fictional*)
Llyn y Cysgodion	The Lake of Shadows
Llyn Hydd	Hart Lake
Llynwen	White Lake
Modryb	Aunt
Mor-forwyn	Sea Maid (*e.g. Mermaid*)
Morla	Bitter, or Marshwoman
Morwyn	Maiden
Mwswgl	Bog Moss
Offrwm	Offering
Oriog	Moody, Inconstant

Pentreflyn	Lake Village (*Meare*)
Plwm	Lead (*metal*)
Pridd	Earth, Goddess of Earth
Prydde	Earth (*Priddy, in the Mendips*)
Pwysi	Bouquet
Salis Plain	Salisbury Plain
Tan	Fire, Goddess of Fire
Teg	Fair
Tresglen	Thrush
y Tylwyth Teg	The Fair Folk, fairies
Wirrheal	Hill of Myrtles (*Wearyall Hill*)
Vivian	Giver of Life, the Lady of Avalon
Wye	River Wye on east border of Wales
yr Wyddfa	The Tomb, Mount Snowdon in Wales
Ynys Bragwair	Isle of Moorland Grass *(high ground west of Meare)*
Ynys Calchfaen	Limestone Island *(Meare in Somerset)*
Ynys y Cysgodion	The Isle of Shadows
Ynys y Ywen	Isle of the Yew, Iona
Ynys Llefrith	Ilse of Milk *(high ground west of Meare)*
Ynys Mawr	Big Island
Ynys Mon, Mona	Mother Isle (*Anglesey*)
Ynys y Niwl	Isle of Mist (*Glastonbury*)
Ynys Witrin	Isle of Glass (*Glastonbury*)
Ynisig	Little Isle, Morla's Belly

Acknowledgements to the Second Edition

It is not possible to write a mythology spanning millennia without involving a few other people along the way. I am especially grateful to Emma Restall Orr of the Druid Network, my colleague and co-author of *The Apple and the Thorn*, who originated the character of Fianna, the phrase *Marsh Tales*, and the first version of *Morla's Tale*. I thank her for the kind permission to further develop those contributions in this second book, and for the inspiration she has provided to me. Many thanks go to authors Bobbie Pell and Wendy Webb, who critiqued my work at the Campbell Folk School in North Carolina. To supplement my meager knowledge of Welsh, I made much use of the *Searching Lexicon* and Mark Nodine's *Welsh Course* online. I thank Cardiff University for making such a valuable resource available to the public. To my children and step-children Jennifer, David, Drew, and Tom, I give thanks for the hours of reading J.R.R. Tolkien and C.S. Lewis aloud after dinner and at bedtime, helping to keep alive a love of myth and mystery into my adult life. But mostly I am thankful for the love, support and companionship of Glyn Lorraine Ruppe-Melnyk, my wife of twenty-two years, and the love of my life, for believing in me, inspiring me, and teaching me the wonderful mysteries of womankind.

In the second edition, published in 2010, the title is changed to *Tales of Avalon: Wisdom of the Ancient Marshes*. Thanks to Wayne Avanson for that suggestion, and also for his work as artist for the new cover, and the map of Affalon. Thanks also to Anita Shaw for her magical portrayal of the Lady of the Lake on the cover.

Walter William Melnyk
Spring Equinox, 2010

Also from Walter William Melnyk

The Apple and The Thorn
with Emma Restall Orr
Thoth Publications
ISBN: 978-1-870450-68-3

The Apple and the Thorn stands upon the tradition of two mythical characters: the Lady of the Lake, and Joseph of Arimathea (Eosaidh, in this tale.). Yet the land itself is a living character in the tale, as is the surrounding marsh, the invading Roman legion, and a very special cup of blue glass that unites them all.

This story is not true in the sense that most people use the word. It emerges out of the mists of time, rooted deep in the heritage of Britain. It is a weave of mythologies, theologies, and histories. It is the story of two people, and a story of all peoples. It has no beginning and it has no ending.

As the tale unfolds, Vivian and Eosaidh debate the story of Eosaidh's young nephew, Jesus, exploring questions of God and the gods, humanity, gender, honour, hope, history, ethics, spirituality and, always, the underlying presence and meaning of the land. They alternately succeed and fail in understanding each other. The growing depth of their intellectual connection is matched by the growing depth of their friendship.

For the authors, there is much in this tale that emerges from their own separate stories, brought together here in a literary collaboration to craft a mythic tale of human struggle and hope in the midst of a violent world.

Melnyk and Restall Orr draw deeply from their own lives to tell a fresh version of the Avalonian myth, yet one that seems the most ancient of all - of a woman and a man who seek honour, and find love. But readers will find only themselves in Eosaidh of Cornualle and Vivian of the Marshes.

Available online through bookstores everywhere.

5076605R0

Made in the USA
Charleston, SC
26 April 2010